Marcia Duncan Shining Bright
Lynn Cavendish
ISBN: 978-1-8384686-4-4

Published By: -

i2i
PUBLISHING

i2i Publishing. Manchester.
www.i2ipublishing.co.uk

Preface

The day Marcia found out the truth about her best friend Molly's sexuality was a day she thought the world was going to end. Some people may have seen the signs but for Marcia, those clues were blinded by a mixture of ignorance, naivety, and a cloak of friendship and love so strong, it made many a person jealous.

There were the rumours of course, like any that scurried around the estate at the speed of light. It was odd, it was said, 'The likes of her, taking up with someone like that.' And 'wasn't it strange Molly's never had a real boyfriend? - not that anyone would be interested in that scrubber!"

Things would quieten down for a while, as their attention was diverted to the latest scandal, then run full circle. Not that it was confined to Marcia and Molly, everyone had their turn; that was the way of Chalksbury, and no one was really bothered.

Marcia had heard a few things; she wasn't at all perturbed. Everyone on the estate got called something or other at some time in their lives, and as for a scrubber, that's what they called Mrs Marchent. She was slightly mad, but harmless enough relentlessly washing her steps. Before her passing, her mother Lily continually told her to, 'turn deaf ears, our Marc, you'll hear much worse before you die.' Marcia always wondered why she should turn her ears. She tried it once, in Watchco's, when Sheila was having a go about her dad, Bernie, not being right in the head, she could not move them. It made no difference, even waddling indiscreetly nearer, some of the conversation was still muffled.

Thus, through Marcia's eyes life was relatively simple. Surrounded by family and her 'bestest' friend, doting on her daughter Tanya, and caring for Bernie, her ailing father, she was perfectly content.

There was, however, an extremely small core of Molly's limited social circle that either knew, or had an idea, but they were confined to her 'clients', who had no interest in disclosing any facts, for fear of publishing details regarding their private lives. In any event, the 'friends' were kept to a very loyal few and the special relationship evolved between them, no outsider would understand.

As for any immediate family, there was Dylan, Molly's father, who was confined within a sixties time warp. Continually away with the fairies, he had long since dismissed any opinion regarding his son's chosen lifestyle. Floating along with 'the flow of love, sunshine and peace,' he was totally unaware of time and space and, in fact, anything normal in the world. After the initial outrage and the 'ousting of one or the other', he obliterated Martin from his mind and accepted Molly the way she was. Her mother, Patricia, had left years ago, and upon learning of her passing, and discovering the existence of her 'posh, upper-class' estranged family, Molly was even more determined to keep secrets to herself. Thus, complications of life were buried, and the years had tootled along with no real problems... except, of course, dealing with Marcia, who was a law unto herself.

Molly was quite happy and content to live the life she chose without taking it any further. There seemed no reason to upset anyone, she had long decided it would do more harm than good for anyone to know, at least not yet. She had thought about confiding in his consultant, Mr Jameson, at one point, as he continually badgered about family every time she attended hospital appointments as Martin. The heart condition was relatively stable now, but returning into the comfort zone, when him became her, always changed his mind. What was the point? It was only on rare official occasions he had to suffer reverting to his biological sex.

Marcia certainly would not understand the battle he had fought within for many years. The overwhelming desire to rid his body of the male physique, the likes of which, much to his dismay, occasionally involuntary showed itself.

Even if Marcia was able, at some point, to take it all in, how was he supposed to explain what happened the night he fished her, half-drowned and paralytic, out of the fountain. They had both consumed enough gin to sink a battleship, and the details were fuzzy, but he seemed to recall babbling to Marcia something about almost losing her, wishing he wasn't what he was and declaring his profound love. He would never forgive himself for the act that followed, and he was ever thankful that Marcia had no recollection of it. Marcia was Molly's best friend, and that is all she would be, and Martin had betrayed her.

The guilt he felt for this drunken mistake lay heavily on his heart, though with time, it had been somewhat strangely alleviated by the love he felt every time he looked at Tanya. If he could turn the clock back? Now he did not know the answer, for today, his life would be worthless without either of them.

Despite his outwardly feminine appearance, looking into the mirror each morning, Martin was conscious of the increasing time he spent making up, acutely aware that as the years slipped by, the baby face features were slowly disappearing. Already, the huge array of hair removal equipment was having a limited effect; the five o'clock shadow was ever appearing at three. His 'friend' Charlie had 'obtained' hormone tablets, which Martin had been taking for a while. He certainly felt plumper in the chest but apart from that, no noticeable difference, and it was dangerous, not knowing where they came from, but for now, it would have to do.

Marcia had no idea; to her, Molly was perfect, and to be honest, compared to some of the girls on the estate she was. Marcia was dependent on Molly, and who was he to shatter her illusions? Of course, what he was not admitting to himself, was he was desperately afraid he would lose the love and friendship of the only two people who mattered in his life, Marcia, and their daughter Tanya, neither of which had any idea who he really was.

As it happened, fate took a turn for the worse and there was no choice in the matter, the truth had to be revealed.

Chapter One
Drama in Clover Close

Marcia rammed her fist hard on the red button for the umpteenth time, to no avail – the chair would not shift. "Damn this bloody thing", she grumbled.

Mildly frustrated but used to her inability to conquer any kind of smooth movement, Marcia looked at her dangling feet with resignation. Her size 3 poised for landing above the fifth step and the size eight pendulum swung wildly, threatening to demolish the hallway wall at any minute.

"Now what? Tan! Tan?!! Moll!! Shift your asses from that tele. Tan! Come and give yer mother a hand!!!"

Molly stretched out her long legs and yawned, "Can't you wait Marcia? This is the best bit!!", she shouted, "And you know you are not supposed to be using that 'till Tom's looked at it."

Marcia felt a little guilty, but her deteriorating spine condition combined with ever increasing weight gain made it difficult to mount the stairs these days. The last few times she had managed the task it took so long that Tanya had offered to make her some sandwiches to eat along the way. She remembered the 'fizzytherapist' said she must try and use her legs more, because she will get that 'muskylateridge' thingy, and to use it as a last resort. Marcia replied she had no intention of taking it on holiday.

She would not have had the lift at all if it hadn't been for Mrs Benton's son ceremoniously dumping it in his mother's garden with a note; 'Free. Don't take if you get car sick'. Her nephew, Tom, had instantly spotted a 'bargain' and whisked it away on his truck. He did speak briefly to Mrs Benton, not really worrying her husband had been propelled up and down non-stop for an hour, at treble the normal speed. Norman's vertigo was so bad now, he flatly refused to go upstairs; she had to make up a bed in the lounge and buy a commode.

Tom was everybody's saviour. He was the one that begged and borrowed, making a few pounds when and where he could. If anyone needed anything, from toilet to garden swing, Tom was the one that found it. Consequently, the chairlift was something he was sure he could 'fix up a treat' for Marcia, which of course he did… you just had to wiggle the switch a bit.

Wiggle the switch Marcia did, several times. Her cumbersome manner not helping at all, it had finally given up the ghost.

"Moll! Tan! I'm stuck, help me out! I'll be ok once I get on the step!", she shrieked.

"In a minute Mum… the cat has just come back from the dead!" Tanya piped up.

"What cat? Molly! What are you watching? Hope it's not one of those horror things again, Tanya's only eleven years old!" Marcia squirmed. "Come on! The faggots are nearly done, and I need the lav an all!"

Molly winked at Tanya, "Sssh…", prised herself up, paused the video and poked her head around the door.

"It's called Pets Cemetery, it's educational, teaches kids to deal with death!" Looking at her best friend dangling in mid-air, she couldn't help but laugh, and was half-tempted to leave her there.

Marcia huffed, "Well! We ain't got no cat, nor are we getting any more pets. Tanya was heartbroken when the canary went up the vacuum."

"Oh Marcia, that was your fault, I told you not to wave the end around, you should have waited till I got here!" The vision of Marcia flat on her back shaking the vacuum attachment around above her head was more than Molly could bear, feathers were flying all over the place. She dissolved into hysterics. "And you thought it was still alive because it was singing - Oh Marcia, it was the cleaner whistling to say the bag was full..."

Marcia swung her legs and sniggered. "Er yes.... well.... don't tell Tan and get me down 'fore I pee me self."

Molly skilfully skipped up the steps and grabbed Marcia as best she could. It was becoming impossible to get her arms around the ever-expanding form. "You'll have to help Marcia!" she giggled. "Or do you fancy a cup of tea until it starts again!"

Marcia put her size three on the step and with Molly's guidance managed to manoeuvre the size eight sideways, so it more or less secured itself. Marcia slid off the chair, the majority of her torso pushing against Molly, whose legs finally gave in.

"For Christ sakes Marcia, grab the rail or something, I can't lift you up!" Molly engaged her shoulder in Marcia's ribs and heaved her towards the wall.

"Okay okay! I got it Moll; I can do it now!" Huffing and puffing Marcia pulled on the rail and like a hungover sloth, dragged herself to the top of the stairs, tripped over the last hurdle and fell flat on her face.

Molly followed, still shaking with laughter. "Come on, you silly bugger, get yourself up, God knows we are going to have to get a lav put in downstairs soon."

Marcia pushed up her arms and straightened her legs, she now looked like Neanderthal man after a fight with a mammoth, but eventually, struggled to her feet.

"Think I'll have a bath while I'm up here and lay down for a bit, can't face going back down just yet!" she gasped.

"Well, watch you don't get stuck in there either, your sticks are by the side and if you need some help bang on the floor... oh and not too hard, Tom's just filled in the crack in the ceiling from the last time." Molly cheered with her usual joviality, being well used to Marcia's antics.

Tanya sat impatiently; somewhat oblivious as young girls are. "Come on Auntie Molly, I started it again, look at the cat, it's dead creepy!"

Acknowledging with a smile, ever heartened by the term of endearment, Molly so wished to invite Tanya to address him by another name. Her inner thoughts deflated as she sank into the cushions; one day she must tell them both the truth. Marcia was becoming ever immobile, and as for the rest of the situation; the longer she left it, the worse the expected backlash and alienation would be. She felt her chest flutter and breathed deep after the effort. Something would have to be sorted out soon, at least for Marcia; maybe she would speak to Audrey, she would look at Marcia's benefit, or the council and see what they could do.

Molly was spending most of her spare time at the Duncan's house. It had its pros and cons. On the one hand, her practical help was invaluable, and she loved her time with Tanya. But it did nothing to encourage Marcia's physical independence and the battle to persuade her to seek medical advice was relentless, she definitely took after her mother in that respect. If it weren't for the fact, she had to be assessed every so often to review her entitlement to financial assistance, she would not go at all. It was almost impossible to persuade her to go to the physiotherapist after she fell off the treadmill attempting to press the button to 'snail's pace' and upped the speed to 'gazelle' by mistake.

"Well, our mum didn't think I needed the Docs! She always said I am what I am, and she don't want no more interference and them making decisions an all... They'll end up taking me away, that's what she said", her favourite argument ringing in Molly's ears. "Just get me some more of those Pannydolly tablets, they're just the job when me back hurts."

The countless times Molly had tried to reassure her that no one was going to take her away, seemed to make no difference whatsoever. Her thoughts continued to wander and despite Tanya's relentless enthusiasm for raising the dead, Molly felt unusually lethargic and sad. Her head mildly throbbing, she closed her eyes and drifted away from the world.

Molly awoke to the sound of whirring. The video had long since finished and was singing its usual tune, refusing to switch off after rewinding the tape. Tanya had retired to her bedroom to indulge herself in the latest fashion magazine. Even at her young tender age, Molly's influence was having a great effect, and Tanya's interest in beauty, clothes, and make up seemingly reached beyond her years.

Looking at the time ticking away on the old brown clock, Molly was surprised that she had slept so long – it was not like her at all. She immediately hoped that Marcia was not in any imminent danger of drowning and quickly rose, clicked off the video and, not bothering with her shoes, proceeded to the hallway, only finding herself suddenly dizzy and clinging to the banister. Her occasional palpitations swung into action once more. Cursing herself for getting up too quickly, and thinking she must be getting old, checked herself and concentrated. A tablet would sort it out, they worked wonders.

"You ok? Marc? Sorry fell asleep ages ago!", Molly coughed.

Laying on her pink candlewick bedspread, wrapped in her old dressing gown, dozing in the land of nod herself, Marcia barely heard the sound.

"Whaa...?" came a mumbled groan.

"You ok? Marc?" Molly repeated.

Marcia stirred. "Yeh," she shouted, am Ok ta, laying down for a bit."

"I'll sort the tea then, shall I? The faggots will have to be reheated now."

Without waiting for a reply and still without her shoes, Molly ran her fingers across her sweating forehead, sighed and walked unsteadily to the kitchen. Seeing her open bag on the table, she rummaged amongst the array of lipsticks and mascaras. Pulling out the small bottle of pills, she quickly unscrewed the cap and popped one into her mouth. It would take a few minutes to work, thus Molly sank upon the kitchen chair and looked at the stove.

Thankfully, Tanya had the sense to turn off the oven. Although still young, she was so much more switched on than Marcia, and unlike other children of her age, through necessity more than anything else, had become quite a dab hand at basic cooking and general chores around the house. However, Molly had long since realised responsibility was the key to keeping Marcia focused and, more importantly, moving, frequently reminded Tanya to leave it to her mother when at all possible.

Steam still arose from the pan on the cooled hob, and seemingly feeling a little better, Molly raised herself and moved uneasily towards the cooker. Lifting the lid and surveying the damage, the conclusion was the potatoes were just about edible.

She was about to recover the remains when the pain hit Molly's chest. So sudden and intense, her right hand instinctively grabbed her left side and the glass lid clattered to the floor and shattered, scattering jewels over the worn-out tiles.

Molly's legs buckled, she fell to floor and lay there, still and staring. Sweat already congealing on her ashen face, in contrast to the red stream, oozing from her knee, turning the diamond glass pink as it wormed its deathly way through the cracks on the uneven surface.

Tanya, hearing the clatter, dismissed it instantly, thinking it was another 'mother moment.' Then realised that Marcia was upstairs, and the noise came from below, jumped off the bed and flew down the stairs.

The sight that met her eyes was devastating.

"Ma!!!!!!!!   Ma!!!!!!!!!!!!!!!!!!" screeched   Tanya.... "Maaaaaaaaaaaaaaaaaaaaaa!!!!!!"

Marcia woke with a start, she did not often hear what was going on below stairs, but she certainly heard Tanya and the panic in her voice, and never did she call her 'Ma!' unless she was wailing about something or other.

"Ma!!!! Come quick!!! It's Auntie Moll, she's not moving Ma!!!!!!!! MAAAAAAAAAAAAAAAA!!!"

Surprised at her own agility which surfaced only when absolutely necessary, Marcia almost leapt out of bed, grabbed her sticks, and with maximum obtainable speed, shot across the landing. Well, it was fast for her, on- lookers would have thought it was more like a tortoise with diarrhoea trying desperately to find the nearest secluded leaf, but she did her best. Looking at the chair dangling halfway down, she briefly contemplated the dilemma and decided drastic measures would be needed.

Throwing her sticks down the stairs, she heard the clatter as they bounced off the wall and landed cross threaded on the front door mat. Grabbing the banister with both hands and turning her body sideways, leaning on the rail to support her weight, she placed her awkward size three on one step then tried the size eight on the lower. Unfortunately, not being able to see the second step, she misjudged it completely, her slipper caught the edge causing her to lose her footing and drape herself over the sloping wood… How she wished Tanya wasn't a dab hand with the polish…

Marcia's limited life flashed before her and she was certain she saw her mother Lily, glaring at her in astonishment as she aquaplaned downwards, hit the stair lift, flew upwards and landed back on the banister reverberating against the final spindle. This in turn, dislodged the loose ornamental ball, hurtling it through the air, propelling it straight through the glass window in the front door, smashing it to smithereens.

Surprisingly, narrowly missing the light fitting, doing a forward roll into the coat rack, causing her see-through plastic mac to surround her like a sausage fit for the Guinness book of records. Any normal person would probably have suffered instant death. But, of course, this was Marcia, seemingly made of rubber and used to reverberation, her body jellied to a halt. Momentarily stunned, she saw little yellow birds fluttering, and heard angels uttering holy words.

"Ma! Ma!!! Bloody get up!!!!" Tanya pulled at the coat and unravelled a dishevelled looking human with her dressing gown round her ears and a very strange look in her crossed eyes.

"Ma!!!" Tanya sat down on the floor and burst into tears, unaware of the tinkling sound as the remains of the glass window showered to the ground. Neither did she hear the rough jangling as the handle was yanked up, and the banging of the front door as it was thrust open. Tanya screamed as two strong hands enveloped her, lifting her to her feet....

"What the fuck is going on?" boomed Tom.

Tanya pulled herself away from Tom's protection and pointed her hand. Sobbing wildly, the words were barely audible.

"Kitch......en.........Kitch.... Moll......", her young shoulders heaved with every laboured breath.

"And your mum? Marcia? You ok?" he stared at the heap on the floor.

Coming to her senses Marcia blinked her eyes... "It's Moll, Tanya said she ain't movin' quick Tom... QUICK!!!!!"

The next few moments were a complete blur to both Marcia and Tanya, neither of them being used to things happening so fast. Tom rushed into the kitchen and put his hand to his mouth, colour drained from his face as he threw himself on the floor beside Molly's motionless body. He put his hand to her throat, there was a very, very faint, dying pulse.

"Tanya!" he shrieked, get on the phone, dial 999 get an ambulance... tell them Moll's unconscious, hardly no pulse, go Tanya go!!!!!!!!!!!!!!!!!!!"

"I can't!" Tanya panicked, "The phone's broke, Mum tripped over the wire and ripped the end out the wall!"

"Then go next door to Sheila's and use hers. Run, Tanya, RUN!!!!!!" Tom bellowed.

Marcia, a little dazed, managed to heave herself off the floor, wobble into the kitchen and stood shocked and silent. Tom's head was resting on Molly's chest, his ear facing towards her mouth. "She's barely breathing now Marcia, Oh God! What to do!!!?"

Tanya ran like lightening, banging on Sheila's door and shouting at the small crowd of nosy people who had slowly gathered around. "Someone get an ambulance!!! It's Auntie Molly, she isn't moving or breathing or nothin' I think she's dead!!!"

In an instant, the whole of Clover close appeared; people dashing here and there, most of them not doing anything constructive except shout orders and suggestions that didn't help anyone.

"We'll get the ambulance Tanya!" someone yelled.

"We'll get the police as well, if she's dead!!" another helpful person suggested.

Sheila, Marcia's next-door neighbour, put her hands on her hips and bellowed. "Well in that case, we better phone the bloody undertaker if you are going to take that attitude!!" Any drama started an argument in the street. "Here's Bernie! Let him through!"

"Go on Bern...!" Mrs Hargreaves raised her voice, parting the waves with her holy stick.

"Let him through there... Let him through!!!"

"Ok! Ok! You don't have to get bloody violent, we ain't glued to the soddin' floor!" Scary Mary from number nine sneered.

Bernie hobbled his way up the path somewhat bemused, despite his failing health, he did realise something was sadly amiss. He had not quite reached the stage of committal – yet – and was visibly agitated at the thought of any mishap concerning his daughter.

"Oh God!" he yelled "What's happened, is it my Marcia?" he cried. "All this at Christmas time an all…"

"Bern it ain't Christmas, it's April…" Sheila raised her eyes to the heavens. "Go and sit with Tanya Bern, It's Molly not Marcia. That's no place for a young'un!"

Bernie stood in the doorway and paused. "Our Marcia is ok then; so, what did I come in here for, maybe it's our Tanya, did I see her back there? Yes, I will go and sit with her, see what she wants Father Christmas to bring her this year…wonder where she's gone?"

Sheila, as did most of the other residents, humoured Bernie the best way they could and had learned, by experience, to know the best things to say to keep him calm. Telling him it was not Christmas occasionally coaxed some sense out of his brain. Today, he was completely confused and aimlessly tottered around the garden.

Thankfully, Sheila had the sense to take his arm and gently ease him away to her kitchen, with the promise of a cuppa and a slice of Christmas cake.

Outside Marcia's dwelling, the local population was rapidly growing.

"I'll get a blanket!" came a shout.

"Is she dead then?" yelled another.

"What's happened? Who's dead? No, never, can't be…so young…" several ladies huddled together chattered.

News travelled fast on the Chalksbury estate, and the 'facts' changed with every onward transmission. An hour later, the story elaborated from Molly passing out, to being drunk and hitting her head on the table. Once it reached the end of the close, she had been murdered in the first degree by mental Delores, Bernie's estranged daughter, who had escaped from the unit, appeared on the scene and accused her of having an affair with her invisible boyfriend.

"Anyone want a cup of tea?" Mrs Hargreaves kindly enquired.

There was so much babbling going on, who knows who said what, such was the commotion. The distance sound of sirens was unheard at first, then grew louder until silence descended on the crowd as the ambulance screeched around the corner.

The paramedics, oblivious to the stares, skilfully concentrating on the job in hand, grabbed a handful of terrifying gadgets and charged into the house. Tanya, ignoring everyone else followed on. George pushed past the audience, threw down his bag and dropped to his knees beside Molly.

His colleague, Cath, stood by, immediately assessing the situation, then addressed the trembling threesome. "Oh, it's Marcia, isn't it?" she briefly paused, "I remember you, and is that the water baby? She's grown!! How could you forget that in a hurry?" Supressing a smile, she thought to herself that this was not the right time for jokes.

"What's her name?" Cath distracted the inappropriate comment.

"Tanya" Marcia answered. "Don't you remember?"

"No, I mean what's her name?" Cath pointed to the motionless body on the floor.

"Oh god!" Marcia screeched gaping at George. "It's Molly and she's my bestest friend ever."

George ignored the rantings and continued, his only communication with his partner.

"Hearts stopped, no breathing - shock I reckon Cath."

Marcia looked horrified. "Course she's in bloody shock, Is she dead?!!! Oh God she's dead!!!! Why's he thumping her like that Tom?" She wailed. "They gonna break her bones like that...Look what they've done, flattened her boobs 'an all. Oh God, and what are they doing now?"

Tom, as were the rest of the group, deaf and blind to comments about boobs, the thought of Molly dying was the only thing in mind. Putting his hand (as best he could) on Marcia's shoulders, he relayed the problem clear and plain.

"She's not breathing Marc, they're gonna put some leccy into her, I saw it on the tele."

"Some Leccy!!!!" Marcia totally dismayed, shrieked. "SOME LECCY???!!!   That's what our Mum died from, they're gonna kill her Tom, STOP IT!!!!!"

Tanya grabbed her mother's arm, "Shut up Mum!!! You're not making any sense as usual... Tom's right, I seen it as well. It's called a defibisomething or other they do it to get her alive again!"

Marcia was even more perplexed." A fibywhat? What the hell is that going to do? She don't tell lies, and even if she did, that don't do no good if you're dead!"

"For God's sake Marcia." Tom grabbed her arms and came close to Marcia's face, trying to ignore the twitch. "Bloody shut up and watch!"

"Stand back!" came the confident and firm instruction, "Ready Cath?" George looked at his colleague.

"Ready, go go! go!!..." Cath raised her arm and with some force, arched it backwards across the onlookers.

There was a loud buzzing, then a thump. Molly's body jerked and her back arched and fell back to its former limp state. Marcia shut her eyes and put her hands over her ears.

Tanya started to sob again. Tom knew he should be removing her from the proceedings, but he too, was unable to move from the spot.

George frowned at Cath. "Again.... go go! Go!! Come on Molly, come on!!"

The process was repeated, again Molly jerked. Both paramedics leant closely over their patient.

George mopped his brow and sat back. "We have a pulse!" he cried. "The eagle has landed!!"

Marcia was totally confused and in panic mode. "What eagle? What's he on about now? Bringing bloody birds into it? What's that gonna do 'cept peck her bloody eyes out!"

Cath turned and smiled, "It's ok Marcia, she's not dead, but we must get her to the hospital now, looks like she had a heart attack."

Far from being comforted, Marcia ignored the paramedic and dropped to the floor, banging her knee and toppling sideways, swiftly followed by Tom, who had grabbed her arm, but unable to sustain her weight, which resulted in both of them tumbling down onto the blood-stained tiles.

"Oh Moll!!! Moll!!!" Marcia cried into her hands. "Don't leave me like me Mum.... MOLLLLLLLLLLLLLL!!!!!!!!"

Tanya's tears still fell as she knelt, being careful to avoid the glass fragments. Of all three, you would have expected a child of her age to be hysterical at the least, but she took a deep breath and hugged as much of her mother as possible.

"Mum.... It's ok, Mum; Auntie Molly's not dead, they're gonna take her to the hospital now. We have to go there.... Mum.... it's ok....come on, we have to get you dressed....

love you Mum." and she squeezed Marcia as hard as her little arms would allow.

Chapter Two
Confidential Disclosure

Dierdre adjusted her glasses and tore herself away from the pile of unfinished paperwork, acknowledging Tom and Tanya's presence briefly, emitting a frustrating sigh, before continuing with the unimportant task before her.

"One moment please." She muttered.

Tom drummed his fingers impatiently, "Sorry, but we have an emergency here!" bending as close as he could without spitting in her ear.

Raising an arm in subtle protest, the hospital receptionist abruptly laid her pen to rest and stared straight at Marcia's face. In fact, Marcia's face was all she could see, as Tom had commandeered the use of a wheelchair to speed matters up, resulting in a somewhat restrictive view.

Dierdre raised herself, "Oh, I see.... accident.... knock on the head.... slumped posture." Sighing, grabbing the form she had completed a million times before.

"No!" Tom furrowed his brow in annoyance.

"It's not Mum..." Tanya joined in, slightly calmer." It's Auntie Molly, she's had a heart attack, she was brought in by ambulance earlier."

"Yeah, It ain't me. I always look like this." Marcia did not take any offence. "It's our Moll; we got here as soon as we could. I ain't as mobile as I used to be and our Moll is all we got, so we come quick!"

Dierdre looked nonplussed. "Oh, sorry, are you relatives?"

Marcia was just about to explain, when Tom grabbed his handkerchief and put it over Marcia's face. "There, don't cry Marcia, we will see your sister soon." Turning to distract

Dierdre, "It's Molly, her sister, Molly Emery."

"But I wasn't...and she isn't..." Marcia spluttered, received a mouthful of cloth and was unable to complete the sentence.

"If you wait over there, I will try and find out where your sister is and get someone to come and see you as soon as possible. It might be a while. There's a coffee machine if you would like some refreshment." Dierdre waved her hand signalling direction and swiftly returned to her files.

The seats were full of people crammed like sardines, and Tanya was glad Marcia had been persuaded to use the wheelchair. She found a cramped spot in the corner, with a space just big enough to accommodate the threesome.

Tom fiddled in his pocket and found some change. "Anyone want a coffee?"

Marcia grimaced, recalling the last time she drank coffee in the hospital. Registering her mother's death still left distraught memories, despite the registrar insisting the stains on his shirt would wash out.

"No thanks Tom," she sighed. "Can't eat or drink till I know our Moll's ok!"

"I'll have a coke if that's alright?" Tanya never let the opportunity of a free drink go by despite any adverse circumstances, "....and a packet of cheese and onion crisps if they have them, if not, a mars bar and if not...."

"Shut up!" her mother glared.

Marcia sank back and reluctantly resigned herself to the fact they could be here for a very long time. Conversation eventually ran out, and the trio sat there in silence, following the paths of brightly coloured darting fish, listening to the trickle of water and humming of the filter, along with the rest of the crowd, interrupted only by the odd cough and the frustrated 'tut'.

Finding it more uncomfortable by the minute, Marcia fidgeted constantly, banging herself up and down, to the left, to the right, unable to find a suitable position which did not cause her any amount of pain.

"Wonder how much longer we're gonna have to wait?" She grumbled. "Our Moll could be dead for all we know, and they ain't tellin' us nothin!"

"I'll get a coffee later, I am going to find someone Marcia, it's not on! Poor Molly all by herself, bet she's wondering where we all are? And I suppose we better tell her dad at some point?" Tom raised himself from the plastic chair.

"Oh, don't you bother telling Dylan." Marcia grimaced. "He's a complete waste of space. He doesn't even know what day it is, let alone where Moll is most of the time."

"Suppose you are right Marc," Tom straightened his jacket. "Leave it till we know a bit more."

"If you are moving round a bit Tom, how about pushing me to the lav, I can manage once I get there." Marcia shifted again.

Tanya looked impatient. "We got to do something; I can't stand all this waiting around. Auntie Molly might be really bad. You go Tom, I'll push Mum, there's a disabled toilet over there, she'll get out the chair okay once she's by the door. Leave our coats here or we'll never get another space."

Marcia put her odd feet to the floor, holding on to the arms of the wheelchair and pushed upwards. The resulting force propelled the chair backwards and she flew forward faster than she had anticipated.

"Christ, ain't there no brakes on this thing?" she shrieked as her body shot forward, feet staying where they were. Landing on all fours, Marcia resembled a distressed bear.

Tanya giggled as two kind people helped her up. "Oh thanks! That's Mum all over, she's always tripping over! Use your stick Mum! Here! I'll open the door."

Marcia grabbed her stick and proceeded to hobble through the wide entrance into the closet. She was in there some time before the alarm went off. Orange lights lit up the wall and the wailing siren was embarrassingly loud. There was no doubt where the emergency was."

Before Tanya could do anything, two nurses appeared and hammered on the door.

"Is everything alright in there? What's the problem? Do you need help?"

Tanya rammed her fist and shouted. "Mum! You Okay?"

A clatter was heard, and the door was about to be wrenched from the outside when Marcia appeared, very red in the face.

"Er, am so sorry…thought it was the light switch… trying to save a bit of leccy for you." Looking at the floor she shuffled past the silent glares and slunk back into her chair.

Apologies were about to be offered, when the events were interrupted by Tom, who appeared a little out of breath and somewhat agitated. Ignoring the scene, he was more intent on partaking of news.

"Molly's alive!" He gasped. "The doc said, but he wants to talk to Marcia first. Something about ID."

Marcia beamed at the news, then looked perplexed.

"What's ID? Is that what she got?"

"Identification Mum, they need to make sure who they got."

Hating anything to do with authority, Marcia dreaded any interaction with officials. Molly always dealt with that kind of thing. Recollections of the fiasco that occurred with the Registrar when Tanya was born, and again when her mother died, caused her eye to twitch rapidly.

Tanya, completely ignorant to her mother's plight, could not contain her excitement at the prospect of seeing Molly, briefly explained to her mother. "Auntie Molly hasn't got any of her stuff, has she? They will want to know where she lives and all that, I expect. We'll come with you, it's nothing to worry about. Come on.... let's go...." Grabbing the wheelchair, she turned towards the clinical corridor. "Which way!!!"

Tom smiled and followed on; his comments falling on deaf ears. "I gave the paramedics her bag, but it'll be nothing much, they have to fill out a few forms that's all. We'll find out what is what and then we can see her!"

Space was somewhat limited in the small consultation room, but all three insisted on sticking together like glue. Tanya and Tom were not persuaded to leave Molly's 'sister', though that would have been the hospital protocol. The consultant, assessing the visitation, was not totally inflexible and condescended that a group meeting would be acceptable under the circumstances.

Mr Jameson shuffled the papers in the file and looked kindly at Marcia. Firstly, apologising for the delay, he carried on to explain that the on-call doctor felt it best if he came over after surgery and spoke to the next of kin."

Tom looked grave. "So, it's bad news then?" his face crumpled.

Mr Jameson took a deep breath. "Well, it was certainly a heart attack, but with the right treatment, the condition should be managed. In the meantime, we are giving a bit of a hand with breathing. Hopefully, everything will be sorted in due course. For the minute, there's a few things we have to establish to make sure he doesn't have another."

Marcia stared at the floor, praying the formal man in the white coat was not going to address her. Her prayers were not answered.

"Now then, Marcia, you say, you are, as you informed us, 'Molly's sister'." Mr Jameson carefully selected his words.

Marcia nodded, still without eye contact.

"And her name is Molly Emery", he continued.

Marcia lifted her head and nodded again; it was abundantly clear that she had no idea what to say.

Mr Jameson leaned forward and smiled, hoping to reassure them all. "It's important you tell me the truth Marcia, there are some things which need to be cleared up. I have to tell you we can find no records of a Molly Emery anywhere."

Tom, sensing Marcia's distress, stepped in. "Well actually, she ain't Marcia's sister, we only said that so's you would let us see her."

"Yeh." Tanya joined in. "She's sort of my Auntie, but not my Auntie, she's not my real Auntie, but Mums best friend and she looks after us. She ain't got no one else."

Marcia burst into tears. "She's my bestest friend for sure, and if anything happens to her, I won't know what to do!! She's going to die isn't she!!"

Tom put his arm around Marcia's lop-sided shoulders. "Marcia listen - she isn't going to die, think what the Doc said."

Mr Jameson looked kindly on, handed Marcia a box of tissues. "Do you know anything about a Martin Emery?" Marcia mopped her face. "What?" She asked.

Mr Jameson repeated his question, this time directed to them all. "Do you know anything about a Martin Emery?" Tom answered quizzingly. "Martin is Molly's brother, if you are trying to find him 'cos he's family, then you'll have a hard job, he left years ago, no one's seen him since, have they Marcia? She has a dad if you want us to get him, but he's a druggie and don't care about Molly."

Mr Jameson mopped his brow; things were more complicated than he had imagined. He had no choice but to break confidentiality, the facts had to be established, if treatment was going to be effective. The patient – unconscious and wired to life saving equipment – was the Martin under his care. The bank card and medication found in his handbag proved as such, along, of course, with the obvious examination revealing Molly's true physical form.

"There's no other way to put this. Normally, a patient is entitled to withhold any facts from his family, let alone friends, but in this case, you need to know, particularly if you think his father will be of no help. We have found traces of a hormone drug in the blood tests; it is a drug that is sold under several names and can vary slightly in strength and component. It is not legal and can have disastrous consequences for someone who already has a heart condition. It is essential we find out, as soon as possible, exactly what they were and what dosage he was taking."

Mr Jameson checked himself, he was not making much sense, and came to the decision that, with or without Martin's permission, someone had to be told as his patient was not going to survive this ordeal without help.

Tanya, Marcia and Tom stood speechless; they had little comprehension of what Mr Jameson was saying.

Silently contemplating the consultant's words, Tom digested the information and formed a conclusion.

"You mean 'she'. So, Molly was taking some kind of hormones, that doesn't surprise me, her looks are all important to her. They'll be in one of her bags or other, I can find them for you." He offered an explanation.

Drawing nearer to Tom, Mr Jameson pulled up another chair, "No, you do not understand, you better sit down."

"Molly is not Molly. I mean she is, sort of, that's what I guess she calls herself. Molly is Martin. She was born Martin and looks like has been living his life as a woman. Transgender is one term, but there are many. Martin is obviously happier living as female, it's more common than you think. He is still your best friend Marcia. Still the same person."

Marcia spluttered. Tom put his head in his hands, and Tanya dropped her bag onto the floor.

"Don't be bloody ridiculous!" Marcia shrieked, struggling out of the wheelchair. "You got the wrong person, that's for sure. You take us to our Moll NOW!!"

Mr Jameson sat calmly and looked at Marcia. "I am sorry, it is a shock, had you no idea at all?"

Tom raised his head, and his expression of disbelief was evident.

"Of course, we had no idea!" He answered for them all. "Don't you think we would have said when the paramedics came? Are you sure? I mean, ARE YOU ABSOLUTELY SURE?"

"Did you not notice anything strange when they were administering CPR?"

Tom shrugged. "Not really, it was all happening so fast, I don't think we were taking anything much in."

Mr Jameson, reluctant to interfere further, drew the subject to a close.

"Why don't you come and see him? I mean, her, well Molly, for a few minutes. Come back to the office and see me afterwards; I will answer any questions you have. I really need you to find the missing medication that he has been taking; I think it caused the heart attack."

Martin lay still and seemingly lifeless, attached to countless tubes, nose and mouth cruelly masked with clinical breathing apparatus. The regular hissing of the intake of air filled the room, disturbed only by the regular bleeping of the heart monitor. His eyes closed and his face pale, devoid of beauty; darkened only by the unfamiliar shadow daring to expose the eruption of new growth. The hospital gown, slightly gaped, revealed a multitude of tangled wires, taped to his flattened chest with no sign of the pert breasts Marcia so envied.

Drawing herself closer, Marcia steadied her torso against the safety bars, stretched out her hand and placed it on Molly's forehead. "It can't be, it's a mistake, this is our Moll, boobs or no boobs, who cares if they were falsies!"

Tom raised his arms and frowned. "This is crazy, it's definitely Molly. We would have known; she would have said... wouldn't she?"

Tanya leant against the bare wall, surprisingly calmed. Unflustered, flippant as any normal young girl, taking it all in her stride.

"Well, there's only one way to find out for sure Mum, look under the gown, if she has a willy then my Auntie is my Uncle!"

"TANYA!" Marcia shrieked, "Don't be so bloody rude!"

"Why not? It's the only way to find out for sure. I'll do it Mum! I never seen a real one before, but I know what it looks like; Bella showed me a picture in school the other day. She said they're called dicks, but Michelle said they're called willies, and that's what Brian Wainwright called his in the playground. He said his willie was itchy. That's why he was scratching it down his trousers. I think willie is a better name for it than dick." Tanya straightened, without any embarrassment sauntered towards the bed.

"Wha….?" Marcia's jaw dropped, brain frozen, she could no longer comprehend what was happening and slumped, in a daze, into the chair beside the bed.

Immediately Tom intervened and stepped into Tanya's path before any more damage was done.

"Leave it out Tan! Give her, sorry, him…. er…. Well, it…. Oh, fuck I don't know…. Give Molly a bit of privacy!!"

"Well! I am sorry for being interested, but Auntie Molly's been there since I were born, and if she's a Tranny I want to know!"

Regaining some sort of consciousness, Marcia became even more confused.

"A Tranny? What's music got to do with it? Anyway, Moll's more interested in our old record player, she ain't one for the radio."

"Marcia! Tanya doesn't mean a transistor radio, she's talking about a transsexual, transgender or whatever they call it!"

"A what?" Marcia squeaked in dismay. The situation was becoming worse by the minute.

"A man living his life as a woman, like the doc said." Tom endeavoured to explain in more detail.

"I ain't stupid; I heard of people like that, but not what they are called. Uncle Robert was one when he got older, cos he changed his name."

Tom had no idea what Marcia was talking about. "You only met your Uncle Robert twice – as far as I know. Once, when you were a baby, and once in the hospital when he was ill, before he died. Lily hardly ever talked about her brother and, from what she said, you were lucky to be allowed at the funeral.... And that was only because if you hadn't, there would hardly be anyone to wave goodbye."

"Yeh, I know; but he changed into a woman, and he changed his name, Mum said so lots of times, and that's why we never saw him."

"He didn't Marcia! He was still Robert until the end, unless there is something Lil never told me or Grandad.... which I doubt."

"You are quite wrong Tom' He was called a 'Miss' not a 'Mr'."

Fascinated by the thought that there may be two 'Trannies' in the family, Tanya spoke up.

"So, this Uncle Robert bloke, was called Miss Roberta, or Miss Bobby Duncan?"

"No, Tanya. Granny said, he changed his name to Miss Guided. She said lots of times - 'Uncle Robert became Miss Guided'. I didn't really think about it 'til now."

"For God's sake!" Tom threw his arms in the air. "Give it a rest! It don't help matters now does it. It's no good, it's got to be sorted and it's a man's job!" Tom marched over to the bed. "I am going to do a quick shifty and we will know for sure - don't you dare look."

"I can't see it then. Oh, come on, just a little peek?"

"No way, Tanya! Don't be so disrespectful, this is serious stuff!"

"Spoilsport," Tanya grumbled.

Tom peeled back the covers and slid his fingers to the edge of the gown, pulling it gently, hoping it would be high enough to achieve the objective without causing any grief. Looking at Molly's unmoving face, he continued, flipping it up quickly.

"Fuck that!" he yelled, closing his eyes tight, dropping the gown and blanket at lightning speed.

Marcia and Tanya stared in anticipation of a result.

"Well?" They chirped together.

Tom's face was redder than an overripe beetroot. "The doc's right..." he whispered.

"So, Auntie Molly has a willy!!!??? And she's a Tranny???!! COOL! Wait till I tell the kids at school!"

Marcia gulped, reality sinking in. "You'll do no such thing Tanya! Molly is our Molly, we must do what she wants, don't be so bloody selfish and think about it. Your Auntie is here, badly ill."

"Your mum is right Tan, it's all a huge shock, keep it quiet. If Molly's kept it secret all this long, she won't want it blabbed. She will have reasons and we mustn't do anything until she comes round.... If, she comes round." Tom turned to look at the being led there, sad and vulnerable, clinging on to the very existence of life.

Looking at the floor, Tanya apologised shamefully, as the severity of the situation sunk in.

Marcia, once again, moved close to her friend. Whatever had happened, she knew her heart would break if she lost her soulmate. Eyes filling with tears, drops overflowed in abundance, winding their way past her odd features and onwards to mark the crisp sheets. Turning to Tom and her daughter, she whispered between the sobs.

"This is our Moll... This is our Moll... an' we don't care what she is... she is our Moll, and we need her."

Simultaneously, Tanya and Tom rushed over to Marcia, flinging themselves to her odd shape, crying and hugging relentlessly.

In some other distant place, Martin dreamed of Angels, enveloping his fragile form with protective, caring arms, and distant voices singing gently, resounding their love.

It was some weeks later, that a reluctant Molly accepted the invitation to reside in Clover close whilst she regained strength and confidence. There was no chance that Molly could return to the tower block and the unpredictability of her father was a danger in itself. Tanya, not impressed with being ousted from her room and lumped in with her mother, eventually accepted the situation on the promise it was 'short term' and soon, Molly would be back to her usual flits between the hovel of the flat and safety of Marcia's small abode.

The only saving grace, in Tanya's eyes, was that her Auntie was really her uncle, and it was an exciting secret to be kept... allegedly. How long she would be able to keep her mouth shut and not brag to her mates that she had major 'gossip' one would never know. Her constant bombardment of questions wore her aunt out, and Marcia soon had to step in to put a halt to it all.

"How do you keep those boobs on? Do you shave your legs? Do you get hairs on your chin? How do you go to the toilet? Do you fancy the postman?" and her constant frustrated reply of; 'I was only asking!' was, quite frankly, getting on every one's nerves.

The last straw came when Tanya flicked over the page of Cosmopolitan and showed Molly a new range of revealing underwear and asked her how she kept her willy in that.

Marcia's angry reaction told her that she had pushed the boat too far. From then on, she resolved to be 'nice'.

Whatever the attitudes, all the family were immensely pleased to see that Molly's progress was good and all the ongoing tests were proving positive. Mr Jameson was pleasantly understanding, and new, safe medication was prescribed to alleviate depression and supress certain areas of unwanted manly natural responses. Martin, mortified and embarrassed, slowly realised that he should never have doubted the love and support that he received from all that now knew of his chosen path. He knew he should have told them a long time ago; however, he still had not been able to come clean with the remainder of his burden and once again, hid behind a wall of self-protection.

Thus, the months uneventfully passed, worries buried; wounds healed; acceptance embedded and some sense of normality – if that was at all possible – returned to Clover Close.

Chapter Three
The Holiday

For Tanya, the months of monotony took its toll; nothing seemed to be exciting anymore. Auntie Molly seemed well enough and her mother - just plodded along as usual, content in her little world. To be honest, Tanya was a bored teenager. So, it was on one particular sunny day, in her infinite wisdom - not to mention the peer pressure from delectable 'Michelle,' who was off to France yet again - Tanya decided she wanted a holiday. After a week of making the whole family's life a complete misery, Tom decided he would try to sort something out. It would not be France, but he had one of his 'brainwaves' that might keep everyone happy.

It had not even crossed Marcia's mind that they would ever spend one night away from the house, let alone a few days. Funds were the major issue, along with the fuss and bother of transportation and accommodation. No-one on the estate had proper holidays, except of course, Posh Pru from number seven. Her husband was always going on holiday, or so she said. For all her airs and graces, everyone knew he had been caught yet again and gone to see the queen.

The day came when Tom, full of his usual enthusiasm, burst through the front door of Marcia's tiny house with a huge grin on his face.

"You never guess what I got hold of today!"

Marcia, being used to all and sundry useful and useless items appearing, turned her head away from the TV. "What now, Tom?"

She did not mean to be ungrateful and was truly thankful for all the support Tom gave her, but there was a kitchen full of gadgets, supposedly to make their lives easier, none which she had any idea how to use properly. She did try using the blender once. Tanya had showed her how to put bananas in, together with a cup of milk. All you had to do was 'turn the knob one click' she said. Marcia's ham-fisted lack of skill only resulted in turning the knob full circle. This, coupled with the fact she had omitted to replace the lid, had disastrous consequences. Suffice to say, her hair styled itself into spikey albino dreadlocks and Tom had to repaint the ceiling.

Tom plonked himself down in the chair opposite Marcia.

"It's mint Marcia, just the job for a holiday!"

"I quite like mints, though no reason to go on holiday, I'll just eat them here."

Tom laughed. "No Marcia, it's a saying, 'it's mint' means it's fantabulous!"

"Ooo... I like fantabulous things, what is it, Tom?" Marcia was now curious.

"A tent Marcia, a great big, lovely tent! So now you can have a holiday!"

Marcia grimaced. "A tent? A TENT?? How we gonna manage that then?"

"Aw come on Marc, I got it special, I got it all planned out, you won't have to do a thing!"

Marcia was not at all keen, but as soon as Tanya found out about Tom's plans there was no turning back. Even Molly changed her mind; the Doc said she needed a break. The pair of them were well up for it and had already packed enough clothes for three years, even though they weren't going for a few weeks yet. Marcia took some persuading, but being satisfied with all the safety issues, namely use of a wheelchair, donated by Mrs Benson, eventually, started to look forward to the event...

"You sure Mrs Benson don't mind me using this chair? it's a bit of a squeeze. What if it breaks?" Marcia was panicking before she even got out of the house.

"Marcia, I told you a thousand times!" Tom raised his eyes to the ceiling. "She don't want it no more, Norman died a few weeks ago, I told you remember. Died on the commode! What a hoot!"

"I know he died. It's not funny Tom; poor bloke."

"What's not funny?" Tanya poked her head around the door, beads of sweat on her brow and slightly out of breath.

"What's up with you?" Tom was still laughing.

"Nothing! Just lumped me suitcase down the stairs, not that YOU noticed. If you wouldn't mind putting IT in the truck!" She retorted haughtily. "Have I missed something then or what?"

Marcia looked at her daughter, Tanya's behaviour was becoming more like Molly's every day. She loved them both, but everything had to be just so, right down to the very tiniest of detail, sometimes, they were both such hard work!

"We were only saying poor old Norman died on the commode." Tom couldn't stop giggling. "Oh, come on, you have to laugh; arse stuck in the hole, they couldn't get him out. Surprised rigor didn't set in, then he would have been buried in an L shaped coffin."

That was it, Marcia and Tanya cracked. The thought of Norman being stuck in a commode, stiff as a board, trousers round his ankles was too much. The three of them creased up in hysterics. Marcia slid to the floor beside the wheelchair and Tanya held on to the doorframe to stop herself slithering to the ground.

Tom crouched into a sitting position and contorted his mouth, emitting groaning noises. Wonder what...sort... of grave...stone they would put on that!"

Marcia gasped for breath. "F….For Christ sake, stop it Tom, any more and I'll pee myself!"

"I can't help it" he wheezed, "Here lies the body of N…Norman B..Benson, D…. died on the lav with no pants on!"

Such was the hilarity they did not hear the totter of heels trotting up the garden path. Molly appeared, donned in a bright orange shift dress, with matching shoes and handbag. Not the apparel for a camping holiday, but Molly was Molly and that was that.

"Come on! You lot!! I'm ready for the off! Suitcases in the back! What you all doing down there?"

Tom heaved himself up, gave up on the wheelchair transportation, folded it expertly and tossed it into the back of the truck, along with Tanya's heavy suitcase.

"Sticks it is then Marcia, come on!" he shouted. "Moll and Tanya will help you!"

"I'm not that stuck, I can walk a bit you know!" Marcia chuckled. "Might need a bit of help getting into that truck of yours though!"

"It's not as small as the old blue one Marcia, there is a bit more room; it will be fine."

Marcia remembered the old truck only too well, being stuck in a mattress in the back was far from fun and the ensuing birth of her daughter in the river even less so!

The aging pick-up had served them well, until one fateful day it decided to give up the ghost completely and no tinkling around by Tom could force it to do otherwise. It was a shame it all happened outside Mrs Marchent's house.

'Mad' Mrs Marchent, as everyone cruelly referred to, was a quaint old lady in her late seventies. Dressed in her famous flowery apron with her hair pinned high, she had lived for an age, in the same house, content with spending her time washing the steps of the front porch several times a day. Over the years, this had progressed to cleaning the path, fence and gate, together with a variety of concrete squirrels, birds, dogs and gnomes. She used enough soap to clean the barnacles off the Titanic.

Marcia was very fond of her, and totally forgave her for causing her mother's coffin to paraglide down the garden path on the day of the funeral. In the main, everyone accepted her for what she was – a harmless old lady, who liked things clean.

To say Mrs Marchent was a little upset when Tom's truck popped to a halt outside her haven was an understatement. The resulting explosion caused her to jump so high, she lost control of her work tools and the precious blue bucket of fresh soapy water flew into the hedge. It was only fate that she avoided the piece of rusty exhaust pipe catapulting across the grass. Had it been a few minutes before it would have been more than her garden gnome that lost its head.

To make matters worse, the offending piece of metal was enveloped in a cloud of black dust, thick enough to conceal a polar bear on an iceberg. Poor Mrs Marchent was so shocked, she just sat there, looking like a dejected chimney sweep, surveying a whole garden full of escaped soot.

It took Tom a whole week of pacification, three new buckets and ten multipacks of Watchco's extra fragrant deluxe soap, before she eventually calmed down.

No amount of tinkering and jigging around could persuade the old girl to get going, so sadly, it was destined for the crush pot.

His 'new' vehicle looked more like he had negotiated an unsuccessful swap at the scrapyard. It's dark green exterior dented and scratched was no improvement on its predecessor. However, despite the outwardly appearance, the engine was 'sound' and despite the grim appearance of tattered and worn fabric of the interior; it was indeed bigger and more comfortable…for two or three people at most.

With a pop and a squeeze, and a heave and a shove, Marcia and Molly squashed into the cab, followed by Tanya, who plonked herself on Molly's lap. Tom climbed into the driving seat.

"You can't sit so far up Tanya, you'll have to slip forward a bit, I'll get done good and proper if we get stopped!"

"Where am I supposed to sit then, on the bloody floor and ruin this skirt?" Tanya shrieked.

"TANYA!" Marcia snapped, "Tom's doing his best, it's either there or in the back on one of those old chairs Tom has to drop off on the way back….and mind you don't step on those Watchco bags, Tom's Becs got all that food for us, and in her condition and all!"

"Oh, she's ok, glad to do something, I think. Still got a few weeks to go yet, she's right fed up now." Tom paused for thought briefly. He and Becky had only been together for a year, they doted on each other. Though unexpected, and daunting, he was nervously looking forward to becoming a father for the first time… Or as far as he knew, he often jokingly bantered.

Molly shifted this way and that, eventually jamming herself upright and backwards, enabling Tanya to half sit on the edge of the seat between her legs, which were stretched wider than a midget riding an elephant.

"This is not funny; my dress is almost above my waist."

"Well, we wouldn't want your bits showing now would we, or me squashing them even more than you already have!" Tanya shrieked with laughter.

"Shut it!" Marcia piped up, glaring at her daughter with a disapproving look...well... as much as she could muster with two odd eyes.

Molly smirked, "It's ok Marc, you know what she's like, it's quite a laugh, really!"

"It's only a couple of hours, we can stop off and have a stretch." Tom pacified his passengers, started the engine, and chugged off with ungainly leaps, sending them all forwards with a jolt, then back again.

"Be ok in a min, clutch is a bit iffy to start with."

Tanya lurched forward and banged her face on the dashboard. "Bloody hell, steady on Tom," she yelled.

Marcia, too busy shifting herself back into her seat, ignored the swearing and was beginning to wonder whether it was all worth it. She would much rather sit in front of the tele munching chocolate.

In fact, the journey itself was not that bad, albeit a little uncomfortable. Once the vehicle had stopped all the jerking and banging, everyone began to relax. The sun was shining and as they drew near the coast, the fresh air and smell of the sea lifted their spirits. Marcia leaned towards the window pressing Molly and Tanya sideways.

"Watch out! You'll be havin' us out the door in a minute." Molly moved sideways as far as constrictions would allow.

The gentle breeze flowing through the cab, regenerating life into the stale, battered interior. Marcia breathed deeply, savouring the unfamiliar odour.

"Don't that smell nice? Bit different from our old house ain't it?" A crooked smile spread across her odd features, perhaps this was going to be a good holiday after all.

"Here we are!" Tom beamed, "Up this lane and your house awaits!" How he loved making his family happy.

Marcia briefly hoped maybe it was a house, and not a tent. Still, a holiday was a holiday, and she had never had one, so she too, was gratefully excited.

The truck bumped up the dirt track and turned left, through an old wooden gate, into a large green field dotted with a few brightly coloured tents and a couple of splendid caravans.

"This is it!" he couldn't contain himself; he was in his element and couldn't wait to see the reaction. "Wait till you see it!"

"See what?" Molly enquired gingerly.

"The tent! Told you I would sort it! Me and a couple of mates came down yesterday and fixed it all up for you."

Marcia was lost for words. She never failed to be astounded by Tom's generosity and kindness and was always full of thanks, whatever he turned up with. Tom would just shrug it all off and his answer was always the same, 'family is family, that's what we do.'

"So, we don't have to put it up?" Molly grinned.

"Course not, how the hell do you think we would put up a tent?" Tanya clambered her way over Molly, completely disregarding the stare of disapproval and flapping of hands, grabbed the truck door handle, threw it open, promptly lost her balance and fell onto the grass. Not being in the least bit bothered, up she jumped, pulled down her skirt, and howled with laughter. The anticipation of the days to come was too great to worry about anything.

Waving her arms impatiently Tanya beckoned the rest of the clan. "Come on. Hurry up. Let's go!"

Tom grinned and started the engine again, "It's over there, behind that hedge, all private and everything, follow the truck Tan."

"We're all going on a summer holiday!" He sang at the top of his voice, joined by Marcia resounding her high pitch squeak, until she banged her head on the roof as the wheels dipped into a trench and forced their way out.

The truck trundled its cumbersome route across the field, bouncing on the uneven surface, causing unrhythmic thumps of old wooden seating, a fine enhancement to the chorus of constipated owls, echoing across the meadow.

Janet plumped up the cushions on her spanking new sun bed and proceeded to drape her torso across the yellow stripes. She had been careful to pick the design and colour; it perfectly matched the large awning which protruded magnificently from the shiny white caravan, or 'mobile abode,' as she called it.

"Another Martini my sweet?" Roger handed his wife the glass, complete with cherries and umbrella.

"That would be fab darling, and one of those brandy snaps if you wouldn't mind? After all, we are on holiday, hang the diet until we get back."

Roger pecked Janet on the cheek and downed a whisky, "You have the eyes of Madonna and the figure of Cleopatra my darling. Gad, this malt is good, I'll just top up and brandy snaps coming u…. what the fuck is that?"

"Language Roger!! You know what we said. Now that you have that new job, we are upmarket people!"

Janet pulled her sunglasses down on her nose and stared at the old pick-up thundering across the field, leaving a trail of smoke as it travelled on. It seemed to be full of odd people singing, followed by a shrieking child, skipping around it like some demented goblin…And what was all that rubbish in the back?

"Oh my God," she blurted. "It's fucking Gypsies."

Having clumsily vacated the truck, Marcia and Molly joined Tanya. All three were motionless and silent, fixed in a trance of mixed admiration and disbelief, staring at the somewhat grubby, but magnificent structure before them.

"Well, what do you think? Isn't it great?" Tom rushed forward and pulled open the large tent flaps, tying them back each side to form an entrance fit for an opening performance of Swan Lake.

Molly was the first to speak, actually, squeak. "It's a marquee Tom, it's massive."

"And it's round, It's brill. Look Mum. Plenty of room for wheelchair and everything!"

Tanya rushed inside, running full circle, twice, and emerged triumphant. "There's a table, chairs and beds, and a rail to put clothes on. There's a little cooker and everything, there's loads of space! Even a little room on the side."

"That's for the port-a-loo, you see, I thought of everything! Got it from the builders up the road, it's a bit taller than the ones you get in the shops, you should be able to manage it if you can't get to the shower block. I put in a light in as well, attached to a car battery, should last you a couple of days at least. I'll be down with Becs and Grandad at the weekend anyway, just for the day like."

"You could stay till Sunday. There's plenty of room. Better put up some fairy lights for Bubbs, and a tree." Tanya joked.

"Not a bad idea Tan. Some little lights would keep Bernie happy that's for sure." Molly chirped in.

"We'll see how he is; you know how he gets." Tom saddened for a moment, briefly reflecting on times when his grandad was compos mentis, before returning to his jolly self. "Come on then Marcia, your boudoir beckons." Bowing before the queen, he invited her presence.

"Boudoir? You haven't gone and bought perfume as well?" Marcia replied.

Molly placed her hand on Marcia's arm, who gently pushed the support away. Using her sticks, she toddled forward with unusual adeptness and stood inside the arena trying to take it all in. There were indeed three small put-up beds, complete with plumped up pillows and pink woolly blankets.

Four white patio chairs inviting guests, grouped around a slightly lop-sided table, upon which stood two plastic champagne flutes. The third having toppled to the floor, rolling onto an old faded, slightly threadbare carpet, which was carefully spread out, ready to be useful once again.

Tom, seemed to have thought of everything, even a couple of old fold up chairs and a somewhat dusty blue umbrella lay waiting to be resurrected, re-born into the sunshine and sandy shores.

Still lost for words, Marcia swallowed hard, tears filling her eyes; this was the best holiday house in the world.

Tanya could not contain her excitement at all. "I'm going to get the food!" she shouted, hurling herself through the entrance and pelting off towards the truck.

Molly, strangely silent, guided Marcia towards the chairs. "Well, Tom has done us proud Marc, let's make some tea and all have a rest."

As the sun wound down the day and disappeared into the sea, Tom, secured in the fact that the ladies were reasonably safe, trundled off in his truck, leaving promises to return with more goodies. Three tired holiday makers, suitably full of tea, sandwiches, and cake, prepared to retire for the night.

The largest of the beds was allocated to Marcia, for obvious reasons. The other two, though roughly the same size, one seemed more level than the other.

"I want this one!" Tanya threw herself onto the more stable looking frame. It creaked as she draped herself across the metal struts.

"Please yourself why don't you Modom!" Molly sarcastically addressed Tanya in her poshest voice. "I'll just make do with this four- poster, shall I?"

Marcia glared at them both. "Pack it in, what difference does it make? Stop arguing, we're supposed to be on holiday."

"Hardly the point Marcia," Molly stretched out, retracted her arms swiftly, grabbing on to the sides of her bed as it wobbled. "She shouldn't be so presumptuous."

"She's not, she don't need a pump, they ain't blow up beds. I am well chuffed with mine...if I can get in it." Marcia giggled, well used to her own clumsiness.

Tanya sighed. "Just sit down on one end and lever your feet over mum, just like you do on the settee, but lower. It's easy." She pulled the blankets around herself. "And quite cosy too."

Never wasting an opportunity to encourage Marcia's independence, and, of course, to savour the entertainment, Molly put her hands behind her head and watched with anticipation.

Sitting down was the easy bit, the flipping up of the end of the bed was something else. Marcia found herself twisting sideways and up, part of her pinning down the pillows, with the scrunched-up blanket piled on her face. The rest of her in remained mid -air, legs flayed desperately as her three and eight looked for an anchor.

"Don't bay bere laughink," she mumbled, pulling the cloth from her mouth. "Give us a hand, or I'll be here for a bloody week!"

"Roll over Marcia, roll on the floor off the t-top, and s-sit in the middle next t-time." Molly shook like a jelly, holding on to the sides of her camp bed to avoid a collapse.

Tanya could not speak, her pink fluffy blanket tight round her face mopping up the tears. She twitched her legs up and down, banging them down to detract from the howls that were escaping from her muffled lips.

Marcia wriggled and squirmed, to no avail, until, afraid of infinite suffocation, Molly came to the rescue. Tugging on one end, Marcia's heavy form holding the other, brute force returned the bed to its level position.

"Phew!" Marcia adjusted her position, re-arranged the covers, took a deep breath, and relaxed. "Actually, it's quite comfy when you get used to it. I could quite drift off." She yawned.

"Thank god for that!" Molly raised her eyes to the roof and put together her hands. "Let's hope it lasts the night."

"Me too," piped Tanya. "I'm dead. We left the light on, and your stick is by the bed, in case you need to get up."

But Marcia was not listening, flaked out, her rhythmic snores resounding in circles as it followed the contours of the jaded canvas.

Janet sat bolt up-right; her paisley padded sleeping bag crumpled around her slim waist.

"Roger?" She hissed.

Her husband, filled with more than a few glasses of Scottish malt, grunted.

"Roger!" Janet hissed louder. "Roger, wake up!"

Roger opened a bleary, blood-shot eye and answered his wife with utter disinterest.

"What?" he mumbled.

"Roger, for goodness' sake!"

"What?"

"There's animals in the field, I think it's pigs. I can hear them snorting. What if it's a wild boar after our food Roger? What about the new awning and my matching yellow cushions? It will all be destroyed. Wake up!!"

"Go back to sleep Janet…" Roger sighed, re-adjusted his position, and closed his eyes. "No boar is going to eat bacon, that would be cannibalism. Anyway, there aren't any boars around here… Go back to sleep…"

Janet pulled the blankets over her face and wrapped her arms around her knees, bundling herself into a comfort position and rocked. "Boar for sure," she mumbled to herself.

Slinking down into her pillows, squishing her Vidal Sassoon foam rollers against her ears. Janet nervously lay as best she could. Far from the expected transformation to a Greek goddess, the curlers looked more likely to accentuate her sponge jelly skin to a full-blown trifle, complete with artificial cream topping. Distant rumbling continued, Janet lay listening, nervously twitching her fingers as they twisted the silky fabric of her gown. There would be little sleep for her that night.

Molly placed her arms behind her head and tried to relax. Marcia's snoring did not bother her. Tanya said it was like having the 10.40 from Bloomsbury zooming round your bedroom, but like many regular disturbances, you got used to the resonance and barely noticed the noise. For Molly, the peace and quiet was blatantly apparent, quite unlike her life at home, but already she was realising the torment of secrets held was surfacing in abundance. Time seemed to slow and beckon the curtain of suppression to unveil, releasing the anguish that dwelled behind.

It was rarely that she cried, but as she watched the sleeping contentment of the two people that were more important than life itself, silent signs of regret trickled down her cheeks. Mournful for the lack of courage and sadness within her heart for the years of cowardly action, preventing the formation of a true bond between father and daughter, she was determined to put it all right - soon.

Save for the odd hoot of and owl, the squeak of a mouse, the snort of a Marcia, the comparative still of the night passed swiftly on, until the first sound of dawn blessed the countryside as the sun opened her eyes and prepared to warm the earth.

"Cock a doodle doooooooo!"

"What on earth is that?" Marcia opened her eyes.

Tanya, already up, full of enthusiasm, folded her wash bag into her towel. "It's only a cockerel Mum, don't you remember? Slimy Sid had one down the allotment - Until it got battered."

Molly stretched out lazily and smiled. "Oh, come to think I remember that. Poor thing, I reckon that old bloke next door did it in. You know, the weird one with the glass eye that glared at you, even when he was asleep outside on that old sofa of his."

Marcia heaved herself to a sitting position, making sure she held onto the sides of the bed. No way was she risking any kind of flight again.

"A cock what? Slimy Sid had a what? What kind of talk is that Tanya my girl? And as for that Fred, his eyes ain't much different to mine, are they? Get me up our Tan, am coming with you, I need a pee desperate and I ain't going to use that potty poo thing if I can help it. God knows how I hung on to it all night, that's a first."

Wrapping her candlewick dressing gown around herself, Marcia accepted the help to aid her mobility, until she was able to use her stick, clumsily banging it on the ground as she linked arms with Tanya and emerged into the country air.

A young scruffy hound levered onto its haunches, one ear perked, whilst the other limply lay. Bright eyes expectantly watched every move as mother and daughter made their way across the meadow.

"What a sweet little dog." Marcia huffed. It took all her efforts to proceed, but being laden with a very full bladder, even more determination to complete the required task. The dog, emitted an enthusiastic bark, wagged its tail, and trotted across the field towards them, staying some distance, pausing every so often as not to overtake.

Thankfully the shower block was not far, it would have been quite difficult to wheel the chair over the clods. Marcia was pleased she managed the expedition without incident.

"These showers are mint!" Tanya screamed. "You have to have one. Look at the spray thing, it's huge, and the water is boiling. Auntie Molly will be love it!"

"Yes, and Molly will stroll over on her own, when there is no one else around I expect." Marcia smiled to herself. Her friend had long since learned to avoid public facilities like the plague.

As for Marcia, she decided to take things one at a time, a shower, yes, later, then she would be happy to smell like Polo mints. For now, she was content to relieve her exploding bladder, muster up some energy to flannel herself down, brush her crooked teeth, comb her straggly locks, and attempt the trip back.

An age later, the pair appeared into the sunlight, ready to face the day. The dog was still there. Tanya stroked its head, which only seemed to make the dog more determined to follow their every step. Perfectly content, the animal sat patiently outside the tent whilst the three ladies ate cornflakes, drank tea, and planned the day's activities.

The trip to the beach did not, as you can imagine, turn out the way exactly as expected.

Tanya looked down at the bag she was supposed to carry. "How the hell am I supposed to carry all that, when I have my own stuff to take?" She protested.

"Well, you have to! And I don't see why you need all that, even I'm not taking makeup, nor nail varnish." exclaimed Molly. I have the picnic bag and the chairs. You are in charge of the towels and the cossies. Your mum has the brolly."

"I need it, I am on holiday, I never been to a beach, and I need it all, I seen it on the TV on Baywatch. I am allowed nail varnish now; I am thirteen after all!"

"Thirteen or not, you don't need to take it to the beach!" shouted Marcia. "I am sure that David Huskydog person didn't have all this stuff, and I don't see why I have to have this wonky sun brolly, strapped to the wheelchair, it looks like a flaming helicopter. The prongs are sticking out one side."

Molly dropped the bag and chairs to the ground and put her hands on her hips, creasing the shiny satin beach dress in the process.

"Look you two." Her face was stern. "If you want to go to the beach, that's the way it is. I have no idea how far it is; you will need the brolly cos of the sun; the cover has just slipped off a bit that's all. It's going to be bad enough wheeling the chair up to that path, let alone carry all this lot!"

"Well, sorry to be a bother, I will just stay here if it's too much hassle!" Marcia retorted haughtily.

Molly softened. "Sorry Marc, it will be ok, tell you what, you walk to the path on your sticks, and I will push the chair with all the stuff in it. You can sit in it once we've got on the tarmac. Ok with you MADAM!" her voice raised in crescendo as she glared at Tanya.

Tanya looked down at the ground, screwed up her face in defiance, and reluctantly helped to load up the wheelchair, refusing to relinquish her pink raffia shopping bag, crammed with bits and bobs that no one would need on a beach.

Negotiating the uneven grassy ground was not as bad as Marcia first thought. Her stick got stuck in a hole which nearly sent her boomeranging back to the tent, but apart from that she was proud of herself to reach the path without further issue.

Of course, Tanya was miles ahead of them all and stood further down the path waving her arms so enthusiastically, her bag slipped down to her shoulders.

"Come on!!"

Marcia was thankful to heave herself into the chair, whilst Molly held it still. Being a little heavier than Norman Benton, the seat groaned as it moulded into the strangest shape it had ever encountered, it was not used to being lopsided. To top it all, with two different sized feet plonked on the base, it must have wondered how many people it was carrying.

"You ok Marc?" She asked, loading all the bags on her friend's lap.

"Yeh, fine. Not much space left for anything else," she chuckled.

"Maybe not but looks like this little fellow wants to tag along." Molly turned as she heard the barks of their new follower. "Ah, we can't leave you there, hop on."

"There's really not much r…." Marcia objected. Too late, the dog had readily accepted the invite and pounced onto Marcia's lap, licking her odd features in immense gratitude.

"Okay okay! Squash yourself down here before you stick all the hairs up me nose, and we lose everything." Marcia was shrieking with laughter. Who could resist cuddles like these?

"What's his name Marcia? He has a collar on, though he doesn't seem to belong to anyone does he? I reckon he's not very old. He's taken a shine to you that's for sure."

The dog did not resist as Marcia hooked her finger under the frayed blue collar. "There isn't a tag, there's a metal bit on the edge though. I can't read it, but it begins with a J, it's very faint."

Molly leaned over, scratched the dog under its chin and was rewarded with a slobbering tongue.

"Well then," she kindly said. "What's your name? It says Jacobs, Marc."

"He can't be called Jacobs, surely."

That's what it says." Molly giggled. "Jacobs it is then. Off we go Jacobs; onwards and upwards to the beach!"

The path to the cove sloped gently down. Marcia breathed in the sea air, tasting the unfamiliar salty traits as the sun warmed her bones. Looking down she could see the sand, shimmering, gleaming, dotted with the black spots of seaweed discarded by the waves on their retreat. It was all that she had imagined, all that Molly had told her it would be and more. She thought to herself she was the luckiest person in the world.

Molly stopped for a minute, taking in the view. "Oh Marcia, it's fabulous, so peaceful, have you ever seen anything so beautiful?"

"It is, Moll, I don't know what to say, it's wonderful."

Peace didn't last long. Tanya, having reached the beach and was charging her way back up, shrieking with delight.

"Come on. It's mint. Not many people at all! Hurry up!!"

Marcia wondered how a beach could be mint. Tanya thought everything was mint, it was all very odd, but she could see her enthusiasm and was eager to join in.

Giving the wheels a helping hand, the chair moved forward without Molly's help.

"See Moll? I can do it all by myself." Marcia giggled and pushed the wheels again – with a little too much vigour.

Molly could only watch in horror as the wheelchair gained momentum, veering from left to right over the small path as Marcia tried unsuccessfully to control it. Jacobs sat upright, barking loudly as it continued to travel rapidly in Tanya's direction.

"Where's the bloody brake!" Gone was the wonder and excitement, Marcia was now in a state of sheer terror.

"What brake!" Molly shouted. "I don't know!! Try that lever on the side, quick Marcia QUICK!"

Marcia leaned sideways, which only made the wheelchair tip onto one wheel as it scooted round the bend past Tanya, pelting her with the picnic bag in the process. "Great catch Tan!" Molly was now helpless, slumped on the ground creased up with laughter. "G...get the brake M..m...a.... that lever by the w-h....ee...." Tanya could hardly speak. Marcia grabbed the grey catch on the side of the chair and pulled hard; too hard - SNAP! Off it came. "What? The f...nnnnnnnnoo!" she screamed.

Janet stretched out her long legs and lay back on the yellow striped sun bed. Although perfectly protected by a strategically placed lemon-fringed parasol, adjusting her hat and sunglasses to complete the overall picture of perfection was essential. Stretching out a pre-tanned hand, she reached over to the crisp blue cool box and delicately picked up the flask.

"This is fabulous darling," she drawled, and took a sip of cool martini, allowing the ice crystals to caress her plump red lips.

"Isn't it just my sweet!" Roger drank deeply from his matching dispenser. "It's so peaceful, so quiet, just look at that sea, so clear, so blue, one could be in the Bahamas don't you think?"

"Yes, it is, away from everything and everyone. That horrid Mr Berwick is going to be so jealous when we show them the photos." Janet curled her lip.

"Who cares about Mr Berwick, he's still stuck at the office, and we are here." Roger stood up and stretched back his arms, thrusting his flabby chest and ballooned stomach forward.

The force of a bag full of ham sandwiches and several cans of coke rammed into his neck and knocked him for six. Trying to stop himself falling, he ran, bent, arms flayed in front of him like a demented ape, before plummeting face down in the sand.

Janet spluttered and dropped her flask. "Good grief! What the hell is that?" She turned and stared unbelievingly at the scene, disregarding the cries for help from her husband.

Down the ramp it hurled. A demonic creature from the blue lagoon, in some sort of air transportation; blue parachute sheets flapping wildly as they tried to hang on to the crooked spokes.

Tanya jumped up, chased behind, leaping up and down like a frog on a trampoline, still laughing, oblivious to the potential consequences.

"Geromino!" She shrieked, "Go for it, Ma!"

Marcia knew she was in trouble when Tanya called her Ma... throwing her arms round Jacobs she clung on to him for dear life. This did her no favours when she hit the boardwalk leading to the beach. The wheelchair banged into the edge and stopped abruptly, springing violently up, then back.

Marcia flew through the air, faster than a circus performer ejected from a smoking cannon. Over the ramp she flew and somersaulted on to the soft sand. Jacobs landed on all fours and charged manically around, barking continuously, loving the game.

Molly kicked off her shoes and ran as fast as she could, past Tanya, who was still doubled up with laughter.

"Good God Marcia, you okay? What hurts?"

Rolling slowly onto her back Marcia groaned. "Just about everything. Good job I got all this blubber on me, or I would have been buggered for sure. Me arse hurts a bit."

Molly grabbed Marcia's hands and gently – or as gently as she could, given her size – and helped her to stand. She had survived falls before and this one wasn't much different. With the exception of a massive bruise on her behind and a shiner of a swollen eye, it was a miracle she came out relatively unscathed.

Tanya managed to fold the battered wheelchair. That too, had escaped major damage, but of course, it now had no brake. Carefully carrying the wonky contraption over the bumpy sands, she joined her aunt and mother.

Eventually, after numerous towels, garments, bags and other bits and bobs were collected, all three managed to collapse onto the picnic rug and burst into shrieks of merriment.

"You s...hould h....ave....see...een your...self mum...You should be.... In...the.... olym...pics...."

Molly couldn't be cross; she rarely was when the usual disasters happened. Over the years, she sort-of got used to it.

"I can see the funny side alright! Shall we have a sandwich? Oh, where's the bag?"

Roger, laden with the yellow sunbed, matching parasol, pale blue cool-box, and a large red and white striped beach bag, struggled towards the path. Janet held the offending weapon in one hand and a mangled sticky flask, covered with sand in the other and walked haughtily towards the three hysterical ladies.

"I think this is yours?" She sneered, throwing the Watchco bag onto the blanket as she passed. "And another thing; you keep that dog of yours under control or I will report you to the site manager. It actually peed on my sunbed leg. Have you any idea how much these beds cost in Harrods? Be prepared for a bill coming your way, and if it's not paid you will be hearing from my solicitor."

"Harrods my arse!" shouted Marcia, "They've got them in Argos, I seen them in the catalogue, and they're on offer. Our Tom was gonna get one for our holidays, but we thought they were too common, and we wanted something nice!"

"You tell 'em Mum!" screamed Tanya, "Get a life you stupid woman!"

Molly stifled a giggle and tried to calm the situation down. "Don't push it, Tanya."

Standing, facing Janet directly, lowering her voice to her near manly level, Molly spoke firmly and clear. "I am sorry Jacobs peed on your sun bed, and I am sorry if we spoilt your day at the beach. But if you don't pack it in, I will be the one reporting you to the site manager for harassment you snobby little bitch!"

Janet, totally taken aback, gawped at Molly for a minute, opened her mouth, cricked her neck and tried, unsuccessfully, to emit some sort of verbal response. Retreat being the only answer, she stuck her nose in the air and stomped off up the beach.

"Roger! ROGER! Get on back and pack up. WE ARE LEAVING!"

"Well, this is turning out to be a very enjoyable day." Molly returned to her seating position. "Anyone for ham sandwich?"

"Er, I think we might be too late for that," Marcia smiled. "Jacobs has munched the lot. Never mind, we'll treat ourselves to fish and chips later. Tom said there's a van come round."

The three holidaymakers, laid out the towels, made themselves comfortable and savoured the rays of the golden sun in their new-found paradise, content and relaxed.

Marcia sighed; How much happier could life be?

The following day, Molly and Tanya determined to make the most of the sunshine were mad keen to repeat the expedition. Marcia, on the other hand, thought she would give it a miss, at least for a day; her bottom still ached, and her eye had blackened. Tanya took great delight in telling her mother that she looked like she had been in a boxing match with a kangaroo.

Molly did not help either, jokingly saying it matched her other eye perfectly and no one would notice the difference. Marcia, used to their mocking, ignored their jibes.

"You sure you won't come Marc?" Molly moved the chair to the entrance of the tent.

"No, you two go, am okay here with Jacobs. We'll just sit in the sun and relax. Tom will be here later anyway; think he's bringing Dad, if he can prise him away from the Christmas tree."

"Yehhh!" Tanya twirled around. "Can't wait to see Bubbs."

"You got a drink, and we bent the brolly back as good as new, in case you get too hot!" Molly pushed the umbrella stalk further into the ground. "Sit down and see if that reaches your head."

Marcia plonked herself into the chair, which swayed to one side before the legs secured themselves awkwardly into the clods. The sun 'parasol' slipped sideways. "It's okay this side!" Marcia grumbled. "Don't cover me lopsided shoulder on the other side."

Molly leaned over and fiddled around with the flaps, knotting them to the protruding spokes, until her friend was shadowed, making her eye look even darker. "There, that'll do, just push it round a bit if you need to."

To be honest, much as she loved her best friend and daughter, Marcia was looking forward to a bit of peace and quiet. Jacobs had taken an extreme liking to her and lay comfortably at her feet, looking at her now and then, checking to make sure she was still there. Marcia sipped her drink, chewed the straw, and stared at the two girls as they skipped off towards the path.

Molly, not quite so spritely as Tanya, resigning to wearing a pair of pink flat pumps, still moved with utmost grace and style even though the surface was uneven. Her long dark shiny hair, waved from side to side, caressing her shoulders with its curls. Marcia sighed; even at thirty, the years didn't seem to have dented Molly's beauty…. how can someone be perfect, so loving; So caring? Why would she bother with her at all? She could quite easily hook up with someone else; someone who was less trouble and more able. The reasons she would never know, but whatever they were, Marcia was ever glad.

Then her Tanya, prancing around with her endless energy; her identical browns locks flaying uncontrollably in the air. Indeed, a young gypsy free and wild, just as Molly would have been when she was a child. They could, quite easily, be mother and daughter.

Now Marcia was not one for putting two and two together; her limited ability to logically combine indications with observations hampered any kind of questioning. The issue of finding Tanya's father was never really a problem, and, apart from the very outset of her pregnancy, had never been mentioned. After all, single parenting was the norm for the majority of women on the estate.

All these years she accepted Tanya as a follower of an idol, mimicking the characteristics from a role model upon which, they both become to rely. Marcia did not have the gumption or the opportunity to look at both of them in together in close proximity for any length of time.

However, watching the fading portrait of the pair disappearing into the distance a strange thought tottered across her mind. Dismissing it in an instance, Marcia put down her drink and spluttered.

"Silly cow," she muttered to herself. "No way, not possible, don't even think about it Marcia, opportunity was never there, and Molly was Molly. Man, or no man, something like that would be impossible."

Laying back in her chair, breathing in the salty air, feeling the warmth of the sun on her face, Marcia's eyes closed, and drifting off into dreams of perfect existence, the idea pushed into the deepest grave, buried for now, but not forgotten.

Tom and Becs, simultaneously, flew their arms out of each side window of the truck as it grew to a choppy halt.

"There she is! Marcia, Marcia!" Becs beamed with delight.

"Heh! Marcia!" Tom screeched.

Bernie sat upright and stared through the windscreen across the field. "Well, I'll be, it's our Marcia isn't it, Tom? It's our Marcia!! What is she doing here?"

Tom jumped out the cab, ran around to the other side and helped a very pregnant Bec's down the step to the ground. Ensuring she was stable, he turned to his grandfather. "Of course, it's Marcia, I told you, they are on holiday, and we've come to visit. Remember?"

Scratching his head to retrieve the memory, Bernie vaguely remembered where he was supposed to be. "Oh yes, you said, I remember now. Did you bring the presents as well then?"

Marcia was dreaming, she was back in the river, her size eight stuck solid and size 3 dangling around like a flaying shoelace. Tanya was not a baby, she was thirteen years old and splashing around in the water shouting at her mother, whilst Molly was on the grassy island shore, chopping up a boat. This was it; she was a 'gonner', destined to be drowned in a sea of demons. A loud familiar voice boomed from the bank, rescuing her from instant death and awakening her with a start.

"Marcia! Marcia! Look who's here! Marcia!!"

Such excitement ensued; the chair rocked dangerously sideways as the family gathered round. All were gabbling at once; exchanging the latest gossip, news, together with demands for instant description of holiday activities partaken; what happened to her eye; the whereabouts of Molly and Tanya and, of course, where did the dog come from? It was as if they had been parted for weeks, not only a couple of days. Marcia was giggling so much; she could not say anything at all, and tears of delight trickled down her lopsided cheeks.

Becs pottered around, waddling from side to side, like some obese duck, taking the need for sustenance in hand, making tea and sandwiches for everyone. This included Jacobs, who instantly recognised the chance of a few tit bits from a new-found friend.

Marcia re-seated herself and eagerly watched Tom and Bernie set up a small, camouflaged ridge tent nearer the hedge.

"What do you reckon? Marc?" Be okay for a night or so for me and Santa Claus eh?" Tom slapped Bernie on the back.

"Oh, its wonderful Tom, you always come up with nice things... and it's green and everything, matches in the with the hedge!" Marcia was delighted, realising they were intending to stay a day or so.

"Yep!" Tom grabbed the tent pole and wobbled it back and forth. "Army surplus, got if off that chap in the high street, said he couldn't sell it."

Becs handed the love her life a cup of tea. "That's probably because there's a bloody great hole in the back Tom." She smirked.

"I know, I know... It's all sorted... bit of Duck-tape and it's proper fixed."

Marcia grimaced briefly. After all these years she still remembered the time Duck-tape saved the day at her mother's funeral. If it had not been for Tom, Lilly would have ended up with more than a piece of shroud sticking out the side of her coffin.

"You okay Marcia?" Becs handed her a piece of cake.

Marcia smiled, the funeral had long since been the butt of light-hearted banter and no offence was ever taken. Her wonky grin spread across her face.

"Yeh, am very good thanks. Get that other chair and come and sit down; you look like me after a trip to the shops."

Becs was grateful for the invite and manoeuvred her heavy form until she was a comfortable as possible. The pair looked strangely similar, of course Becs, being younger and a lot prettier, but their legs parted, and feet splayed caused some hilarity from the men.

"Look at you two!" Tom shrieked. "You look like two elephants waiting for the circus to begin!"

Bernie put his hands on his knees and howled with laughter." "Yeh! Two Christmas puddings!!"

"Oh, shut up and get on with sorting everything out before the girls get back. Go on." Bec shooed her hands in mockery. "Get those lights up, and that little tree... chop, chop!"

Marcia spat out a mouthful of tea. "Oh! my gawd, don't tell me you're going to chop trees down as well."

Tom winked. "You'll see me dear... You'll see, it'll all be done in a jiffy."

And - as good as his word; it was...

Molly and Tanya were so engrossed in sunning themselves in paradise, they almost forgot the time. The sun was low in the sky, casting its golden rays across the bay, causing ripples of dazzling lights dancing across the waves.

Molly stretched. "Good grief, we've been here for ages, hope Marc is alright. Come on, we better head on back."

Tanya yawned. "'Spose so. She'll be wondering where we got too, surprised she hasn't wobbled down here!"

Reaching the top of hill and turning onto the path, both of them stopped dead in their tracks.

"Bloody hell, you ain't gonna lose your way in a hurry with that!" Tanya pointed her finger at the magnificent display.

Molly put her head back and roared with laughter. "I guess Tom has arrived!"

Sure enough, even though it was still dusk, the tent was lit up brighter than the castle at Disney land. Glowing strings of pearls draped around the entrance, across the circular frame, and dotted around a small tree, anchored to the ground and tied to a large lorry battery.

Tom was waving his arms and yelling at the top of his voice. "Come on you two. Party time!"

Tanya leaped in the air. "WOHOOO! Can I have a lager Auntie Molly, pleeeease."

Molly grabbed Tanya's arm. "No chance... lemonade it is! But first, toilet block - if it's party, then dresses it is."

"You brought party dresses?" Tanya's eyes grew wider.

"Of course! Never go anywhere without a party dress Tan, remember that always."

It was when Tom switched on the music that the small number of people that could bear the presence of 'gypsies' started to gather. In fact, they weren't exactly gathering they were forming an orderly queue at the tent entrance.

"What are you all doing?" Tom waved a bottle at them. "Come and join in, I bet you all got some drink in your tents.... Go get it, bring what you want and let's have some fun!"

A middle-aged man placed his arms around his wife and drew her close. "I would rather not lose my place in the queue just yet. We want to get a good seat."

Marcia poked her head around the canvas. "I am sorry, we ain't got no spare seats, if you'd like to get some of your own or sit on the grass, you be very welcome!"

"No seats?" The man raised his eyebrows. "No seats? How much is it then, with no seats."

"How much is what?" Becs linked arms with Marcia and the pair toddled outside to find the source of the commotion.

"The circus." The man looked quizzingly. "What time does the show start?"

"What circus?" Marcia was totally confused.

"The circus." The man repeated. "You know, acrobats, performing animals and all that. I see the clowns are ready, and that clever dog looks a bit of alright. What's its name?"

Jacobs sat holding up his paws, eager for a little sympathy and possibly some food.

"What clowns? What dog? What's he on about Becs?"

Becs looked Marcia up and down, then repeated the process with herself. "I say Marcia, we do look a bit of a state. You with that black eye and me with me huge belly and hot flushed cheeks!"

Marcia, not at all offended replied. "Yes, we do, and what with me feet being all odd an all, they are a pair of wonky flippers that's for sure!"

Tom continued to wave his beer, finding the whole situation extremely funny.

"He's called Jacobs, and it ain't no circus, though it ought to be! It'll be the tent what fooled ya! Got it from old Cyril. D'you remember Marc? Cyril and his brothers... the dwarves... you know, the one who fished you...."

"Okay, OKAY! You don't have to remind me, I know...I know." Marcia interrupted.

"Why is he called Jacobs?" The man looked at the dog, who was twirling round like a spinning top.

"Because he's crackers." Tom dryly replied, before enticing everyone to get 'with the beat' and enjoy.

Having suddenly dawned on everyone that there was not a circus, swings, big wheel or anything else around that resembled a fairground. A small titter became huddles of chuckling strangers, and as exchanges grew happy and louder, a barrage of happy holiday makers filled the quiet country air, drowning any sounds of emerging night wildlife, as darkness descended to cover the earth.

The party was indeed, in full swing. A small number of people, airs and graces disarmed by the warmth of several glasses of alcohol, laughed and danced. Others drowned in beer, screamed at silly jokes and elaborate stories, told by inebriated folk enjoying their new-found audience.

A teenage girl sneaked round the back of the tent and drained the dregs of an almost empty can. She was joined by a small boy, dressed in a bright red football shirt and scruffy jeans.

"What you doing?" he asked.

"SSh...." said Tanya, "It's only a drop."

"Can I have some?" He reached forward.

"No! Certainly not, it's only for big girls and boys. Go away. Where's your mum and dad?"

"Dad's gone back to get some drinks, and Mum's gone to see if that gypsy will tell her fortune."

"You better go and see them, don't want them snooping round here." Tanya grabbed the boy's hand and dragged him back to the proceedings.

"There she is!" He shouted. "Mum!!"

Deirdre patted a bemused Marcia on the shoulder and walked unsteadily towards her son. "Oh! There you are! David. Is this your new friend?"

Tanya released her captive, gave a wave and trotted back to her hiding place behind the marquee. Lifting the flat, she pulled through a bag of necessary provisions and dared to open a can.

Molly poured a large glass of gin and gave it to Marcia. "There get that down you, it's a party."

Marcia rarely drank, she had seen enough of that with her mother. But she was on holiday so what the heck? One would be alright.

"She seemed a nice lady," Marcia accepted the drink. "Bit odd though, kept talking about divorce and tall dark strangers and gave me a quid. How strange. She doesn't need to pay us for anything does she?"

Molly drained her glass, hiding her amusement. She was only too aware that on occasions Marcia was still oblivious to many things. But then, if she was, it wouldn't be Marcia, would it? She loved Marcia the way she was and would not change her for the world.

"Fancy a dance?" Molly jibed.

Marcia, legs not really abiding, waved her arms and to-and-fro, completely out of sync with the music, but giving it a go.

Hours later, suitably fed and overly watered, the numbers dwindled one by one. No one really remembered what time they went to bed, or how they got there, but suffice to say, a good time was had by all.

Marcia lay face down on her blankets, one leg hanging over the side of the bed, the other bent upwards towards the sky. Molly wondered how on earth she could balance, until it came crashing down with a bang. Not a jolt, not a stir; the snoring continued.

Tanya had been sparked out for the last couple of hours. It was strange, she normally had the energy off fifty people. Molly assumed it must be the sea air. Becs lay sleeping, cuddling her unborn baby, exhausted but content.

Checking outside, Molly stared at the littered cans and wrappings, not in disgust, totally the opposite. The night air was still warm and silent. She lay on the grass and looked in awe at the shining stars, wondering if others were returning the gaze. Life was perfect at that moment... closing her eyes in contentment, she wished the problems away and drifted off into heaven, serenaded by those familiar angels.

"GOOD KING WENSLESLAS LOOKED OUT, ON THE FEAST OF STEPHEN. WHEN THE SNOW LAY ROUND ABOUT, DEEP AND CRISP AND EVEN...BRIGHTLY SHONE THE DOO DAH DAY....!"

Molly woke with a start. "What the hell?"

Tom flew open the tent flaps, charged outside, completely forgetting he had removed his belt. In his drunken state, trousers around his ankles, he fell flat on his face. Making matters worse, he rolled over, got his legs and pants in a complete muddle and was totally unable to move.

"Mol..lls, I believe I am s...stuck." He could hardly speak. Howling with merriment, he tried to reach Molly, who by now was crumpled up herself.

"Serves... yyou... rrright. What the hell is going on? Who's making that dreadful racket?"

Tom kicked his legs, ensuring his predicament was permanent. "It's Grandad... "

Molly could hear Bernie but could not see him anywhere.

"GATHERING WINTER FU---EE−LLLLL!" came the shouts.

"Oh my God, what's he done now!" Molly struggled up and peered into the darkness. She could make out a groggy shadow a few feet away.

"BERNIE! BERNIE! SHUT THE FUCK UP YOU'LL WAKE THE WHOLE CAMPSITE!" If it was possible to whisper loudly then she did her best.

Tom shrieked. "Oh, leave him be, he will come back in a minute... everyone is out for the count - it don't matter. It's bloody funny though."

Molly moved forward and watched the stumbling shadow, head facing upwards, singing at the top of his voice.

"Be...be...tter b-bring h-him back I suppose, and h-help me get out of this, am well jammed in!" Tom was howling with laughter.

Molly couldn't help but shriek out loud and sat down on the grass, unable to keep upright any longer.

"I will, I will... in a minute.... when he's finished."

"F..f..finished w..hat?" Neither of them could form their words properly.

"Finished p- pee-ing, which is what I.... am going.... to do... any minute... He's p-pee-ing in the h-edge and singing f-f – kg Christmas C-Carols!"

At this point, Tom was rolling around so much, his legs mummified, and he was completely trapped.

Molly was shrieking, Tom was in hysterics, Bernie was singing... It was a good job everyone was so consumed with booze; they were either dead to the world or could not give a dam.

"Oh Tom!" Molly yelled. "W-W-hat a h-oot! You're buggered, Bernie's mental and now I've peed me pants!"

Bernie, unconcerned by any predicament, still holding one hand between his legs, bumbled towards the little tent, narrowly avoiding Tom who was pinned to the ground, with strappings of tangled fabric.

Head held up to the night sky, Santa Claus stretched out his arms to the stars; his underpants falling to his ankles, baring all to God and his cherubs.

"MERRY CHRISTMAS!" he bellowed... then turned, tripped over his feet and plummeted head-first, through the tent flaps and landed on top of a screwed up sleeping bag.

"What a shame we have to go home." Tom muffled. "What a shame... and we really need to do something about Bernie."

The little dog curled up by Marcia's bed was thinking exactly the same thing, determined to stick to his new friend, there was no way he was going to leave this family.

Chapter Four
Ruby

Ruby Carson stood solemnly in Bloomsbury cemetery staring at the small grey headstone. It was insignificant compared to the gleaming pristine white of the ornate shrine situated several yards away, but her parent's simple grave was neat and lovingly cared for.

With a little difficulty, Ruby bent low and discarded last week's flowers, even though they were not totally over. Replacing them with fresh freesias, she breathed in the aroma and smiled. They were her mother's favourite, and she loved this time of year when they were available in abundance. Her father never really liked flowers, but in death as in life, he had no choice in the matter. Freesias are what her mother loved and if her dad did not like them, he would just have to put up with it.

Reaching into her pocket she pulled out the delicate lace handkerchief and rubbed it gently over the brass lettering, carefully eradicating the smudges left by the recent rain. It had been difficult to think of any words to adorn the memorial, but the ones chosen, clearly portrayed the heart felt tragic loss.

After all these months, she still felt numb and empty. Visions of the crash still dominated her dreams and the guilt of survival constantly preyed on her mind. Yet, there was another void lying deep within, masked by many happy childhood memories.

Wiping away her tears, Ruby sniffled promises of her weekly return, bade her goodbyes and walked along the short path towards the cemetery gate. Pausing at the magnificent Henley memorial, she marvelled at the shiny marble and the glorious carvings. The flowers, regularly laid, were usually expensive, orchids or lilies. However, on occasions, she had noticed small bunches of daffodils, or sometimes tulips, placed beside the ribboned bouquets. She did not know why but she was strangely drawn to the monument.

Once, a while ago, she had seen someone, standing there, staring at the epitaph. She remembered the well-dressed man, and his dark eyes as he momentarily glanced in her direction. Not that he noticed her much; indeed, he quickly resumed his vigilance, but the young man had looked at her briefly again, before dismissing her presence, turning, and walking solemnly away, lost in his own grief.

Looking at the inscription, as she had countless times before; the Henley names meant nothing to her, but she wondered why she felt compassion for these people and what stories they could tell.

The bus ride into the village was short, but Ruby still felt fatigued as she turned the key and opened the door to the small, terraced cottage and stepped into the lounge. The décor had once omitted a warm and cosy aura, the pale colours perfectly complimenting the darkness of the oak, and the deep blue velvets softly flowed as the calmest sea. She remembered the heat of the glowing logs, warming her toes, as her father pointed out dragons and monsters in the flickering orange flames.

Now it was dreary and bland, the charred remains of the unclean grate now hidden by the modern log effect fire, unwelcome and cold. The part drawn drapes cast eerie shadows across the room, playing tricks in the dark corners.

Moving slowly to the mantelpiece, Ruby looked into the once ornate mirror; sculptured surrounds now tarnished with age and lack of care. The person returning her stare had pain etched on her skin and sadness in her eyes. She was alone, no aunts or uncles near; no grandparents to spoil her; no real friends to speak of; no lover to hold her close; no one to show her the way; no one to right her mistakes and no one to mop up her tears.

It was not as if her life had been totally sheltered, her parents had been meticulous in ensuring a good standard of education and always encouraged her to mix with other beings. The school was excellent but did not hold particularly good memories, and Ruby was conscious of her looks, or lack of, as the bullies of the class had frequently reminded. The cruel name-calling, the sniggers and jokes were vividly recalled, as 'Chubbs' once again, came last in the sack race. Her protests of 'Can't do it miss, my leg hurts' had fallen on deaf ears as Miss Gibbs bellowed the command to take part and to 'stop fussing and get on with it Ruby.'

Of course, there was some element of truth in Ruby's statement. Her leg did cause her some pain, but not enough to prevent participation in any task she perceived difficult. Ever since she had fallen from the large oak tree at the bottom of her garden and resulted in a considerably severe fracture, it had never totally recovered.

It was the impact of the crash that had compounded the old injury and the subsequent unrepairable damage had left her with a minor impairment. This resulted in enough discomfort to cause a slight limp to frequently to rear its ugly head – or rather – leg. Thus, Ruby had always been happy in her own company and was content, at the time, to potter around, listening to music, reading the odd book or two. The faster pace of life eluded her, partly through disinterest, partly through reluctance to participate in activities any normal young lady would relish.

It was thanks to her mother, that she had any kind of outside contact at all. The part-time position secured for her within a small local catering establishment was not ideal; but gave her limited contact with the outside world. Despite working on her own and being lumbered with the monotonous task of preparing endless piles of sandwiches, she enjoyed the peace and quiet and generally kept herself to herself.

Ruby turned away from her reflection and, still lost in thought, wandered aimlessly to the kitchen. Filling the kettle, she gazed through the grubby window and across the uncut grass, reminding her of the numerous jobs she must get down to completing.

Forgetting the present and the clumsiness she now despised. Ruby saw herself squirming on the old swing, clinging madly to the ropes to keep balance, her skirts billowing in the breeze as her mother pushed her gently under the shade of the tree. She saw the laughter as she tried to ride her tricycle, her feet slipping from the pedals. She saw herself drinking red fizzy lemonade and eating crisp sandwiches; her mother laughing at her cheekiness, as she poked out her crimson tongue. She saw her father, squirting the hose, chasing her as she shrieked, and her mother trying to look cross because the washing was drenched.

Smiling as she stared, her heart was filled with love and happiness, Ruby could not have wished for a better upbringing, and how her parents coped with her through the difficult times, she would never understand. They were good to her and had nurtured Ruby from a timid child to a woman, capable of contending with the trials and tribulations of general life.

She was truly grateful, but the uplift was brief; her stomach churned, and her insides wrenched, as the reality of loneliness and grief swamped any positive feelings. Thoughts that had been ignored were now resurrecting; guilt added to the roller coaster of emotions which constantly flooded her mind. She watched her parents as they laughed and loved; but tears welled in her eyes as she wondered what it would have been like if it was her REAL mother that pushed her on the swing and if it was her REAL father that soaked her with water...... Maybe it was time to find out.... Maybe, it was time to act on the limited information John and Sarah Carson had left her.

Chapter Five
Mobility Gained

Marcia sat defiant, risking the wrath of twin queens of Sheba, neither of which, had any intention of taking 'no' for an answer.

"Mum, you have no choice, you have to go. They said in this assessment thingy." Tanya pushed the letter under her mother's nose for the umpteenth time.

Marcia grimaced. Many moons ago, she would have obeyed without question; nowadays, such was the level of confidence, painfully achieved over the last few years, she was able to make her own decisions, some of which were unpopular and frustrating for the other members of her household.

This was one of those occasions where Marcia's stubbornness and reluctance of any involvement in matters of authority resulted in all-out War.

"Well, I ain't, and that's that. You know what happened the last time, I nearly killed me-self."

Molly frowned and supressed an inappropriate smirk. Normally she would have joked about the situation, but some things had to be done, and this was one of them.

"So, you fell off the treadmill. That was years ago, and that stupid nurse woman, should have been there to work the controls. Too busy, she was farting around that young, fit looking guy."

Crossing her arms in annoyance, Marcia defended herself. "What young fit guy? It was a bloody phsywotsit place – no one fits in there I can tell you. Things they put you on, not big enough for a ruddy mouse!"

Tanya's interest diverted at the mention of the opposite sex. "There's fit guys as well at these places, Auntie Molly? We definitely got to go then."

Molly threw her arms in the air. "For God's sake, I give up with the pair of you. Marcia: you either go to this appointment; or you get no more support."

"I got me support; I got me sticks and the wheelchair, which is fine now Tom's bent the bottom bits back. Sod that stairlift, fed up with getting stuck on that one."

"Oh, come on Mum, it'll be a right laugh. Hunky blokes as well."

"Shut up Tanya...You aren't helping at all." Molly reverted her scowl to the sour faced invalid who was determined to ignore all sane advice.

Marcia was sufficiently strong enough to ignore jests and jibes about her looks and condition. Thankfully, snide remarks were few and far between, her being no different from many other 'odd balls' on the estate. However, behind the wall of self-protection, there was a child, scared and embarrassed to face outsiders and one who shied from any form of prognosis.

Molly hated these situations; there was no other option, home truths had to be told.

"What I mean Marcia; is that you are getting worse. Unless you want to end up completely disabled and stuck in that chair for the rest of your life, or end up in some bloody care home, when we can't look after you. So, you WILL go to this physiotherapy assessment. They will sort out your benefit, and who knows, even a new wheelchair and stairlift. God knows Tom does his best, but you could have new ones Marc... just think about it!"

Molly took a deep breath and continued before Marcia could protest. "In fact, don't think about it. I got a taxi booked for Friday and you are going and that's that!"

Tanya threw the letter to her mother's lap. "That's settled then, schools out for Friday!"

Marcia looked unusually angry. "You ain't coming m'girl, you stay in school, you got your exams coming up."

"One day isn't going to matter, is it? And I already have a job, in the salon."

Marcia was extremely proud of her daughter; no one in her immediate family had ever finished school at the appropriate time, let alone secure a 'proper' job. Granted, Molly had her bits of 'biz' as she called it, but a proper job! That was something else and she was not about to hamper any opportunities by allowing her daughter time off school. Her defiance reluctantly relented, and a compromised solution suggested.

"Okay, okay, I will go…but only if you come Molly, and YOU stay in school. Oh, and I ain't getting on no trod mill. Tom can take us in the truck."

Breathing a sigh of relief, battle won, Molly grinned. "It will be fine, I promise. Tom can't run us everywhere, he's busy working and looking after Daniel. Becs can't do much now, you know that, her being sick all the time with this new baby an all."

"I suppose. I remember feeling like that, sick as a dog some days. I thought it was marshmallows didn't I – silly cow I was. Hope it stops, she's only just pregnant ain't she?" Anger depleted; Marcia resigned herself to the dreaded event she would have to endure.

"That's what happens when you're up the duff." Tanya snatched the letter and threw it onto the sideboard, as she marched out of the room. "No time off school then, that's not fair, is it? I'm off to my room, to look at those new mags you got Molly. Thanks, and no thanks!"

Marcia gritted her teeth and grunted an incoherent response.

"Ignore her, Marc." Molly sat on the arm of the chair and took her friend's hand. "She's a stroppy teenager, I told you before. I guess we were a bit like that?"

"She maybe like you were Moll, but if I spoke like that, Lil would have clipped me right round the ear 'ole! Get us some tea, I'm parched, I ain't thinking about it anymore."

Marcia rarely thought about her appearance. Unless it was one of those extremely infrequent outings, to which enthusiasm emerged from its sleepy bed, it was deemed unnecessary. The old mirror, with its chipped wooden frame and blotted glass, turned inward, reflecting the faded paintwork of the bedroom wall, resigned to a limited purpose.

Using one hand; the other firmly grasped around her stick; pulling on the comfortable, oversized sloppy jumper was relatively easy. Marcia arranged it to cover as much of her upper torso as possible. The ample fabric of flowered skirt hung limply from her middle, draping unevenly over her calves, not quite brushing the odd size, slip on trainers.

Tanya, flippant as ever, poked her head around the bedroom door. "Am off to school then…unless you changed your mind and I can come, like I wanted to in the first place. Where's those shorts? The letter said shorts Mum."

The look on Marcia's face told Tanya the pink shorts, unworn and folded neatly in the drawer under a pile of disarranged underwear, were not going surface this time.

"Don't know why you won't wear them; they been there for ages. You wouldn't even put them on when we went on that holiday."

"I told you, I ain't going to look like no upside-down candy floss." Marcia curtly replied. "I'll stick to my normal stuff thank you." The vision of the brightly coloured apparel gracing her ungainly form, dousing any interest in new costumery.

"Suit yourself then, but you might get hot. Why don't you put them in your bag, just in case?" A glimpse of empathy thrusting a path through the cheek.

"I'll be fine as I am. I ain't going to be running a mile."

Tanya emitted a grin of surrender; swung her bag over her shoulder and thundered down the stairs. Echoes of 'Okay - See you later alligator,' faded into the morning sun, as the buoyant young lady skipped into the fresh air, narrowly avoiding a collision with her aunt.

Retrieving herself from a forced seated position on the garden wall, Molly muttered several negative phrases, before strutting up the path and trotting into the hallway. Dressed in navy slacks and white cotton top, casual attire for most; the shiny patent stilettos managed to accentuate her long slim legs and turn the outfit into catwalk material.

"You ready Marcia? Taxi's here! You want some help down the stairs?"

Marcia grabbed the banister and slowly began the descent to the ground floor.

"What? In those shoes? We both be on the floor." Puffing, she paused halfway. "You know what? I don't think this is a very good idea, maybe I'll give it a miss."

Molly frowned. "Not a chance. Taxi's here and paid for, you got no choice."

Indeed, Marcia did not have an option. As much as she hated the idea, deep down, the awareness of the progression of her condition was not totally forgotten. Disgruntled, apprehensive, and secretly afraid, she made her way out of her comfort zone, to the waiting carriage of death.

Thankfully, the physiotherapy department was strategically placed on the ground floor of the medical centre. Situated away from the main hospital, nestling between a group of modern offices, it was easily accessed by persons of lesser agility. Marcia gazed around at the clinical surroundings as she awaited her fate. Recollections of previous visits to various clinics splattered across the establishment flashed through her mind as she observed several practitioners, uniformed in stiff white coats, ushering to-and-fro, consulting flapping papers loosely pinned to rigid blue clipboards. They were not altogether good memories; the registrar, the broken ornaments, the coffee stains on his shirt; Molly, laid out, still and pale, linked to life by wires and tubes. Then there was Tilly, soaked in violently expressed milk, as Marcia struggled to grasp the act of breast feeding.

Marcia stared blindly at the bright abstract, adorning the bare walls; colours ignored, as her mother's image shimmered before her. No longer the drunk, inattentive parent, but the loving grandmother, rocking baby Tanya and smiling proudly at her daughter.

Water invaded her eyes. Sadly, for Marcia, although acceptance of her condition came naturally over the years, there was still an element of worthlessness; normally successfully supressed and accepted with no question or self-consciousness. Today, reminders of perceived inadequacies were high on the list of worries. In fact, it was one of those infrequent occasions when she felt completely useless.

Molly, seeing her friend's plight, sidled along the bench and moved closer. Taking a hand, she stroked Marcia's palm.

"It'll be alright. They're only here to help you, Marcia; they can do things; make you move better. You want to move better don't you?"

"How?" Marcia blubbered, tears freely flowing. "Look at me, I ain't worth bothrin with. They will look at my weird face, my fat body - they will say how bad my back is, laugh at my feet and tell me I'll be in a wheelchair forever."

Molly stroked Marcia's brow lovingly, gently brushing the invading strands of straggly hair across her forehead.

"Now you look here Marcia Duncan; you are not going back to those thoughts. Those doctors won't do any of that. You haven't got that much worse, have you? You can still walk with sticks. Don't you worry, whatever they tell you to do; we'll do it together, cos that's what soulmates do."

"Soulmates? What's that then?" Marcia wiped away her tears with her baggy sleeve. "Like you mean, shoes? Your shoes are lovely, mine aren't, so we can't really be mates about that."

Cuddling her 'soulmate', Molly smiled. "No, Marcia, not soles, you are funny. Souls is in your heart, and if you are soulmates, you never leave each other, ever."

"Marcia Duncan?" The young nurse glanced at the files, re-checking the name. "Marcia Duncan?"

Molly helped Marcia to her feet and the pair of inseparable friends followed directions, as the nurse patiently guided them to a screened section of the room.

"If you could take off your jumper, change into your shorts and lay on the bed please. Remember me? I'm Helen. Nice to see you again, how are you doing?"

Raising her eyebrows, Molly looked at Marcia, as the nurse disappeared. "What's she on about? It's years since you came here."

"Perhaps she remembers me falling off the trod mill." Marcia grunted through wool, as the cosy jumper was discarded. "I'm keeping me skirt on... help me hitch it up a bit when I lie down."

"Hardly; she probably wasn't even born then. She looks like she would still be sat on a potty."

The thought of the nurse being sat on a potty certainly raised glum spirits. Marcia's fears, temporarily dashed, lifted her mood allowing a few giggles to present.

"Actually, when you fell off the trod mill – oh sorry – you got me at it now – treadmill, you have to admit it was funny." Molly hooted, tucking the blooms around Marcia's thighs.

Marcia relaxed and joined in the frivolity. "Yeh, you remember? Right on me arse, legs stuck in the air. Completely lost me size eight."

"Oh, Marcia! That bloke's face, when it whopped him across the head.... priceless!"

"Were we supposed to pay then? Ooh, we got away with that one; like we used to do in the disco's" Marcia lent forward, hand on hips in mockery.

Their fun was abruptly interrupted by a rather large lady, squashed into a tabard, six sizes too small for her frame. Her hair, tightly crunched into a bun on the top of her head, did no favours for the sour-face features. Eyebrows furled and slanted, haunting a menacing, scowling expression as the cracking sound of a scary looking rope slapped against her muscly thigh.

Marcia and Molly, joviality immediately doused, became motionless; two naughty schoolgirls, caught in the act of disobedience. Leaning sideways, stiff as a statue, eye contact supressed, Molly veered towards the victim, pushing her friend sideways in similar stance. They looked like two stuffed owls, nailed on the branch of an overly large tree.

Being well used to speaking without moving her lips, Molly muttered loud enough for Marcia to understand, soft enough to escape the massive lug holes of any potential attacker.

"Bloody hell, it's Hitler's mother."

Marcia had no idea who Hitler was but by the tone of Molly's voice – and the look of the assailant –, the name seemed rather apt. Thankfully she found this comment hilarious – it could have so easily gone the other way.

Laying down on Marcia bit the inside of her cheeks and placed her hands over her face.

"Hello there again Marcy, I am Helga. I have come to check movements."

Molly's eyes filled; knuckles clenched, nails digging into her palms to control her actions. "She...she went this m...morning."

Marcia kicked her legs up and down, alternately banging each odd foot, thumping hard on the vinyl mattress, until the size eight missed the side of the bed entirely, and nearly took the rest of her body with it, to the floor.

Helga had no idea what was going on, jokes were not learned in her English class. Instead of questioning the proceedings, she put down the rope and clapped her hands.

"Bravo! Bravo! That's very gooood. Much better than last time."

Molly, by this time, was stamping her feet on the ground, in an attempt to distract the howls escaping from her mouth and retain some sort of decorum.

Directing her speech to her patient's companion, the vacant physiotherapist put down the rope and moved towards Marcia, who was struggling to lift her leg back on to the couch. Not attempting to help her patient in the least, she turned her attentions to Molly.

"If you would care to pull round curtains, we see what movements Marcy has... And if you need toilet, it is near entrance."

Molly grabbed the drapes and yanked them around the rail. "Okay, thanks. Be back in a minute...'Marcy'."

Rushing off to the Ladies room, she was grateful to escape, before dissolving into wobbling jelly. Her legs gave way, stilettos skidding on the shiny tiles, her whole form slid against the cubicle partition and keeled to the floor.

Helga carried out her assessment with ultimate precision. Marcia did not realise she could be manoeuvred into such painful positions; at one point she was sure her bent spine was going to snap. It was the final straw when her size three and her size eight were forced into a massive rubber band. Not in a million years could she co-ordinate the two, let alone stretch the ridiculously tight elastic.

Having composed herself sufficiently enough to take most of the session seriously, Molly made her way back to the treatment area. The groans and grunts of an animal in pain, resounded around the room for all to hear.

"Oh! my gawd; I can't do it.... Oh! my gawd.... Ow.... Me leg's going.... Me leg's going.... Oh, my gawd!"

Helga, seemingly ignoring Marcia's plight, nodded with encouragement, scribbled notes on the paperwork adhered to the enormous clip-file clasped in her hands and poked her head outside the fabric screen. "Good, there you are. You help Marcy dressed. We check to walk next and bicycle."

Being put through the mill was an understatement. Marcia was almost bent double as she wavered from side to side, clinging onto Molly for all she was worth.

"Can't do no more Moll; honest; am done in."

"Come on, it's only a few more minutes, then we'll be out of here. We'll go and get some of those nice cakes for tea."

For once, Molly was in agreement with her friend – who looked completely worn out.

Standing in front of the row of static bicycles, Marcia surveyed the equipment with dismay. She well remembered the last time she stood inside a rack full of cycles; recalling vividly the grim sight of the melted saddle on Graham Beneton's mobility trike and charred twiggy remains of Miss Biddle's Raleigh Shopper basket. A cigarette had not passed her lips since.

Helga beckoned her victim to the larger of the contraptions. "On please. We take time and help necessary."

Marcia's mouth opened wider than a hungry hippo, before protesting, "Waaa....? That one? The big one with THOSE peddally wotsits?"

"Can't she have a go on that little one?" Molly pointed to a small exercise cycle, situated away from the main bunch of torture weapons.

Helga managed half a smile. "Oh no, they are for little people, and we have one on next moment."

Hitler's mother was not giving up. With a heave and a shove, Molly on one side and Helga on the other, Marcia was manhandled clumsily on to the offending object.

The picture was not one of delight. Body bent forward, hands wrapped tightly around the rubber grippers for grim death, her straggly strands dripping sweat onto her flowery skirt as her head drooped downwards, Marcia was far from delighted. Each irregular leg stretched out, stiff and immobile; the size three pointing directly at the wall and the size eight outright on the opposite side, Marcia was adamant – this was as good as it gets, and she wasn't moving anymore; whatever anyone said.

Cyril, being incredibly small, due to a birth dwarfism condition of 'Russell- Silver' syndrome, re-fastened the lace on his child size trainers, pulled up his oversize shorts to his chin, and hopped onto the small exercise machine. He had been summoned occasionally to physiotherapy to keep his thinning bones strong and prevent further deterioration and potential breakages. Unnoticed by most of the audience who were attentive to the current entertainment on the neighbouring contraptions, he began his rotations without effort. Looking at the familiar figure, literally petrified, motionless on the neighbouring contraption, there was no doubt in his mind, who the terrified woman was.

Marcia, with whom he kept occasionally in touch, and seemed to meet every time she was in mortal danger, was here again and in just as much trouble by the look of it. The first time he had met this sorry creature was when he was fishing one sunny day on the Banks of the River Ellis. It was the biggest fish he had ever landed when his scooped the new-born Tanya out of the water in his landing net. Since then, he had befriended the family, though having more contact with Tom than anyone else these days. His cunning abilities gathered during his career with the circus turned out to be invaluable in obtaining almost any object desired -

from the smallest bouncing ball to the largest marquee. He certainly was a perfect complement to Tom's habit of nabbing anything – preferably free – that would come in 'handy'.

"Go to it Marcia!" Cyril shouted. "Nothing to be scared of, it's easy; see? Watch old Cyril!"

Marcia turned her head and grimaced an acknowledgment, grateful for any support during the current crisis.

"Cyril! What you doing here? Look Marcia, it's Cyril! He's on the bike fine. Go on – you can do it – put your feet on the pedals!" Molly tried her best to encourage.

Marcia cricked her neck enough to spy her past saviour whizzing his legs without effort. The look on her face would have scared away a roaring lion. Panting, partly with exhaustion, partly with fright, she gasped.

"Cyril? I... is th...at you? I'm bloody well stuck here again. I can't bend me knees like they want. It's a fizziwotsit impossible doo dah."

Molly pushed on Marcia's left leg, whilst Helga attempted manual manipulation on the other. The result was a total imbalance of body mass and Marcia slid sideways off the saddle and landed legs apart and rigid, her head and shoulders on the ample chest of Hitler's mother's bosom.

Helga had no option but to place her strong arms under Marcia's armpits and drag her unceremoniously to the safety of the rubber floor covering. This was not in the training notes, but dignity was all essential it said, don't get fazed, it said. That did not help, Helga the magnificent, was 'fazed', this part of the assessment was a complete disaster. Glaring in horror at the crumpled mass on the mat, it was difficult to decipher which was the top and which was the bottom as limbs presented themselves here there and everywhere, protruding from an immense mound of knotted flowery fabric.

Cyril jumped off his cycle and sat on the matting, attempting to straighten Marcia into some sort of order.

Helga, slightly embarrassed and admitting defeat, defended her actions. "Think we leave it today Marcy, I give you some exercise to do at home." She muttered, running her hand over her forehead. "I send report to doctor soon."

With that, Helga the Great grabbed the clipboard and scuttled towards another victim. A gaping patient briefly stared in disbelief, before donning his jacket and with renewed vigour, rapidly vacated the premises before she had a chance to say 'Velcome'.

Molly put her hands on her hips and shouted after the dragon. "So, you going to leave her here like this then?"

Helga raised the board above her head, and without turning, replied. "She be fine. Good session to be repeat; but no bicycles next visit."

Marcia managed a seating position and placed her hands on each side of her head, shaking it slightly to regain some kind of composure, whilst Molly furiously yelled after Hitler's mother.

"Well, there isn't going to be any next time! Don't know who you think you are putting my Marcia through that. You are one hell of a class bitch that's for sure!"

Marcia wailed tearfully. "Molly! Leave it, I am okay. Had more falls than this in me time, ain't I Cyril...? Been in a lot more trouble than this! But I hurt me back, me bum feels like it's been slapped with one of those big belts with metal studdy bits on. Me legs are like jelly. I'll be okay. I want to go home now."

"You sure have Marcia." Cyril grinned, "and here I am again, to rescue a fair maiden in distress!"

The audience, seeing the proceedings coming to a conclusion and all parties were relatively intact, one by one returned to their own tasks, grateful for the interval. An elderly gentleman, grinned, and removed the heavy band bound constricting his calves throwing it to the floor. Waving his arms in the air in delight, he addressed the remaining victims of restraint, as an old thespian would.

"Well said, Oh lady of the night. The peasants are revolting! No more I beseech thee woman! No more will thou blacken my thighs with weapons of torture or burden mine arms with heavy bricks of persecution. Be gone Satanic lady.... For thou are not welcome in this prison of mortal destruction."

Cyril grabbed Marcia's arm and attempted to help her rise. Unfortunately, he was not much use, being less than half the size of everyone else in the room. Molly intervened and with a bit of organising, Marcia was returned to her un-normal self.

"What the hell is he on about?" Cyril, making himself of more use, returned Marcia her trusty sticks.

Molly smirked. "Think he's had enough of Hitler's mother. Come on, let's get out of this place, it's nuts. Where's that nice nurse gone? I reckon a word or two might be in order!"

Supporting an aching Marcia, Molly on one side, Cyril on the other, holding her elbow as best he could, the three toddled slowly out of the physio room, and past the reception desk.

The young nurse rummaged through the pile of paperwork heaped on the desk and retrieved the notes for the next patient. Blissfully unaware of the problems Marcia had incurred, she happily continued with her mundane job – seeing people in and seeing people out.

"You finished then?" She smiled. "See you soon."

Marcia lost for words, screwed up her face and portrayed her gloomy mood. Whilst Molly, not wishing to cause another scene, calmed, then replied with false and sarcastic politeness.

"Not if I see you first. Thank your torture queen for her time. We are utterly delighted to leave."

Helen, not fully understanding the underlying statement, nodded an acknowledgement and resuming her welcoming manner scanned the waiting room.

"Mr Smith please? Mr Smith? No?" Perhaps he is in the bathroom, she thought. Ever efficient, she ruffled the papers again and called for the next person.

"Miss Harper? Miss Emily Harper? Is that you Miss Harper?"

The small lady, dressed in a blue tabard, replaced the soiled mop into the bucket.

"No, it's Gwendoline, the cleaner; thought I would start early. Everyone left just now."

Helen shrugged her shoulders. "How strange is that. Ah well, time for a cup of tea then."

Gwendoline raised her eyebrows. "Yes, very strange... mine's two sugars if you please."

Chapter Six
Ruby's Quest

Ruby sat uncomfortably on the cold plastic chair; one of several identical bland seats, uniformly glued together. She wondered why? It was not as if someone was going to pick one up and stroll blatantly along the labyrinth of corridor and sneak it away unchallenged, past reception, through the translucent revolving doors and scupper along the street, mingling inconspicuously within with the crowds.

Contrary to this part of the building, the foyer itself was quite impressive. Soft beige carpet lay calmly wall to wall, complimented by glorious leather chesterfields; buttons gleaming as the sun pushed its way through the immense glass windows. She had sat there for a while, watching people coming and going, and her apprehensiveness was somewhat alleviated for a moment, as she watched a group of people, unrecognisably knotted together, tumbling down the steps of the medical centre. She had been there, it was not pleasant, she felt sorry for them, but the scene was uncannily comical. They reminded her of the awful visits she periodically endured and was not looking forward to the next physiotherapy appointment.

Here now, the jaded magnolia walls, dotted with dreadful abstracts of unimaginable forms, faced Ruby expression-less. Even the flippant gesture of the vase, full of dusty, artificial flowers, roughly placed next to a heap of random leaflets, strewn across the small off-white side table, did nothing to make any visitor feel welcome.

Taking a deep breath, Ruby closed her eyes and thought of the brightly coloured, fresh freesias, dancing in the wind around her parent's gravestone, releasing their pungent aroma to comfort restless souls. What would they think of her, parked apprehensively outside this clinical adoption office? Would it be a dreadful betrayal despite the limited information they left her? But then, they would not have said anything would they? Guilt haunted her every day, but the hole in her heart would never be filled, until her questions were answered.

A pamphlet brushed lightly against her leg, fluttering aimlessly to the floor, dislodged by the draught of swaying skirt as a well-dressed being, armed with a pile of flaying papers, rushed past without acknowledgement. Ruby leaned awkwardly forward and picked it up. The face of a child, with sad pleading eyes returned her gaze. 'Help me,' he silently cried.

"Maybe one day I can; maybe one day I will, like Mum and Dad helped me."

Mrs Hanover removed her large spectacles, rubbed her tired eyes, pushed herself back against the lumpy contours of her seat and sucked her pen. The ever-increasing pile of paperwork lent precariously towards the edge of the old wooden desk, unable to find a secure place amongst the mound of letters overflowing the wire mesh trays of 'ins' and 'outs'. No doubt the next appointment would be the same as countless others. It would most likely, be one of three reasons. A benevolent social worker, hopeful of a placement; a distraught young unmarried mother; or a lost soul, searching for unobtainable roots.

Either way, she would feel frustration with mindless bureaucracy and restrictions, hampering her caring nature to achieve the job satisfaction promised on her acceptance of the position. Of course, the promises were mainly false, it was once again, the result of a cost cutting exercise. Promotion or demotion, that was the choice.

Broken promises were not on the agenda in her mind. Information she gave her clients was factual and given with as much gentleness and conviction as she dared. Giving genuine hope was her aim, not direction to impossible dreams or aspirations.

Some days, like today, the overload of clerical tasks, the constant ringing of the phone; the depressed faces of childless couples, filling form after form, enduring assessment after assessment, overwhelmed her normal positive mood. Yet, the occasions, where she was able to see the process to the end, lifted her to the moon. To see a delighted couple, loving a new child, or the re-union of long-lost family renewed her faith in the crumbling structure. At least there was a system, and help she would readily give, as much as she was able.

No doubt, her mood would change when she clapped eyes on the next sad being that sat nervously in front of her, looking forward to, or dreading answers, which one way or another, would change their lives forever. Leaning forward, she checked her list for names, and sieving amongst the files, found the old, tattered wallet, retrieved from basement cobwebs, patiently awaiting attention.

The contents were nothing out of the ordinary: standard adoption to a Mr and Mrs Carson. Baby girl, Daisy, given up for adoption at birth, re-named Ruby. It was a miracle the files had survived. Under normal circumstances it would have been destroyed after twenty-five years. Thanks to the lack of funds and failings of the authorities, the new computer system was far from complete and countless little lives, locked away in rusty cabinets still fought for their existence.

Ruby jumped, as the buzzer interrupted her empathy of parentless children, and shone its flashing green light across the closed door. 'Enter' it intermittingly instructed.

"Enter at your peril." Ruby muttered to herself, stuffed the leaflet into her pocket, picked up her stick and politely tapped on the portal to fate, before opening the entrance to another part of her world and responding to the warm smile and beckoning hand.

"Ruby? Hello, I am Mrs Hanover, or Julie to you if you please."

Ruby felt a little more at ease. It was no ogre or wizard about to cast an evil spell on her future. The lady seemed quite human and more importantly – kind.

"Before we start Ruby, do you have any Identification? A driver's licence, or passport? A household bill? I guess you have no birth certificate?"

Driving had never occurred to Ruby. Her dad had always taken her anywhere she chose to go... not that she went anywhere much. Apart from the expense, the confidence to enable such a skill was beyond her capabilities. As for a passport, the thought of travelling anywhere outside Bloomsbury hardly crossed her mind; a birth certificate had never been needed, at least, by herself. Content she was, in the little cottage, tucked away in a country corner of Bloomsbury.

"Am, afraid not. The only thing I have is the appointment letter you sent me, and the bits of information that Mum and Dad left, but nothing official; just to say where I was adopted and the name of your centre. I have the bills for the house though. They are all paid through my bank, Dad – er, I mean Mr Carson, had the solicitor man, sort it out; he put it in the will, in case he and Mum.... well.... died, which they did.... My allowance covers it all, so I don't really see them,

not good at that kind of thing - Dad did it all you see...."
Ruby could hear, but not stop herself, gabbling like a lost
goose.

Julie Hanover, glanced at the documents, in no particular
order, unceremoniously thrust one by one, onto the table.

"It's okay, Ruby. They will be fine. Now then, I have all
the information here. There isn't much I am afraid, but it will
give you a start."

Ruby's heart sank. A start? A start for what? Would there
be more worry, more roads to go down before she found the
truth?

Julie passed her a small magnolia envelope, opened, its
flap clinging on to the certificates, pinned to a thick official
letter, with two bright orange paper clips.

"Do you want me to read it to you Ruby?" Julie kindly
laid her hand over the shaking fingers of her client.

"No, it's okay.... I can read, well, not great, but I can....
then I don't know if I dare. Maybe you could tell me, or not
tell me, I don't know. I don't know why I came. I don't know
anything anymore." Ruby spluttered and burst into tears.

Grabbing her trusty box of tissues, frequently
replenished from her own funds, Julie came to the rescue, as
she had with many.

"Don't you worry Ruby. You are here for a reason, aren't
you? Tears will fall, it's natural. Listen now, let me tuck
those papers away and look when you get home. I will tell
you what is in them. A certificate with your date of birth;
your original name, your mother's name; her date of birth;
her place of residence; the date you were adopted and the
agency - that's us by the way, that handled it all."

Ruby blew her nose in the sodden tissues and mumbled
through the layers.

"....And my dad? I mean....my real dad?"

"Sorry Ruby, no record of your dad. Maybe that's the reason your mum gave you up. Who knows? You could try and find out another way."

"How? I don't know what to do next."

"In the large letter, there are details of a place called the GRO. It's a way to go but they have records of births marriages and deaths. If you go there, they will help you look for your mum and any other members of your family. Then, if, and it's a big IF Ruby, you find anyone, you might be able to get some answers. But Ruby, please remember, you may not like what you find out, or it may be a very happy re-union. Are you prepared for that? Have you got anyone that could help you?"

Ruby shook her head. "Not really, I haven't told anyone about it; Mum and Dad never really talked about it much. Not that they ever lied, I knew I was adopted; they just never talked about it, no need to, I guess. I could go, they will help me, won't they? I just have to find out, even if it's bad. I need to know."

"They should do Ruby but watch out; if anyone asks you for money for help, don't give it to them. See only the officials at the office. The only thing you might have to pay, is for copies of any certificates you want. I wish you the best Ruby. If you get stuck with anything, give me a call."

Clutching the envelope tightly, Ruby mumbled her thanks and slowly walked from the room, repeating her gratefulness as she left.

Mrs Hanover replaced the tattered file in the dusty wallet and smiled to herself; genuinely wishing Ruby would find solace, suppressing doubts, as she knew, many during their searches, fell on stony ground.

Pouring herself a welcoming cup of tea, Ruby glanced at the unopened envelope, glaring her name to warrant attention. 'Ruby Carson', it said; of course, she wasn't - she was never really Ruby Carson. Ruby was a girl who lived in a fictitious fairy land, full of magic, love, and candy floss. Ruby was a girl who adored the people that had showered her with rainbows of affection that would forever colour her heart; but now the fantasy world had disappeared, vapoured away by the wakening rays of the sun, soaking up the morning dew.

She cupped her hand around the mug and sipped the hot brew, hesitant to continue with exploration. After all, as Julie had said, who knows if she will find anything, or anyone? But could she continue her meagre existence with anonymity, content to hide behind the wall of protection her adoptive parents had built? Or should she follow her heart and break down the chain of stones that hung heavy around her neck. It was a question that had surfaced and kept her awake throughout the night.

Swallowing hard, Ruby put down her cup. She was in no doubt, she could not rest until she knew. Gingerly she opened the letters and read them one by one, then re-read them, again and again. Most of it was general information about the GRO and what she could expect to find out about her mother and maybe even her father. However, this was briefly digested as a few words stood out in all their glory. She had a mother... and she wasn't Ruby...she was Daisy....her name was Daisy and she had to find her mum.

Ruby was not looking forward the long train journey to Southampton. Telephone calls had proved fruitless, being shifted from one department to the other, then back again, she came to the conclusion a visit in person, as Julie had advised, was the only sensible option. It wasn't as if she had not ventured far from Bloomsbury; her parents being fortunate enough to partake of a holiday on the coast now and again, but the ever-increasing necessity to deal with official bodies on her own was taking a toll on her mental health. However, needs must, and determination drove her to overcome her fears.

Swaying with the rhythmic sound of the train as it clicked its way along the track, her head moving gently against the window; Ruby watched the trees dance in the wind; their autumn colours wilting as the showers spattered dying leaves to the ground. She was glad she had chosen a warm, woollen coat and fur lined boots, even though it was a little early for winter wear.

It seemed hours before she finally reached Southampton station and stood in a daze on the platform with a crumpled leaflet clutched to her chest; Ruby had no idea which way to go. Thankfully, a fellow passenger emerged from the second carriage and nudged her elbow, making her jump and pull her bag closer.

"Oh, sorry, didn't mean to startle you, but you looked a bit lost. Maybe I can help you?" The man smiled.

Ruby stuttered, embarrassed at her own inadequacy. "Er, y..yes, I am a bit. I am trying to get to the GRO, but these directions on this map are so confusing and I am not sure I am up to walking a long way."

"Well, you are in luck, I am going there myself; I work there you see; only in the afternoons like; getting all the post together and stuff. It's a bit of a walk, about twenty minutes in the rain or ten minutes on the bus." He laughed. "It will be here in a few minutes - stops outside the station, or you could take a cab if you are feeling flush."

Ruby was feeling very flushed, and not through richness of the purse. The attention of any man was a rare occurrence. It was something that hardly crossed her mind, having long since perceived that no one would be interested in helping her do anything at all.

"Oh, that would be wonderful, the bus will be fine...just fine. I have to go and find my mother." she babbled.

"No problem! It doesn't matter if we miss it, they run every ten minutes or so. Where is your mother? In the Ladies, is she? I can wait if you like?"

Ruby found this strangely funny and relaxed a little. "No, you don't understand, I need to find my mother.... I mean.... find who she is.... I mean.... I know her name... but not if she's alive, married, dead or whatever."

"You are certainly going to the right place then; but it's a minefield, and that's where yours truly, Philip Turner, can help you out Madam." Philip took off his woolly hat and bowed.

Finding herself involuntary giggling, Ruby attempted a wobbly, ungainly curtsey. "Thank you, kind sir, I am Ru.... Daisy and pleased to meet you."

"Very pleased to meet you too Miss Daisy - very pleased indeed."

Chapter Seven
The Mobility Scooter

Molly lounged lazily on the sofa, stretching her long legs over the patchy cloth. One hand behind her head, she flapped the letter in front of her face with the other, the remaining pages tossed randomly to the floor.

Marcia, uninterested and unperturbed that her private correspondence had been infiltrated, continued to stare at the television, fascinated by a very overweight chef demonstrating how to do the perfect Sunday roast.

"Hey, Moll, what you reckon? We could do a Sunday lunch like that, looks better than that frozen stuff we get."

"Mmm? What?"

"That Sunday lunch thing, we could do that. Why do they call it Sunday lunch d'you reckon?"

"Because people eat it on a Sunday." Molly glanced briefly at her friend, before returning to the communication.

"Oh. Well, we could, that's if we remember if it is Sunday; can hardly remember which day it is these days, they all seem the same." Marcia giggled.

"Mmm..." came the flat reply.

"Those roasties look scrummy. Not sure 'bout those green grassy things, or those little carrots. Julian can keep them, ain't big enough to fill a mouse."

"What grassy things?"

"Those long green things with thistles on the top. Aspygrass."

"Asparagus Marcia; it's Asparagus."

"Give them a miss then, bet you and Tan could do the roasties, I can easy do that chicken. Bit of butter on the top and lob it in the oven."

Molly, at the mention of the word 'oven', placed the letter on her stomach and answered with a tinge of sarcasm.

"You aren't going near any chicken, or the oven. You and ovens don't mix. Anyway, it's still all black from the last time; it stinks when you put anything in it. Sheila will be round in a flash, accusing us of cremating the dog again."

Marcia huffed. "Am alright with faggots ain't I? It don't smell that bad now. Looks easy enough to me... aw come on, if you stay with me, I'll be okay."

Not wishing to dampen any enthusiasm, and actively encourage Marcia to gain any level of skills, Molly relented. But there were limits; the history of kitchen disasters spoke for itself.

"Alright, if you want. As long as I am there to make sure you don't blow the whole house up. Will get the stuff from Watchco's on Friday, but you can forget the roasties. Out of the bag is a lot easier, and safer."

Marcia smiled. "Fantabulous! Don't get those aspidistruss things though; those big peas in a tin we always have are nice."

Molly grinned. "Marrowfat peas, yes, those big ones in a tin. We'll stick to them. Changing the subject; there are some forms for you to fill in."

Ignoring the comment, Marcia tried in vain, to divert the issue. "Don't think we'll do the gravy like that though, that granule stuff is better, just add hot water. I know it sometimes comes out weird but it's alright."

Reacting to Marcia's delaying tactics had become an art form. If there was one thing Marcia was good at, it was selective hearing and ability to escape from anything to do with clerical tasks. Molly had long since discovered that perseverance usually resulted in success.

"Your gravy makes slurry look appetising." Molly reluctantly moved herself to a seating position, picked the papers from the floor and grabbed a pen from the side table.

"What's slurry?"

"It's a posh name for mushed cow pee and poo."

"Cow pee and Poo!!" Marcia immediately distracted from crispy chicken. "Who the hell would want cow pee and poo?"

Tanya, returning from a hectic day at the beauty bar – namely, sitting around, filing a few nails, and gossiping about the local male talent, as usual – did not want to miss out on anything. Flinging her jacket across the stair banister, she flew through the door faster than a feather whipped up by a tornado.

"Why you talking about cow pee?"

Molly smirked. "Hello. Nice to see you, how was work? You seem to be very happy these days. I was comparing your mum's gravy to slurry if you must know."

"Yeh, it was great!" Tanya flashed her pampered fingers, purple glittering as the evening sun shone through the open curtains, then reduced the fleeting ambience to the normal level of basic aura.

"Mum's gravy and slurry - not much difference there then." Tanya taunted. "Both of it, liquid shit!"

"TANYA!" Scolded Marcia. "Don't talk like that. Me gravy ain't that bad."

Tanya still grinned; she knew her mother would not take offence at any joke aimed at her ability. In fact, the reaction was usually totally the opposite.

"You must admit mother, it's either so thick you can stand a spoon in it, or so thin you can't even see it on the plate."

Marcia found the whole thing amusing. "Yeh, 'spose you are right there!"

Much as she did not want to spoil a good laugh, Molly was glad that she had managed to prise Marcia away from the television.

"Right then, to these forms.... Do them now, or they won't get done at all."

"What forms?" Tanya and Marcia spoke together.

"Disability stuff, because of the report from Helga Hitler what's-her-face."

At the mention of physiotherapy, Marcia's face drooped. Seeing her friends expected un-enthusiasm, Molly continued to explain that the report from the hospital said that mobility had not really improved, and she would be entitled to some extra support and helpful aids...and wasn't that good?

Of course, what the report actually said, was that Marcia's condition had continued to deteriorate as expected, albeit slowly. Although still able to move independently with sticks, it was felt that further mobility support would enhance quality of life and encourage Marcia to partake in outdoor activities more often. Therefore, it was suggested that an application should be made for increased benefit and possible provision of relevant appliances.

"Why have we got to do that then? Can't we take them to Audrey? She knows how to wangle all that stuff?" Marcia frowned.

"Apparently, it's all changed, some benefit called DLA is coming in and you have to send this lot off in the post. Audrey's getting on a bit now Marcia, the office shut ages ago, I told you. She might help if we get stuck, but I think we have to try first."

Grimly, Marcia resolved herself to attempting the dreaded task.

"I'll help as well." Tanya volunteered.

Knowing Tanya, as Molly did exceedingly well, the input from an over-zealous, cocky sixteen-year-old, would not be helpful.

"It's okay, we'll do it. You can make another cuppa if you would."

"Okey-dokey. Will do your nails later Auntie Moll if you like!"

One of the advantages of having someone in your household working in the beauty business was heaven for Molly, however, for now, other things took priority.

Flipping through the papers, Molly sighed. "There's loads of questions Marcia. I'll do the ones you can't."

"That's just about all of them then." Marica winced.

"How many metres can you walk without your sticks do you reckon?"

"Depends where the meters are, might be able to walk from ours to Sheila's, I think hers is in the hall, same as us."

"Right!" Molly raised her eyes to the ceiling and circled the lowest possible answer.

"Are you able to carry out household tasks, for example preparing meals, personal needs? If no, describe your difficulties."

"What do they mean? Are they saying I can't make a bloody cup of tea or go to the lav? Course I can. I ain't that thick."

Tanya had ears like a bat and could pick up any sound yards away, especially if there was something interesting going on.

"Chances of you making a cup of tea without flipping the tea bag across the room Mother, are pretty slim. Just put 'impossible without falling over', Moll." She shouted.

Marcia retorted. "That's great then; make out I am some idiot then - tell the whole world..."

"Never mind, I will jot something down. Don't fret so Marcia, the worse we make this look, the more chance of some extra money."

Being content with her lot, Marcia was not bothered about finances, and indeed rarely thought about her immobility; until of course, it was highlighted in black and white and propelled her out of her comfort zone. Whether she would get extra benefit or not, the forms were unimportant.

"Are you able to make small trips outside of your house independently? For example, shopping, hospital, post office etc. If no, please describe how your disability prevents this." Molly continued unintimidated.

"Why are they asking that? They know all this from the last lot of rubbish they sent me. I reckon I can get on a bus, with me sticks. If Mrs Hargreaves can do it, I can, and she's at least a hundred years old."

Tanya returned with three mugs of steaming brew, two of which slanted dangerously as they chinked together, insecurely held with two cupped fingers.

"Put them down there m'girl, haven't I told you to use the tray?" Anything to redirect away from the interrogation.

"Be fair Mum, you can't properly, not on your own. The Last time we went, you fell off the bus and crushed that Peter kid against the fence. He was well miffed about his sausage roll; squashed to bits it was, all over his face...and it was one of those extra-large ones from that new Greggs. Told you I should have got off first."

Unrelenting in her defence, Marcia crossed her arms. "Serves him right; shouldn't have nicked it from Gregg then!"

Molly slammed down the papers in frustration. "You know what? I'll do these myself. You sign the last sheet where the cross is."

Although Marcia's limited abilities had hampered any kind of academic progression, thanks to Tanya – and Molly's encouragement – she had managed to grasp basic phonetic reading skills and was able to scribble some kind of illegible signature. This she did with unusual pleasure on the appointed place, as, of course, it meant she no longer had to bear those intolerable probing questions.

It was one of those occasions, where there was no point pursuing anything. Taking the hot mug of tea, Molly ignored the triumphant look on Marcia's face.

Marcia returned her interest in the television. "Look Tan, look at that lovely chicken. We're going to do one of them on Sunday."

Tanya plonked herself roughly down beside Molly, causing her to spill her tea, splashing it across the paper.

"Oops! Sorry."

Scowling, Molly turned away, placed the spotted documents on the arm of the sofa, and continued to complete the application. The brown marks did not look that bad, and she thought, if anything, it would help the cause.

It was several Friday, Saturday, Sunday lunches – and many desecrated chickens – later that a large letter arrived successfully through the letter box. Not that they had a lot of post, and that which fought its way past Jacobs gnashers usually ended up un-opened in the bin. Both Tanya and

Molly remained vigilant, not necessarily in fear of missing any official correspondence, but far more importantly, any coupons for free beauty products.

The contents of that letter proved to cause a very mixed reaction from all.

Marcia was completely dismayed. "What do they mean, a mobility scooter? I don't want no scooter. Me size eight don't work with me size three. Can't balance on one of them. Tried it when I was a kid and ran over a cat. Don't want one, don't need one."

To the contrary Tanya was impulsively ecstatic. "It's not that kind of scooter, it's motorised. Cor! That's brill, what fun we can have on that!"

Molly immediately dampened the inappropriate enthusiasm. "It would be for your mother, not you Tanya."

"I know." exclaimed the teenager haughtily. "She couldn't go out on her own on it. Can you imagine!"

The thought of Marcia on any kind of motorised contraption filled Molly with horror, but who was she to say that it was an impossibility. No way would she let Marcia out on her own, but with suitable support it would allow them all to go further afield, it would make life a whole lot easier. Supporting Marcia's expanding body was becoming more difficult by the day.

"I think it's worth a try Marcia. Tom's good at all that kind of thing, maybe he can rig it a bit so you don't get into bother. It says her that you qualify for more benefit too, and you can have an allowance for it."

Marcia was horrified. "What's the point? Am happy as I am, sat on me sofa. I use me sticks when I got to go anywhere...And there's that old wheelchair - IF I can't manage. Tell them we don't want it."

"Don't want what?" uttered a deep voice as Tom poked his head around the lounge door.

"A mobility bike!" Tanya hooted. "Aw, come on, it'll be mint, you can at least try. Tom will help, won't you?"

"I don't care what colour it is, I ain't going on one an' that's that!"

Tom's initial reaction was one of petrification, he coughed on his own saliva as the sharp intake of breath invaded his lungs. There had been enough incidents in a wheelchair over the years, let alone on a motorised scooter.

"Not sure about that to be honest. Suppose we could give it a go; I have some safety straps we could put on it. Do you have a choice? Don't you qualify for a car or something? You could learn to drive soon Tanya, I was thinking about it the other day, could give you some lessons."

"Learn to drive?" Marcia shrieked. "Who's got a car round here? Not many, and what we do with a car?"

"I could learn anyway. Might get a car later on if me wages go up. One of those sports Mini Cooper things. Catherine's got one, it's pink and dead cool."

"Who's Catherine?" Tom asked

"She's my boss, at the salon."

Molly decided to curb the discussion and take charge. "Hold on everyone! Let's hit a bit of reality here. Tanya, you aren't getting a car. Tom, you aren't giving Tanya any lessons until she's settled in that job and earned herself a bit and Marcia, you can at least give it a go if the benefits people are offering it to you. Turn it down and they won't give you nothing else. Besides, you can send it back if it you can't manage it. Have a bit of spirit and try it!"

Defeated, and dejected, all gave in to Molly's demands.

And so, it was, a few weeks later, the shiny yellow, Beast of Chalksbury, stood majestically in the front garden of the Duncan's abode. As was with any major event, gossip quickly spread, until half the residents of Clover close, together with all but one of the family, surrounded the vehicle; completely oblivious to Marcia's plight as she peeped out from behind the tired nets. It dawned upon her, there would be no peace until she tried the blasted thing.

The dreaded day of practice arrived all too soon. Marcia was adamant she was not going to get on it with everyone watching, much to the disappointment of the neighbours.

Sheila crossed her arms and leant against the frame of her front doorway. It was incredible how she could talk and still keep her 'fag' stuck on her lips; a skill many people of Chalksbury had mastered without study. "Aw, come on Marcia, Let's have a laugh; gawd knows we could do with it!"

Tom surveyed the cracked uneven pavement; visions of Marcia flying down the middle of the road and crashing into someone's wall came rushing to his mind."

"Maybe, we should take it somewhere safer, away from the road. We could all give it a go then, and Marcia will feel safer. What you reckon Marc?"

Marcia grumbled. "If I HAVE TO."

"Right then, we'll go to the car park by the river. It will be safe there, not many people around this time of day. I'll put the scooter on the truck. Molly, you heave Marcia up in the cab. Where's Tanya?"

At work, she'll be sorry to miss this," laughed Molly. "Think she finishes at three, will leave her a note just in case - she'll probably be off with her mates somewhere or other. I doubt she'll be back 'til tea."

Molly had long since given up on Tanya's whereabouts. Regrettably, she had reached the conclusion some time ago, admitting to herself that Tanya was a blossoming flower; it was time for his daughter to take some sort of responsibility. The few rules that revolved around night adventures were generally respected and an element of trust had been established. There was a determination, not often seen within some families on the estate, that Tanya would at least have a better upbringing than her parents, and drug abuse was the most important thing Molly prayed would be avoided. Not that she would advocate any other kind of predicament, though Tanya was made aware of consequences; she kept the thought to herself that anything else, was surmountable. After all, who was she to judge – but drugs she could not abide.

Marcia on the other hand, was so elated and full of pride that she had actually produced a child that had managed to finish school, gain a qualification and secure a job, no other dangers ever crossed her mind. The make-up of the society on the estate was so varied, every element was accepted as normality of life. Generally, she left the majority of discipline and guidance to Molly, who was absolutely perfect, and able to 'sort out all that kind of stuff.'

Thankfully, Tanya was aware of Molly's father's drug misuse and had chosen not to go down that road; despite several school colleagues misguided choices. She had a decent job and was particular about her appearance. Wanting to make something of herself was important and that path of self-destruction was not, and never would be, the way to go. The delights of other normal activities of teenage rampage, of course, did not totally escape her, but then, that was fun.... and as long as she kept her wits about her, she was not about to disappoint her family if she could help it.

Hoisting Marcia into the truck had become an art form. Tom and Molly, experienced in the matter, had long since learned to secure Marcia's feet to the cab step and give her bottom an almighty shove. This invariably left the poor woman with her face buried in ripped seat covering, and her legs dangling out the door, size eight tangled with size three - but at least, she was in.

Quickly scribbling a note on the front of a dog chewed magazine, Molly threw it on the table and glared at Jacobs.

"You munch this anymore and you are meat."

Jacobs, of course, had no idea what she was talking about and looked dismayed that he was being left behind. His soppy look and little whine had absolutely the desired effect.

"Oh, come on then - but if you fart in the cab again, Tom will go ape. And no running off either!"

It turned out to be a godsend, that, regardless of the warm weather, the car park was indeed, almost empty. Visitors that were fortunate to own a vehicle usually restricted their explorations to the weekends. Those that chose otherwise, were either solitary souls evaluating their lives, or fishermen escaping from the boredom of staid routines and nagging wives.

The gleaming scooter stood in all its splendour, the afternoon light flickering across the polished paintwork, reflecting the odd shapes of expectant audience. Cushions of unblemished, soft black vinyl invited their first customer, anxious to comfort and support. There was no doubt, that this brand-new vehicle was the most expensive, glorious piece of equipment that had ever graced its presence in the

Duncan household. One would have thought this precious gift would have been looked upon with grateful acceptance; however, one person was, initially, not at all impressed.

Molly pulled Marcia's arm, leading her closer to impending death. "Look at it, Marcia, it's brill! It's even got a little basket on the front for your shopping. Listen to Tom Marcia; you just press a button and off you go. It's all done with your hands – you don't even need to use your feet!"

"Good job, cos they don't work anyway. How does it stop then?" Marcia feigned interest.

"Er... don't really know. How does it stop Tom? That's the most important think I reckon." Molly ran her fingers over the controls.

Tom was in his element. Tinkling around with cars, bikes, gadgets, or anything else that technology had to offer, fed his brain with constant sustenance.

"It's easy. Look Marcia, I read all the stuff, I will show you, am dying for a ride, come on!"

Marcia watched Tom mount the appliance with expertise. "You just turn the key like this, and these levers make it go back and forward. This button is the speed and when you take your hand off the throttle it stops all by itself.... and if it doesn't there's this emergency brake button here. Look it's easy! I don't even think you need straps, it's safe enough!"

"I'd like to throttle all of you." Marcia grumbled. "I ain't never going to be able to do it. You remember when I fell off me bike? Me bum was sore for weeks and me size three was swollen 'til it looked like me size eight!"

Her unenthusiasm was completely ignored. Molly and Tom were full of joy and excitement.

"Oh, go on Tom." Molly shrieked. "Have a go - then I can. Ooh it's off... look Marcia. Look at Tom!"

Tom was grinning like a Cheshire cat, as he winged his way in a large circle, then proceeded to spiral this way and that, reluctant to give his new 'toy' to anyone.

"Aw, come on Tom. Let's have a go!" Molly waved her arms and chased the elated driver around, begging him to stop.

The attire that Molly had specifically chosen for the event, for once, was evidently practical. The white, sleeveless roll neck jumper, perfectly co-ordinated her pale green slacks. Mid heels, accentuated the flawless contours of her ankles, somehow reducing the manly size of her feet. Slipping into the seat with utter decorum, she quickly mastered the controls and followed the trail of the master Tom, although a little slower.

"It's pimps Marcia. You have a go now!"

Tom hooted with laughter. "Pimps? That's rich coming from you."

Molly glared at Tom. "Shut the fuck up, that's all done now."

Marcia, not hearing the remark, looked upon the proceedings with utter despair; sooner or later she would have to take the plunge....

"I can't get me leg over! I ain't gonna fit in the seat, me arse is too big. I'm too heavy, the bloody thing will break!"

A little frustrated, Tom knew it was a time to take action, or the project would be doomed to failure.

"Will you shut up whinging and be a bit grateful. It's meant to help you and it's made for people of your build. It's simple.... no, sorry, meant easy - that's the whole point! If it don't work out then it don't, but give it a go. We made all this effort to get it for you Marc!"

Molly, being a little more sympathetic, placed her arm under Marcia's and helped her onto the scooter. "It's okay

Marcia, you can do it - sit in the seat for now; see how you feel."

Surprisingly, once Marcia was seated, she actually felt quite secure. Her feet rested comfortably on the footplates. Even her size eight failed to flop over the edge as she adjusted her position, wobbling her ample form back and forth until she was sure that no part of her body was in imminent danger of departing. A smile dared to grace her hairy lips.

Molly stood back and put her hands on her hips and laughed. "There you go then! That's not so bad, is it?"

"Ooh, er... it's alright I suppose, I don't think I would slip off me seat."

Leaning over the handles, Tom pointed out the controls again. "All you need to know for now is that turning this one makes it go. If you take your hand off it, the scooter will stop, and if it don't then you press this button."

Marcia gulped...part of her wanted to vacate immediately, yet another voice was calling her to surmount the challenge. "What's all these lights for and this bit?"

Tom reassured her that they were things to go over later, and the 'bit' pulled backwards was reverse. "Don't worry Marcia, all you need to do at the moment is move forward and stop. I set the speed on this button, so, you can't go too fast. We will walk right beside you - go on."

Marcia clung on to the handles with both hands. "How do I do that and hang on at the same time?"

"You move your hand like this. You can keep your hand on the handle and turn the throttle at the same time. Don't think about it, just turn it and try and steer."

Marcia leaned forward like a jockey on a horse in the starting gate, ready for the Grand National; her bottom of course, still glued to the saddle.

"Sit back Marcia!" Molly giggled. "You won't see where you are going!"

Marcia nervously raised her head. "Right! Here goes!" Prepared for an ultimate rocket launch, she turned the appropriate control. The mobility scooter did not move.

"Aw! It's not working!" She wailed. "I broke it!"

Tom, who was stood apprehensively close, came to her rescue. "You haven't done it hard enough. Try again."

Marcia swallowed and followed the instructions. The scooter moved forward.

"HOLY SHIT! It's moving... HELP!"

Molly and Tom positioned themselves protectively either side. Walking slowly beside the scooter as Marcia continued to progress in a forward direction.

"That's it, Marcia! You are doing it! Carry on...keep your hands firmly on the steering handles and keep going straight." Molly was exceedingly surprised that Marcia had managed to get on at all, let alone make it travel.

"I'm going, I'm going... Cor! This ain't too bad!"

Changing direction became a bit of a challenge, but with Tom's hands placed firmly on top of Marcia's, turning a circle was eventually mastered. In fact, Marcia went round in circles so many times, she was feeling a little dizzy, and Tom, fed up with the monotony, let go and watched.

"Right....Now...pull that hand back off the throttle and it will stop." Tom instructed.

"What's the throttle again?" Marcia shouted, this time with more confidence.

Molly stood back, jumped up and down and clapped her hands in delight. "It's that big black thing you've got your hand on silly!"

Releasing her grip abruptly, the scooter came to an immediate halt. "Wow! I did it, Moll! I made it move and it stopped!" Marcia beamed with satisfaction. "Let's do some more! Let's go along the path. Aw come on...I ain't pregnant this time, I ain't gonna end up in the drink!"

Molly looked at Tom and shrugged her shoulders, her dark eyes requesting guidance. Not wishing to dampen Marcia's spirits, she was still apprehensive.

"Well? I don't see why not – if we stay close. I don't think the straps will work, they might get tangled, and she seems to be able to master the art of stopping. There won't be anyone around and it's better than trying it in the street. The more practice the better and Jacobs could do with a walk; he'll probably get soaked and mess up my cab, but what the heck? Bit mean to leave him in the truck."

Cyril flicked the rod with the maximum force his little arms could muster and cast his line far into the river. It was a very long time since he had been fishing, but time was on his hands now that the circus was no longer in existence. Contemplating his long enjoyable career in entertainment, he was not sad to retire. His aging bones no longer able to sustain the constant walloping of hunting clowns, or the weight of the sodden sponges as they splattered against his tiny face. Looking out over the water, he chuckled to himself, remembering the time he fished a tiny baby, flaying her little arms and legs as she squirmed inside the landing net. It was a grand day that he would never forget. Forever friends made and that little urchin? Well; little Tanya? All grown up she is, and a bonny girl at that.

The tranquillity of the afternoon was welcoming; peaceful and silent save for the chirp of cheerful birds and the light splash of water as hungry ducks foraged beneath the course. In the distance a faint whirring vaguely whisked through air, not unpleasant and hardly disturbing; some other lucky fisherman casting his line no doubt. Cyril lay on the lush green carpet and closed his eyes.

"That's it, Marcia! You got it!" Molly walked briskly alongside her friend, whilst Tom, tootled along behind, a little complacent, content to amuse Jacobs by repeatedly throwing a boomerang stick, which the dog incessantly retrieved, anxious for more fun.

The look of triumph on Marcia's face was rare, and completely welcoming. Molly looked proudly on as the driver took full control. These small steps of achievement, minor accomplishments to most, were conquering mountains for Marcia, who smiled and dared to take her eyes off the controls. She felt the breeze brush her face, and the cool tickling as it fumbled its way through her tangled curls. It felt good!

"Whoopeeeee! This is fantabulous! Can we go a bit faster now, it's this throttle thing you just turn up a bit?"

Molly broke into a trot, then into a run. "Turn it back a bit Marcia! I can't keep up with these shoes on...."

Cyril rose sleepily from his dreams and checked his line. No bites yet. Reeling it in he wondered should he use the luncheon meat, maybe the fish would be more interested in that. Breaking off a small chunk, he reloaded his hook and prepared to launch again. His actions were interrupted by the increasing volume of engine murmur. Turning his head sideways he saw the cause of the noise, and he blinked in disbelief as recognition came to mind. 'No, can't be; must be seeing things.' Scratching his head, he stood, rod in hand, ready to cast, staring at Marcia, looming towards him.

Marcia, brimming with elation, was far from worried, she

had not enjoyed herself so much for ages. "Hey! It's Cyril! Look at me Cyril! Am on the move like I never before!"

Tom, about to throw the stick for the umpteenth time, averted his eyes as he heard Marcia's shrieks. Lobbing the wood aimlessly, it landed in the middle of the river with an almighty splosh; Jacobs accepted the challenge and plunged into the water.

"Marcia! Slow down!" he shouted, "Take your hands off the throttle!"

Molly kicked off her shoes and pursued the vehicle. "For God's sake, Tom, catch her up! How can something like that go so fast? I thought you stopped it speeding like that."

"I did! She must have turned the regulator by mistake!"

But Marcia did not slow down. Marcia was in control and having a ball.... until she flew past Cyril, much too close for comfort, and his bait of luncheon meat became well and truly hooked on the wire shopping basket.

Beatrice and Elizabeth sat on their balcony, as they had done, most days for the past twenty years or so. Frail old ladies now, they had come to love this daily routine and, weather permitting, watch the peaceful comings and goings of riverside life. They still enjoyed their afternoon tea, occasionally partaking in the Earl Grey if their fancy took them. Long gone was Mrs Witherspoon, maker of the wonderous strawberry jam, but the name carried on, thanks to her daughter Mildred, who had taken on the family business. Thus, they were still able to savour the sweet sticky flavour of the fruits, lavished with thick clotted cream, smothering rich floury scones.

Occasionally, peace was disrupted. The infiltration of those 'noisy council people' was ultimately frowned upon and today was no exception as the crescendo of unified voices spoilt their day.

"Goodness me Elizabeth, look at that. Motorbikes are not allowed along here, are they?"

Elizabeth sipped at her tea, before replacing the bone china cup delicately on the saucer. "Certainly not Beatrice! I do not know what the world is coming to, no respect these days."

"Exactly Elizabeth, I think, once again, the committee must be informed."

Cyril was sincerely regretting choosing a twenty-pound line. Far too thick for the small river fish, it was over-ambitious to say the least. He also mistakenly thought, hanging on to the rod would save his equipment from instant destruction. Sadly therefore, he was thrown off his little feet and dragged along the bank like a demented pike, desperately trying to escape the wraths of human hunters. It was at least thirty metres before the line eventually snapped and poor Cyril catapulted through the air and sploshed deep into the water, narrowly averting a long stringy branch attached to a soggy dog. Jacobs, far from attempting any kind of rescue, proceeded to pounce all over the dwarf, in a vain attempt to entice him to play 'fetch'. The resulting gurgling shrieks, mingled with enthusiastic, slobbery barks could be heard for miles.

It was some time before the poor man gained control of the situation. Seeing that play was out of the question, Jacobs, jaws firmly clamped round his treasure, paddled off towards the small island further along the river. Cyril, up to his neck in water, began to wade slowly to the bank; his thick corduroys and denim shirt, sodden and heavy, hampering every step. He could see Marcia, flying along on the scooter, and, he knew, with despair, what was coming next – and there was nothing he could do about it.

Marcia, feeling the jolt, suddenly realised there could be a bit of a problem. "Molleeee!" She yelled.

"Take your hand off the throttle!!" Shouted Tom and Molly together. "Now!"

Marcia obeyed the command immediately. Of course, she took her left hand off the throttle, and off the steering. The scooter ground to a halt, not before Marcia's other hand, gripped tightly round the right handle, veered the vehicle sideways. Fishing line wrapped around the wheels, it tipped, dangling dangerously on the riverbank, with Marcia frozen to the spot.

Tom and Molly ran as fast as they could; they nearly reached Marcia before she, and her trusty steed, disappeared into the depths.

Hidden by the lush foliage, a young couple canoodled, embarking on a journey of sexual exploration. The island paradise, inaccessible for most, was a prime spot for lovers and birdwatchers alike.

The young beau, daring to go further, cast aside the unbuttoned shirt and caressed his hand over her bare breast. Who could resist those dark tantalising eyes, the impeccable form of her body, and the long bare legs, tanned from the summer rays? Kissing her plump red lips, he moved his unchallenged hand beneath the frills of her short cotton skirt.

She breathed deeply, allowing the pleasure of his touch, feeling the response as he pressed himself against her thigh. Flickering his tongue upwards he followed the beautiful contours of her neck to her jewelled ear. Her heart missed a beat as she heard the inevitable gasps. "Please...no one can see..."

Torn between morality and temptation, she paused her passions for a brief moment. "We mustn't Rich, I don't want to end up like my mum. We'll have to be content with the usual."

"We've been doing the usual for ages, I won't let you get like your mum; I promise; don't you want to?"

"Yes, but..." Her weak protests diminishing, in favour of unrelenting arousal.

"I have something; it will be safe, I promise. Please."

Her voice hardly audible, swallowing hard, she mumbled. "Okay."

Richard did not waste a second for fear of retraction of consent. Leaning sideways, he picked up his jacket and fumbled clumsily in the inner pocket for the item that had been awaiting its debut. His potential conquest lay back, amorous and waiting; watching with anticipation as he ripped open the packet with his teeth and unzipped his jeans.

It was a real shame that the proceedings were completely dampened by the shower of mud and dirty water, violently expelled by soaked fur, as Jacobs scrambled through the undergrowth to greet his owner. Tanya flapped her hands to dispel the torrent.

"What the bloody hell? Oh my God it's Jacobs."

Leaping up, Tanya frantically tried to fasten her top, as the dog lavished affection. Richard had no idea what was going on, but sensing imminent defeat, pushed himself off the ground and stood with his jeans round his ankles - the rise to the occasion having completely deflated.

"Good grief!" Tanya wailed, then reduced her voice to a hoarse whisper. "Fuck! Get down Rich! It's the whole fucking family, and that bloody dwarf Cyril. Duck! For Christ's sake. If I am caught, I'm done for! Shoo! Jacobs - bugger off!!"

Richard, trying unsuccessfully, to pull up his trousers with one hand, crouched in the grass besides Tanya.

"Someone's in trouble though Tan. Look, there's been an accident for sure."

"There's always accidents where mother is concerned; believe me; this river is jinxed."

"Mother?" Richard's face paled.

"Yes, Mother! And worse still, my bloody Aunt! we have to scarper and fast.... Jacobs BUGGER OFF!!!"

"But they might drown Tan!"

"No, she won't, she's used to it." Peeping through the grass Tanya saw Tom and Molly wading to the rescue. Satisfying herself that neither her mother nor Cyril were in imminent danger of instant death, she instructed the terrified suitor.

"Throw that stick as far as you can, and we'll leg it out the back of the island; through the other side of the river and over the fields."

"B...but, we gonna be soaked."

Tanya gritted her teeth. "Which would you rather? A wet arse or a beaten arse, take your bloody pick!"

'Rich' did not need telling twice.

Elizabeth leaned over the balcony and popped the last piece of delicious scone into her mouth. The cream seeped to the corners; chuckling, she brushed if off with the back of her hand.

"I do wish you would use the napkins, Elizabeth. I have mentioned it on more than one occasion." Her sister nagged.

"Sorry, didn't think, but something is going on with those council people. Do you think we should render assistance?"

Beatrice held her cup away from her face, surveying the mayhem in disbelief. "I don't know what they are doing, they could be drunk. There seems to be some sort of contraption steaming in the water, covered in flowery cloth and there is a pair of feet- least I think it's a pair - sticking out the water. A man and a woman are shouting and splashing about. There's a big fish swimming towards them and a red hat floating down the river...Oh, and there's a beaver with a log. There is also something going on by the tree on that island as well - looks like a man with no trousers on. Elizabeth? Elizabeth?"

"A man?" Elizabeth shouted. "With no trousers?"

"Yes, Elizabeth, it's most disturbing and utterly intolerable; a stern letter must be written to the committee indeed. Elizabeth. Elizabeth! What are you doing?"

"Fetching the binoculars."

Marcia had a definite sense of familiarity. She could just about keep her head above water by leaning forward with her head on the side of the steering bar. Thankfully, the scooter had landed sideways, in the shallower part of the river; but still she floundered in mud and fluid up to her chest. Her feet, on the other hand, splayed out awkwardly, unable to find any security. Visions of swirling tides, fishing nets and squirming snakes swarmed her mind. She vaguely remembered the red fountain, and Molly kissing her face and holding her close, protecting her from bloody devils. Third time wasn't going to be lucky, she sure as hell was going to die.

Molly reached the distraught woman first. "It's okay Marc, we got you."

She put her arms under Marcia's torso. "It's no good Tom, I can't get them round – you'll have to go the other side."

Tom obliged without question, and between the two of them prised Marcia from the mobility scooter, dragged her up the bank and propped her up against a litter bin. She mopped her brow and looked blankly at her rescuers, before bursting into tears.

"Look what I done now." She blubbered. "Oh, am useless ain't I? In the drink again, and after all I said."

Molly glared, intending to reprimand Marcia for not following instructions, but her demeanour softened as she surveyed the damage. First, Tom, stretched out with his hands behind his back, trying to catch his breath, hair stuck to his forehead, clothes completely sodden. Herself? Just as bad – the pale green slacks could easily have passed for camouflaged army pants. Her long dark locks, no longer voluminous and shiny, hung in dripping, matted dreadlocks.

Then there was Marcia, slumped up against a litter bin which was full of yesterday's picnic remains. She resembled a rotten sack of potatoes, and about the same colour. How could she be cross? They were all safe and sound, and, after all, this was Marcia. Why would they expect anything else?

"Cheer up! To be fair Marcia," Tom chirped. "It was that fishing line that buggered up the wheels. And it was probably my fault, I should have put a permanent cap on the scooter."

Marcia stopped crying and eyes brightened. "So, it weren't really my fault then? You should have put a cap on it for sure Tom. Good job all that petrol didn't come out into the river; those poor fishes would be dead."

"What? No, Marcia it's electric, there's no petrol." He replied.

"Electric?! Gawd, you never told me that! Look what happened to our mum. I could be electrocutionised."

Cyril slopped along the path and joined the soggy party. "It had to be you lot, didn't it? Can't even do a bit of fishin' without it turning into a war zone! Still, are we all alright then?"

Marcia grinned. "Yep, am alright, I ain't electocutionised. That was lucky, Tom said I would have been okay if I wore a cap."

Cyril arched back his head, fell to the floor and roared with laughter. "Well, you got a cap on now Marc...If I am not mistaken it's half a McDonalds Big Mac."

Sure enough, a polystyrene container – an escapee from the overflowing bin – adorned Marcia's head, accessorised by a lonely strip of lettuce hanging from her ear. Jacobs came bounding up the path and jumped on her shoulders, licking her face, anxious for a piece of the action.

Molly was the next to break down, followed by Tom, who suddenly found the whole episode hysterical.

"Oh. Marcia!" He bawled, "What would the world do without you?!"

Elizabeth was loath to give up the binoculars. Despite pulling hard on the straps, Beatrice was unsuccessful in obtaining the magnifying eyes.

"What's happening now Elizabeth? I think it will be in order for me to assess the situation as well."

Elizabeth eagerly swayed the binoculars left then right. "Oh, it' so exciting Beatrice. It does remind me of that time, years ago, when that girl had the baby, you remember? There's people lying on their backs kicking their legs in the air now, and they are all wet."

"Yes, I certainly do; what about the island? What's happening over there? What about the man with no trousers? We must ascertain his identity and inform the police."

Beatrice grabbed the binocular straps for a second time and decorum flew out the window. Yanking them to her eyes, Elizabeth was nearly decapitated.

"Get off Beatrice! I saw him first. Give them back!"

The tug of war that ensued only sufficed to add to the comical scene; as in the fields beyond, a bare bottom mooned in the fading sunlight; and a pair of turtle doves evaded imminent discovery.

Chapter Eight
Bernie

Having a 'loony' on the estate was no real issue for any of the residents. Such was the varied array of colourful characters brightening the day with their odd ways, the antics of an old man obsessed with Christmas went largely unnoticed. What would appear to be alien to any outsider, was perfectly normal behaviour in Chalksbury. It was only when things deteriorated into complete mayhem that anyone took a blind bit of notice.

There was no doubt that Bernie's mind was not really 'on the ball' as Tom would say. Months gave way to years and the family bumbled along, content with playing along the harmless shenanigans of their aging relative. Marcia was ever thankful her father was still around, and denial, coupled with a degree of ignorance, prevented her from the realisation that Bernie was deteriorating, albeit slowly, in mind, and body.

Tom, on the other hand, was well-aware of his grandfather's irrational state. Having seen his mother sink to the depths of mental despair, was determined that his grandfather would not suffer the same fate and be shipped from one terrible institution to the next. He had visited Delores on very few occasions and hated every minute of it. Trying to have any sensible conversation with her was like attempting sign language to a deaf dog. Jacobs would have understood more.

Despite this, the young man occasionally allowed pangs of guilt, to think that his flesh and blood was locked in prison; stuffed with sloppy mashed potato and cabbage; laced with sedatives, passing life by in a dreamy haze of induced unreality. Tom always defused this feeling, telling himself time and time again, that they tried but even survival within the mad world of Chalksbury was impossible for his mother and she was 'in the best place'. Visits to the outside world were few and far between, and even then, the occasional outings were closely monitored and 'risk assessed' as they continually advised.

As it happened, the risk assessments were clearly made by a visually impaired, amateur, psychotic psychologist, who had probably infiltrated the prison with an ambition to kill off all the patients. Whoever carried out the last one clearly did not realise that travelling the short journey to Bloomsbury on a busy train would severely take its toll on Delores. It took Tom ages to persuade the police that his mother was not a stalker and did not intend to rip the trousers off a fellow passenger, nor batter his face to smithereens. She was just trying to put up her automatic umbrella before fighting her way to the exit. The weather, being warm and sunny, did not really help the situation at all. It was hours before she was carted back to the safety of incarceration.

In no way did he want to see his grandfather cocooned in such an establishment, but he was fast coming to the conclusion that, despite the support and tolerance of the family and all and sundry on the estate, Bernie would soon need the care than only professionals could provide.

The seasons came and went. Spring crocus bowing their heads in respectful retreat as the summer blooms display their colourful frocks, only to wilt once again, as the coolness of Autumn and bitterly cold of the winter temporarily suppress rainbow resurrections. Regardless of this circle of life, in Bernie's happy world, it was Christmas all year round. His enthusiasm for the festivities carrying him through the remainder of his life with merriment and enjoyment.

Thus, it was one rainy day in April, that he came to the decision that enough was enough and somehow Marcia must be made to understand and accept the inevitable.

Each day, regardless of date and time, Bernie's merriment and positivity could not be dashed. There was no doubt in in his mind that soon, his Marcia, Tom and the children would be round with the presents. It was on this particular spring morning, that he stored the beers safely in the washing machine and toddled into the sitting room of his small council dwelling. The dated décor and threadbare carpet hidden beneath a sparkling display of winter cards, sparkly tinsel, and chains of hand-made trimmings, lovingly put together by the children. Clapping his hands excitedly, he looked around the grotto; it was almost perfect...just one thing missing. He was almost ready.

Where he obtained the chestnuts from, Tom would never know. Certainly, Marcia would not have given him any; Marcia would not even know what chestnuts were. The fact remained that whoever came up with the idea of cheering Bernie up with this kind of present was clearly as mad as his mother.

It was the smoke, seeping through the gaps in the ill-fitting windows, choking Rudolf to death that gave it away. The glowing red nose of the sill decoration was all that was left of the poor animal, as the rest of him was enveloped in a thick fog. The putrid smell of burnt offerings seeped into the air as Tom jammed on the handbrake, flew open the truck door, leaped down from the cab and raced along the path into the house.

The fumes, not so dense in the hallway, were still enough to severely hamper his breathing. Ripping his coat from his back he stuffed it across his face and kicked open the living room door. Charging inside, he could barely see as his eyes stung and his chest tightened.

"Grandad! Bernie!" he coughed. "Oh my God! Where are you? I can't see!"

A faint voice struggled to be heard. "Tom? Is that you?"

"For God's sake Grandad! Where are you? In your chair? By the tree? Where the hell are you? Can you see me?"

"Course I can't see you. What you on about? I'm in the kitchen finding a beer. I can't remember where the hell I put them. They aren't in the fridge, silly bugger."

Tom did not know whether to be angry or thankful. Gritting his teeth, he ran out of the room, back along the hallway and pushed open the door into the kitchen.

"You silly sod! Have you no idea the place is on fire?"

Tom ran over and grabbed the dazed old man, who had no idea what was going on.

"On fire? Get off me! What you doing? What's going on? Me chestnuts will be ruined now. Get off!"

There was no time to explain or pander Bernie, Tom pulled his grandfather by the scruff of his little bright red jacket and yanked him out the back door, into the garden, along the path, through the small adjoining tunnel that connected the neighbouring residence and unceremoniously plonked him on Mrs Benton's front lawn. Bernie's feet did not touch the ground once.

This rescue, taking a matter of minutes, did not go unnoticed by the remainder of the street, who were, as usual, there like a shot to witness the drama. Gathered in a controlled group outside the gate, no one was panicking at all. It was as if it was a normal occurrence...which in some ways it was. Many a crisis unfolded in Chalksbury, on a regular basis. Mrs Benton, however, was charging round her garden like a demented medicine man, screaming at the top of her voice.

"Someone help! Someone get the fire brigade. Fire FIRE!"

Maud leant against the wall picking her nails and looked at Sheila, non-plussed. "Has someone phoned the fire brigade then?"

"I expect so, they usually do. I think I will toddle off and get Marcia seeing as Bernie is alright. I suppose you better make that mad woman a cup of tea before she explodes."

The firemen of blue watch piled into the shiny red engine and prepared to do their bit. They would not falter from their duty in their quest to protect the public even though it was 'Chalksbury again.' They were soon at the scene and took charge immediately, bringing the situation totally into control.

Patrick removed his dusty yellow helmet and crouched down beside the two survivors. "You okay? Narrow escape there my friends. Another few minutes and the whole place would have gone up in flames. Just mainly smoke damage as far as I can see. The smell is going to be around for a while. Strange thing is... I could swear I could smell burnt nuts... Hard to tell what happened in all that smoke. We will send someone round when it's all calmed down to see what the cause was. In the meantime, you two are off to hospital as a precaution. Ambulance is on its way."

Tom glared at Bernie. The old man shrugged his shoulders. "I don't know what all the fuss is about. I was only roasting me chestnuts; I would have sorted it after I got me beer; I just left the room for a minute."

"Chestnuts? Chestnuts!? On a gas fire?" Patrick was astounded.

"Roasting your chestnuts?" Tom croaked. "Roasting your chestnuts on what exactly? You haven't got an open fire!"

"I know, I know! I put them on the bars of that gas one, you know.... the one in the grate that you press the buttons and on comes the heat."

Patrick stood up, rolled his eyes and strolled off towards his colleagues muttering. "Chestnuts... bloody chestnuts... anyone would think it was Christmas."

Tom took a deep breath; there was no point in chastising his grandad. Instead, he was blaming himself, he should have seen this coming ages ago.

"Well, it don't matter now, what's done is done. Least we are all alive. My throat is so sore though. Better get ourselves checked out, seeing that nice fireman has arranged it all. You can stay with me and Becs for a bit; we'll sort the house out don't you worry."

Bernie grinned. "That's wonderful, and your Becs, she cooks a good Christmas dinner she does."

Tom's swearing went unheard as Marcia waddled, arm in arm with Sheila, along the street towards her father's house. Having been persuaded by her neighbour that there was nothing to panic about, and everyone was unharmed and safe, she was reasonably calm. Images of her mother's charred body rarely left her mind, but the initial sickness in her stomach subsided, once Sheila has repeatedly informed her that Bernie has been up to his tricks again and no one had died.

Of course, it meant another trip to the hospital, to which Marcia was reluctant, and it was with some relief that Tom insisted that she would be better off staying at home as it was all unnecessary and they would be there for hours.

"Becs will be round in a bit, and in any case, you better let Tanya and Moll know what's happened, speaking of which, the diva doll has arrived."

"So, what actually happened again?" Marcia was trying to comprehend. "He was roasting chestnuts? What's nuts doing on his chest, and why was he trying to roast them? Has he gone completely mad? Look at the mess? Who's going to sort all that out then, council will take weeks!"

Bernie unsuccessfully tried to set his daughter's mind at ease whilst his granddaughter ran to his aid.

"Oh, it's our Marc! And our Tan! Look what your silly old Bubbs has done, nearly set meself and me house on fire. Burnt old Rudolph to a crisp, and nearly lost me tree as well. God knows I'll have to get new decorations now. Christmas is ruined that's for sure. What we gonna do now? I don't know.... I don't know."

With that the old man put his head in his hands and sobbed.

Apart from the time that Marcia had found out Bernie was her dad she had rarely seen her father so upset. He was usually so happy. Placing her odd arms around his shoulders, she gave the biggest hug imaginable.

"It's okay dad, everything is going to be okay... we can have Christmas at my house. You can even bring your breast-nuts if you want."

Marcia did not mind at all having Christmas at any time of the year. Her dad was precious, and she loved him regardless of his craziness. Her childhood memories of the event were not the best, coping with an alcoholic mother; but since the birth of her daughter, things had radically changed. Other celebrations she tended to brush over, even her own birthday. Bonfire night was a definite no-no. The last time they went shopping in November, Molly pushed her in the wheelchair, excited with plans to buy a few fireworks. Then someone kept giving Marcia pennies and she was well miffed being mistaken for a man; she refused to have anything to do with it again.

Tanya, nodded. "Of course, we can have Christmas all the time!" She draped herself over her Bubby, gave a few more hugs; then satisfied that everyone was relatively intact, ignored her mother's unintelligible explanation and sauntered off towards Patrick.

"Where's she gone now? Fat lot of help she is, getting her Bubby up." Tom croaked.

"It's okay, she's gone to give that nice fireman a drink of water." Marcia heaved herself up.

"Should think that Patrick had enough of water!" Tom rasped. "Shouldn't want any more!"

"Well, just for once she was thinking of someone else, cos she said he looked hot."

The ambulance pulled up, no flashing lights this time. George flew open the doors, leapt to the ground and strode towards the sorry party; his many years of experience instantly assessing there was no imminent danger.

"Oh my! Guess who we have here. Not you again Marcia! You be getting your own room in that hospital soon! Come on then, in you all go! Best get you all sorted! Cath! Come and see who it is!!"

Cath climbed from the driver's seat and joined the group. "Well, what a surprise! Fancy that, and me just come back on the job too. Hated that early retirement lark. Now what have you been up to? Looks like someone left a bun in the oven again."

With that everyone burst into laughter... even Marcia, though she had no idea why.

Two weeks later, Marcia prepared herself for one of 'those' dreaded family meetings. It usually meant something official and bad. The aftermath of hospital admittance resulted in the local GP and assessment team becoming involved in Bernie's predicament. There was no more covering up.

The outcome was unwelcomingly clear. Bernie needed proper medication, supervision, and care, none of which he was able to access living on his own.

Marcia tried her hardest to understand. Her dad was going to get worse. It was going to take maybe a couple more years or so, but he was going to need more care than any member of his family could possibly provide. The atmosphere in the small lounge was grim.

"But all he wants is Christmas! He's happy when it's Christmas, we can do that can't we Moll?" Marcia blubbed.

Molly put her arms around her friend. "We can for now, but he can't be on his own Marcia. There's no room here is there? And you barely cope with yourself. Tom has the kids and can't be there all the time."

Marcia's heart sank. She hated being reminded of her limits. Her dad was her life, she'd lost her mum and found her dad. Now she was going to lose him too.

"I can't let him go, I can't! He will hate it." She bawled.

Tom's eyes glistened. "Marcia, I don't think we have a choice. He nearly killed himself. They said they would do his room out like Christmas – tree and everything. Least let's show him and see what he thinks."

Thus, it was three weeks later that Bernie settled himself into his new grotto. It was bright and warm, with tinsel, cards lights and a tree. He seemed quite excited.

"Look Marc, I even got one of those new music things with records and stuff! And I get me meals as well. It will be okay you see; no doubt the elves will be here as well soon."

Tom and Tanya stood back whilst Bernie held Marcia's hand. "How long do I have to stay here too then?"

Marcia tried to remain composed. "Just till Christmas is over Dad... we will have Christmas here, with you, and bring you presents and s...stuff."

"Okay; I'll get some sherry ready, for when you come, and some of those chocolates you like."

"That will be nice. Won't it, Tom? Tanya can bring you a new Rudolph as well, won't you?"

"Where did the other one go then?" Bernie looked confused.

Tanya rushed over and threw herself on her Bubby. "Oh Bubbs, you remember you bur...."

Tom hurried towards the group and interrupted.

"You remember? The silly bugger flew away, out the window. It never shut right, you be better here for a bit, till it's all mended anyway."

Bernie smiled. "In that case, we better light up that tree and make the angel sing. Everything's going to be alright, Christmas is nearly here."

More cuddles ensued, and the family group said their sombre goodbyes and walked, silently, out of the care home door into the warm air, leaving their beloved Bernie behind in Lapland.

Outside, they sat, in a row on the garden wall, each lost in their own emotions; guilt; grief, relief; it was all so mixed. Marcia was in a complete daze and felt sick.

"We have done the right thing ain't we Tom?" Marcia whispered.

Tom sniffed. "We have, there is no other way. It's not as if we can't see him; It's not far, I can call in every day and bring you when you want."

Tanya put her arm mostly round her mother. "It's okay Ma, we can't look after him anymore. He will fall or do something, or set things on fire, or hurt himself."

Marcia's tear-stained face emerged from her hands. "No different from me then." She half smiled.

"No, Mum; no different to you, except you don't think its bloody Christmas every day of the year."

A crazy old man looked at the nurse, her eyes returned his gaze with kindness and compassion. "Here; have something to eat Bernie, then we will put those cards up."

He picked up the red serviette and tucked it into his shirt. "Ooh lovely, Chicken! Can we put the carols on as well?"

Chapter Nine
The Proposal

It was a cold evening in late 1997 when fate lent a helping hand to surface long buried secrets and return broken family ties to ribbon and bows. Tanya burst through the door with such excitement, Jamie could not keep upright, as she dragged him along the hallway.

"Ma! Ma!"

Marcia turned her head uncomfortably. A few years ago, she would have made a best effort to force herself out of the chair and establish the cause of the commotion. Tanya rarely called her 'Ma' unless there was instant danger of death or something incredible was about to transpire. These days, the pain in her back and neck frequently confined her to the large comfortable armchair, where she spent her days watching the television and looking through catalogues.

"Ma! Ma! Guess what!!" Tanya released Jamie just in time for him to miss grabbing the back of the sofa and landing in a heap on the thread-bare carpet.

Judging by the look on Tanya's face, Marcia took a deep breath and prepared herself for the worst. The last time she saw her daughter this excited, Tanya had dyed her hair bright red and came home sporting a tattoo of a sad looking fairy on her thigh.

"What on earth is it?" Marcia's eyes widened. Did I see Jamie there? Where is he? Must be seeing things again."

Tanya threw herself on Marcia's lap and wrapped her arms around her mother's neck and kissed her heavily on the cheek.

"Tanya! Go careful there! What's all this?"

"It's Jamie!" Tanya retracted her arms and slid backwards until she was stood upright then twirled around so rapidly, her long dark locks wrapped around her head, obliterating the features of her beautiful face.

Marcia shifted herself forward and upward, prepared for battle.

"What about Jamie? What's wrong with him? What's he done?"

Two shirt-cuffed hands fumbled their way to the top of the sofa, followed by a handsome head of thick curls, half-covering a pair of deep green dazzling eyes.

"I am fine Mrs Duncan." Jamie stood to his feet and rearranged his jacket to some sort of suit resemblance.

"Honestly, I am fine, in fact I am more than fine." He began to laugh. "Tanya, you will be the death of me I swear!"

Tanya pushed her hair to the side, stroking it with some force, until it rested unaided, draping across one shoulder; a velvet carpet upon which, you would not dare to walk.

"Sorry!" She giggled, "Am too excited for words, you know me!"

"Don't we all," retorted Marcia, relaxing into a crooked smile. "Now, what's this all about? and Jamie, I told you loads of times, don't need to call me Mrs Duncan. I ain't a Mrs anyway, just call me Marcia."

Jamie walked over and took Tanya's hand. "Mrs Duncan.... Er, sorry, Marcia. If it's alright with you I would like to marry your daughter."

Marcia's wonky eye twitched and her mouth dropped open, she was completely shocked and silent.

Tanya leaned forward; her face drooped with disappointment." Mum... Mum... say something, are you mad or what?"

Wiping the seeping fluid that had collected round her motionless lips, Marcia swallowed hard.

"Mad. MAD? Why would I be mad?" Her brain was desperately trying to digest the information. Rarely did anyone get married in her family. In fact, there were very few people married on the whole of the estate. Most of the older generation had committed themselves, her father included, but not to her mother. As for the younger, many seem to chop and change partners like the wind. It was not that wedlock was disapproved, generally no one bothered.

"It's just a bit of a shock, I wasn't expecting anything like this...now, if you had said you were pregnant...." Marcia took a deep breath and exhaled with a sigh. "You aren't pregnant, are you?"

"Mum!" Tanya put her hands on her hips and scowled. "No, I ain't pregnant. For once, I would like to do something proper, and Jamie is proper, aaaa...nd he has a job and everything... and we gonna have a nice house in Bloomsury.... and."

"I'll look after her Mrs Duncan, I promise." Jamie interrupted and put his arms around his love. "And, yes, I want to do it all 'proper'.

Marcia gawped at the doting couple. Her Tanya, a 'proper' lady, with a 'proper' husband and a 'proper' house. It all beggared belief, was it at all possible? A broad grin spread across her face, making her two chins stretch almost into one.

"Well, I think it's fantabulous." She raised her voice. "I think it's bloody fantabulous!"

"Is it alright with you then Mrs Duncan?" Jamie returned the smiles.

"Of, course! Don't know why you are asking me though? Tanya usually does what she likes these days."

"Because, Jamie's proper Ma, he's a 'proper' man." Tanya cuddled further into her boyfriend, as if that were possible.

"That's settled then!" Marcia heaved herself out of the chair. "Hand me my stick please."

Tanya unstuck herself and passed the crutch to her mother, helping her to stand. "You don't have to get up Mum!"

"Not get up!" Marcia bellowed. "Not get up?? I want to give that Jamie a hug, I do. But one thing I say." Marcia tried to feign sternness, unsuccessfully. "You stop calling me Mrs Duncan or I'm going to bonk you on the head with this stick, mark my words! Tanya? Get some tea m'girl. On second thoughts, bugger the tea, open that gin and put some of that banana music you like on. Fantabulous it is, just fantabulous!"

Tanya giggled. "You mean Bananarama Mum. Come on Jamie, fish out Venus!"

Marcia clapped her hands together. "Yes, that's the one I like that! That's that big star thing ain't it? I saw in on the tele - though what's moons got to do with bananas I'll never know, maybe 'cos they're all yellow!"

Molly wearily placed her key in the lock and opened the door of the small terrace house in Clover close and dropped her holdall to the floor. The 'bits of biz,' as she described it, were becoming more difficult to obtain as she grew older. The few regular clients she retained, seemed happy enough; but despite being fully confident in their discretions, one day, it was likely they would either look elsewhere, or succumb to age themselves. Still, for the minute, desires remained secretive and untamed, it would pay the way for a while yet.

The music and singing resounding from the living room, filtered quickly to her ears. Immediately, curiosity overcame her melancholy mood. Someone was having a party; and a party was never to be ignored.

Such was the joviality, no one heard her enter the room at first. Tanya was the first one to spot her aunt and before Molly could question anything, she was dragged into the room and handed a large gin and tonic.

"I certainly need this!" downing the lot in one go, Molly walked to the sideboard and refilled her glass. "Have I missed out on something good then? You all seem to be well gone!"

Marcia replied with a slight wobble of speech. "Yeh, we are a bit. It's special today Moll, right special. Our Tan is getting married to her Jamie! He's here, look. Asked me proper and all that!"

Molly took another giant swig of her drink. "Good God! You ain't been going together long, I hardly know you! But hell, who cares, long as my Tanya is happy." Raising her glass in salute to the handsome young man that stood smiling. Molly laughed. "Nice one Jamie. That's marvellous! Bloody Marvellous!"

"We been together some good few months, Auntie Moll, that's long enough… and to think… Ooooh, I can't believe it! I am going to be MRS TANYA HENLEY!!"

Molly choked on her drink, spluttering it across her new yellow jumper. Immediately composing herself and wildly wiping the dregs away. Taking a deep breath, she prepared to make her excuses. This was the worst nightmare. The Henleys? The Henleys of Bloomsbury? Her relatives??

"You okay, Moll?" laughed Marcia, "You should take it slower."

Determined not to spoil her daughter's day, Molly managed some sort of positive facial response, and topped up her gin once more. Don't panic, she told herself; you don't know anything's amiss yet Molly, stay calm, enjoy the party - sort it later. It may not be a problem; on the other hand, it may be a complete disaster.

Chapter Ten
The Bull by The Horns

Taking the decision, rightly or wrongly, Molly decided there was no option but to make contact with the Henley's and, if necessary, take the unenviable steps of dropping the final bomb on her family. The impending marriage to 'Jamie', whatever the blood relationship, the concealment of Tanya's fatherhood, the burden and guilt he had carried for so long, could not go on.

'Martin' had been putting if off for years, convincing himself any revelations were on a need-to-know basis; thus, avoiding any unnecessary conflict and prejudice. It was far easier to contain his life in the small comfort bubble he knew and loved, allowing acceptance without questions, than risking the loss of Marcia and his daughter. Life without them would be intolerable.

Tucked away within his conscience, he always knew that the longer facts were concealed, the harder it would become to give into the desire to fulfil his parental role, as he forever chose the 'easy' option and invented any excuse possible for not exposing the truth. Even the thought that his heart condition could have passed to Tanya had not pushed him far enough. Constantly monitoring Tanya, for signs of breathlessness or pain, he persistently told himself. 'No need for the moment, she is fine.'

Certainly, he should have at least confided in Marcia concerning the fatherhood of Tanya. There was an inkling within him that she had some idea, but lucky or unlucky, Marcia had neither the gumption nor the curiosity to pursue the matter. The quest to find Tanya's father had long since been dismissed and all were content to allow one day to roll into another, and far too soon the years had passed by without awkward questions.

No doubt the likeness between father and daughter had raised some comments in the past from many on the estate. Such was the makeup of society within this tight knit community, gossip rarely leached itself to one person or subject for any length of time, and unsolvable puzzles soon forgotten and discarded. Even the extremely trusted few that knew of his chosen lifestyle, Martin had refused to be drawn into exposure, the truth remaining in a locked box within his soul, and only he had the key.

Casting the vast array of colourful outfits aside, Molly stripped away the polythene and pulled out the linen suit. Worn only for his necessary official appearances as Martin, the ageless fabric was still crisp and creaseless. For one brief moment, she wondered if Martin should be the bearer of good or bad news, then dismissed the idea. Gently reaching into the inside pocket, she pulled out the letter from its safe box. The letter from Patricia; the sacred document that changed his life; the letter from his mother.

It was with much trepidation, that Molly – protected from the rain by her camel coat – pulled up the collar and stood warily outside two huge entwined, magnificent black iron gates. Staring down the long-gravelled drive, bordered either side by well-manicured gardens, she admired the perfect picture of complimented autumn oils. The actual dwelling, shadowed in the distance, was difficult to make out, but in the dimming light, the grandeur of the place was all too evident.

It was all too overwhelming. Who was she to think her family would want her? A lower-class transsexual, from a two-bit council estate, who had survived on menial jobs and state benefit, topped up by secret soliciting. Even the small inheritance left to her by her mother, put in trust for Tanya, would not be enough to gain any respect; neither would it alleviate the disappointment her family would no doubt feel if she walked through those gates. For the first time in Molly's life, she felt ashamed.

Retreating, Molly dejectedly watched the bus trundle off into the distance. There was not another for over an hour. Fumbling into the dry inner pocket of her outerwear, she pulled out the frail paper, stroking the creases delicately with her fingers. A drop of rain dared to mix with her tears, striking the treasure, blurring the faded writing. Quickly refolding his mothers' loving words, she filled her lungs with the damp air, regained her composure and exhaled slowly. This time, there was no going back.

A shaking hand reached towards the small, glowing light and hesitantly pressed the button beneath. The wait seemed endless; she tried again, with yet no response. Molly breathed a sigh of relief, outcome out of her control, decision made, reprieved; grateful to leave it for another time.

Respite did not last long, ended abruptly by a crescendo of deeply disturbed barking, and the ensuing sounds of blasted ammunition as the gravel splayed across the grass. Finding herself faced with the biggest Great Dane that ever walked the planet, her feet were glued firmly to the ground refusing to obey the orders of her brain. The hound snapped at the air and lunged menacingly, at the protective bars. Molly thanked God for the strong metal barrier.

Emily Henley, although still in her forties, was unable to keep up with her pet. Appearing minutes later, dressed in a long, very wet, green waxed Barbour coat, hood drawn tightly around her face, she walked, in her muddy wellingtons, briskly towards the gates, where Molly was still stood motionless.

"Rosey, down now! Stop that noise, Mummy's here now!"

'Rosey' gave a final defiant, much quieter 'woof' and proceeded to jump around her owner as if she had saved the world from an impending atomic explosion.

"So sorry," she spluttered through the rain. "I was just taking her for a stroll, or a gallop, as you can see."

'Rosey', coming to the conclusion that the person standing at the gate was not Jack the Ripper and all was hunky dory, proceeded to charge around the garden in the hope of grabbing some attention from anyone who would be prepared to listen. Her hopes shattered, off she loped, to find another source to satisfy her unrelenting quest for play.

"We have to have some sort of guard dog you see. she's only two. To be honest, if you had come in, she would probably have knocked you over and licked your nose off! Can I help you in any way? You are very wet."

Molly stuttered, "Only two? She's massive!"

Astounded by the size of Rosey, Molly silenced for a few seconds, then checked herself, realising she had not said a word for the reason of the visit.

"I was just wondering if I could have a word with Mr or Mrs Henley. It's sort of personal business."

Emily glanced over her shoulder and, in the absence of any risk of her baby escaping, creaked open the gates as far, as to would allow a slim, half-drowned, slightly scared looking woman, squeeze through.

"That sounds ominous." The kindly reply came with an obvious hint of amusement. "I am Emily, Mrs, Henley. You better come in. Look at you, you are a little wet I feel! Some hot chocolate is the order of the day."

"Oh, thank you, thank you so much; it's raining very hard. My name is Molly E.." She was about to say Emery, then stopped; having no idea if any of the Henley's would recognise her father's surname.

"Er..Molly." she mumbled.

"Oh right," Emily, suspicious of the stumble, reserved judgement.

Side by side, they walked along the stony drive, silent, save for the scrunch of trudging footsteps etching their marks in the soggy scree. Each, conscious of the awkward lack of speech, but also, each consumed by questions and deduction.

Who was this woman, arriving out of the blue? Who was Mrs Henley? What relation was she to Patricia? Who was Jamie?

The entrance to the house was magnificent. Polished marble steps, adorned each side by tall pillars, reaching high up into the ornate porch covering. Feeling extremely uncomfortable, Molly lagged a little behind, as Emily produced a large bunch of keys, choosing one, without hesitation, and opened the huge dark oak door.

Perceiving the plight of her caller, Emily paused, beckoned, who was she to condemn anyone without evidence. Emitting a friendly smile, she invited Molly to make herself at home, whilst she 'rounded up Rosy.

Stripped of her camel coat; soaked shoes left in the immense hallway of the house; Molly sat in her stockinged feet, on the edge of a very large flowery sofa. Hands together, she nervously rubbed the palms in an attempt to relieve the anxiety that was steadily building, ready to explode like some dormant volcano, awoken from years of hibernation. Her state of mind was not helped by the humbleness she felt, as the richness and perfection of the surroundings caused her to conclude that this, was totally alien and was completely out of her league.

Although extremely spacious, the room was pleasantly warmed by crackling orange flames, set within a huge traditional stone fireplace. The décor was elegant and chosen with much thought and expertise. From the high, pristine white ceiling, caressed by the whisper of glistening candles, twinkling between glass beads, to the pale grey walls, abundant with traditional paintings, the whole effect was stunning.

Framed in silver, photographs of ageless people, grouped in unison on a shiny black piano, waiting, watching with reserved intimidation, wondering why this stranger dared to encroach on their property.

To Molly, the people were strangers. She did not notice Jamie's eyes, remaining unobtrusively to the back of the crowd. It was the large photograph, framed in a band of pearls, placed to the front, that shocked her to the core. As she rose and took a closer look, familiarity hit her like a barrel.

Swallowing hard, fighting back instant tears, her hand ran shakily over the image. Having no photos of her own, it was shocking to see the facial features, the high cheekbones, the purse lips, the long dark hair, all duplicated from her own etched memory. The girl in the picture was young, but Molly was in no doubt, it was her mother, Patricia.

"Do you play?" Emily interrupted her thoughts.

"Oh, no." Molly looked sheepishly, her usual abundant confidence gone. Lowering her head, she smoothed the creases of her skirt. "It's very nice. I was just looking at the photographs, sorry."

Emily placed a tray on the coffee table. Steam billowed from the mugs of chocolate, as she beckoned Molly to sit.

"Hope you don't mind mugs, it's not the same in china is it?"

Forcing a smile, Molly returned to the sofa, and accepted the drink. Warming her hands around the mug, she stared at the friendly lady sat opposite. Trying to keep her composure was difficult, especially when the person she was looking straight at, had the same beautiful dark eyes, as her mother.

Emily sipped her chocolate. Looking at this nervous young woman, sat tensely on her sofa. It was obvious that this was no ordinary meeting. Something, deep within was nagging at her conscience. She did not know how, or why this feeling was erupting, there was no logical explanation; but she felt suddenly drawn to this stranger that had unexpectantly arrived on her doorstep.

"Well?" Emily replaced her cup and leaned forward. "You've come for a reason, I can sense that, you don't need to be afraid of me, I am not going to bite your head off, whatever the problem is."

"You might when I explain the circumstances of my visit." The anguish evident in her speech was not lost on Emily.

Molly had no idea where to begin, the countless hours she had spent over many years, rehearsing the inevitable meeting, seemed pointless and irrelevant. The confident person she was, able to deal with any situation with tact and decorum, slithered into oblivion.

Swallowing hard, trying hard to regain some sort of composure, she began to talk in a small squeaky voice.

"Firstly, Mrs Henley..."

"Oh Emily...please." The anxiety portrayed by her visitor now disturbed her greatly.

"I- I don't know where to start really." The quake in Molly's voice could not be disguised.

"The lady in that picture, the one on the piano in the fancy frame; it is Patricia, yes?"

"Yes, it is indeed, my sister-in-law, and how, is that of interest to you?"

"She is my mother." Molly put her head in her hands, refusing to view the reaction.

"She's your what?" Emily gasped.

Molly looked up tearfully. "She's my mother."

The genuineness of this woman was only too apparent, but Emily stared in disbelief. "You must be mistaken. Patricia only had a son, at least as far as I know; Martin I think his name was, he is long gone, god knows where."

"I know where he is." Molly sobbed and retrieved the letter from her pocket. "I am so sorry, please, read this."

Emily stood from her chair and sat beside the shaking person that 'claimed' to be Patricia's daughter and carefully opened the thinning paper. Picking up her glasses from the coffee table, suitably attired, she began to read.

Dear Martin

I have left this letter with the solicitor in the hope he may be able to locate you. I have tried so often to find you but to no avail. The contents are not intended to be offered as an excuse or an expectation of forgiveness, and there is nothing I can say to convey enough apologies. It is a matter of giving you some kind of explanation, and now that you are mature enough to bare responsibilities. I think you should be the one to know a little bit more and come to your own conclusions. I did not want to pass on without giving you some family history at least.

There were many reasons for my leaving all those years ago. My life with your father deteriorated and despite all the ambitions we had, he was content to stay on benefit, laze around and smoke his way to death. To say the least life took its toll and I could see no future for us as a family, save for a repeat of a dull life existence and financial struggle in a dingy flat.

I had to leave and build a better future, which initially sent me into squalid digs, no place for children there; it was worse than the situation you were in. I managed, after a while, to get a job in a florist, cleaning, tidying and watering etc to start. But I did well, and I learned the trade, worked hard, and earned enough to rent a room in a large house in a decent area.

Four years ago, I opened my own florist, a few miles away near Torling, doing weddings and funerals and things like that, my health held me back this last year, but it was a successful business, so after it was sold a few months ago, I have a few bob to leave as some sort of inheritance.

I tried to contact you, but my many letters remained unanswered and the visit to the flat was a disaster, your father slammed the door in my face and told me that I wasn't seeing anyone and to stay away.

So, when I could, I used to sit in the park and stroll around the area, but I never saw anybody going in and out the flat, so I thought you must have moved.

My love has never faltered, and it was truly my intention to put things right. Maybe the small legacy I have left will make amends and help to secure the future that I always wished for us, and I know, as a trusted son and a grown adult, you will execute it well.

My ashes have been laid to rest with your Granma and Grampa Henley in the cemetery in Bloomsbury. I prayed they would welcome me back, so that was the best thing I could think of. As far as I know, your dad does not know his parents, so Henley's are your historical family.

I say goodbye now, please don't think too badly of me, and let me into your heart as you have always been in mine.

Your loving mother
Patricia Henley.

Returning the letter to its owner, Emily remained quiet, expressionless, for a moment.

"Just a minute." Emily walked over to the large rather daunting bureau, drew down the wooden hatch and floundered around, discarding a mound of books, files, and paperwork, leaving them in a heap on the deep pile of the carpet. Producing a small bundle of envelopes, she took one, and returned to the couch.

"Let me see that letter again?"

Molly gingerly handed over the document, no words seem appropriate.

The room was eerie, disturbed only by the tic toc of the grandfather clock, stood with fine glory in the corner of the room. Molly breathed heavily. The last time she felt like this was when she was stood in front of Mr Jameson, awaiting a prognosis.

Emily placed both letters on the plump cushions. The writing was identical, the signatures were the same. This had to be written by the same person, Patricia, but still, nothing made any sense.

"This is Patricia's handwriting, no doubt about that. I am very confused. Where did you get this from and where is Martin? I don't know much about him; Edward – that's my husband, Patricia's brother – doesn't talk about it much.

There are those letters, but there isn't much practical information there. Only pleas from Patricia to come home... which she did, sadly, in the end."

Molly, grappling to come up with some sort of verbal exclamation, sniffed back the tears, opened her handbag and took out her wallet. Emptying every single compartment, she displayed all the ID she could find.

"These are Martin's, bank cards, national insurance card, and social security statements. I also have documents from my solicitor if you want to see them."

Emily scrutinised every document that was laid before her.

"It still doesn't make any sense?" Emily was flummoxed. "This is all Martin's," She held out her arms in disbelief. "Are you telling me he is dead?" She looked very closely at Molly's face, those dark eyes, those cheekbones, the image of Patricia's. "Are you, his sister?"

Molly composed herself as best she could. 'Go on girl, you got this far, too late to stop now.'

"Emily; Aunt Emily. Martin is dead, well sort of... Aunt Emily, I am Martin. I was born Martin and still have his identity. I live my life as Molly, have done since I was a teenager – after mum left. Dad, I mean Dylan, sorry Raymond, went berserk and vowed to kick me out unless I sorted myself out. So, I did, I became Molly, and he accepted it eventually; once he had got it through his thick drugged, dopey brain."

Molly grabbed her bag and battled with the zip compartment. Shaking uncontrollably.

"I got medical notes here as well... I'm not making it all up, I promise!"

Putting her hand across Molly's sodden cheeks, Emily wiped the tears, pushed back the long dark curls and gazed into her 'nieces' eyes. Her beauty was astounding, as was her mother's. Running her hand downwards, across the lips, and down to the chin, she could feel the slight roughness of manly skin daring to peak beneath the make-up - then onwards along the shapely arms, to the wrists and finally to the hands, larger than average, though not blatantly obvious. She was in no doubt that Molly was certainly family.

"But why now, why after all these years? Why did you not come to us before?" Emily's eyes watered. "We wondered where you were Martin, I mean Molly. We thought you went the way of your dad. We thought you took Patricia's money; we thought all sorts of things! Edward looked for you for a while, then drew a blank and quite honestly thought the worst."

Molly wept. "I don't know, I really don't know. Mum never said much when I was a kid, not that I remember anyway. I was ashamed I suppose, I didn't want you all to be disappointed and I didn't want another rejection. Mum rejected me, she left; she left me with a monster of a father. She left me to fend for myself, despite what she's written in that letter!"

It was the first time Martin had shown any aggression towards his mother. Of course, he didn't mean it, he had long accepted the reasons behind the disappearance, but such was the emotion of the day, years of pent-up frustration overflowed and burst out in a babble of incoherent voice.

"She left me, Auntie Emily, and she's dead. She's dead and I will never see her again. Dad's permanently in cloud cuckoo land; you will probably chuck me out now. Marcia is going to kill me and....our Tanya might be ill; she's going to marry Jamie, and I don't know what to doooo."

Emily did the only thing she could think of; She put her arms around Molly and held her as tight as she could.

"Molly, my darling Molly. I have no idea on half of what you are talking about. Listen to me." She retracted her arms and placed her hands on the shaking shoulders.

"Look at me, look at me Molly, look straight into my eyes."

Molly lifted her face, crushed and defeated, eyes red with tears, make up dissolved.

"I am your Auntie even if it's by marriage, am I not?"

All Molly could manage was a nod.

"Aunties help their nephews; sorry I mean nieces do they not?"

Another nod.

"You are family, Molly. You are FAMILY, and you are OUR family. You must never, EVER think that you are not part of Patricia, part of us. I am so glad you are home Martin - Molly... so glad.... Oh, and Edward? Don't you worry about him either, he's a nice old fart, he will be extremely glad to see you and unravel some mysteries that's for sure! We'll sort everything you see. Oh, Oh Molly!! I could squeeze you until you break."

And that is exactly what she did. Both cried and hugged, hugged and cried. They did not even hear Rosy, bounding across the carpet, eager to join in the fun. Her mummy did not say no, so join in she did, hurling herself at the pair of them, pushing the sofa backwards, landing them all in a heap on the floor, and to further add to the palaver, licked both their faces alternatively, until all the tears of happiness disappeared into a vat of slobber.

"Well!" shrieked Emily in between the washes. "I think we both need a clean-up and rescue from my cosmetics; to say nothing of a couple of very large gins! Get OOOF Rosy! Daddy will be here soon. GET OFF!"

Molly, out of breath, sat on her heels, ran her sticky hand through a tangled mop and laughed. "Oh my God Auntie Emily, OH MY GOD!"

Suitably freshened, made up, hair brushed neatly (or as neat as it could be after being ruffled by a monstrous animal) the two ladies, calmed and composed sipped their gin. Edward, as Emily had promised, digested the news with elation. However, being more practical than his wife, it took a long time for him to register all the details. Of course, he was anxious to view the letters and the documents, but, as Edward always did, looked at every aspect and took everything in his stride. He wanted to know all about his nephew, now his niece. He wanted to know all about her connection with Marcia and Tanya. Unintentionally intimidating, the questions went on and on relentlessly.

Molly tried her best, but by the time she had figured out what to say about one thing, he was off on another tangent.

"One step at a time, Edward," Emily was light-hearted with her husband. Charming as he was, she knew he could be very overbearing. "Fill the glasses, we all need it!"

Edward obliged and continued. "Right then Molly, let's take it bit by bit. I am so glad you are here, and so very, very glad you have come to us. But there is one thing I am really not getting. From what you have told us, why would Marcia be annoyed with you? She knows who you are, so Why? And Jamie? What's he got to do with it, Tanya is a lovely girl, despite being totally wild."

This was the six-million-dollar question, what will she do now. Molly racked her brains, she had to find out about

Jamie, but it was not the time or the place to divulge the most sacred of secrets, and certainly, Marcia had to be the first to know.

"There's so much going on." Molly collected her thoughts determined not to dig a bigger hole than she was already in.

"Marcia, naïve as she is, will be fuming I haven't told her that I am related to the Henley's. She thinks I do not have any family. Now Jamie is intending to marry Tanya, I have to tell her about the money I have put by for her, and how I am related to him and also about a heart condition that runs in the family. Has anyone else got it? Only Mum? She won't be happy I have kept that from her I can tell you. It's all my fault, I should have done it ages ago. There's other stuff too that there is no time to go into now, stuff I have to sort first."

"We can talk about the heart condition, but that is not an issue as I will explain. Is it the money you are worrying about Molly? We are very well off, and I am glad you have Patricia's inheritance safe, but you may need it yourself?" Edward's face clouded for a minute. "Jamie will get full entitlement to the estate after we've passed. It's all written up and legal, no one will contest it. He has good prospects and will look after Tanya; I can promise you that."

Molly's face quizzed his response. "The money? That's far from my mind, really it is. I am just concerned about Tanya. Sorry, if this sounds bad, but, like me, she's not exactly upper class, is she?"

Emily tried to alleviate an awkward moment. "It's okay Molly, we like Tanya; I must admit she takes a bit of getting used to. Edward says she reminds him of Patricia when she was young. Taming of the shrew and all that."

Molly knew exactly what she meant but didn't elaborate on the comment. "I am really not worried about the money; Tanya will have some of her own." She repeated herself.

"Am sure you are not, we are just saying that if you are worried about Jamie's stability, he is well taken care of if something happens to us. You see, there are certain members of our extended family that would see Jamie penniless. Oh, I am getting myself into knots here…and I don't really know why we are mentioning it now, but heck, I've said it. Jamie is my son. He is not Edward's. We have no other children. I will explain it all another time, it's not really appropriate now, he is not at risk of any heart condition to my knowledge. All you need to know now, is that Tanya, who appears for some reason, to be somewhat adopted and brought up by yourself, will be looked after financially and emotionally. Jamie is a kind and loving person, even though I say it myself." Emily shifted a little uncomfortably.

Molly dropped her mouth, not quite taking in what she had just heard. "You mean Jamie is not a blood relative of mine then?"

Edward coughed, slightly embarrassed. "No, he isn't. It's not something we have ever hidden, but not exactly broadcasted either. There is no need for anyone to gossip about it either. Does it matter? He is still part of the family."

The grin that spread across Molly's face was indescribable. "Does it matter? Of course, it doesn't matter. This is the best day ever. I have my family back… whoopee!!!"

Slightly bemused, Edward raised his glass. "In that case, a toast! A toast to families entwined!

Molly smirked, unable to hide her amusement. 'You have no idea what you have said,' she thought. 'No idea at all.'

Chapter Eleven
Another Proposal

The chance meeting with Phillip turned out to be one of the best things that occurred in her young life. Never in her wildest dreams did she think any man would be interested in her; 'Chubbs' the ugly girl with the dodgy leg; but here he was, devotion apparent.

At first, Ruby questioned his attentiveness; but there was no obvious reason, other than herself in all her glory, to invite his attraction. There was no wealth to speak of, other than the cottage, and in any event, Phillip had his own impending inheritance. As time passed by, Ruby had grown to accept his love as genuine and rejoiced as the relationship blossomed.

He was certainly a great help with her quest for her biological family. Ruby had been, indeed, out of her depth as she waded through mountains of logs, lists and legal papers. If it were not for his persistence, she would never have found the details of her birth mother. Discovering that her only link to her past had died, and no marriage was recorded in the archives, came a bitter disappointment. Burying the papers for a number of years, reluctant to continue the search outwardly portrayed her false acceptance to; 'let things be as there was no point in going any further.

Phillip, on the other hand, without force, had gently encouraged her quest. He thought the world of his partner, and when Ruby agreed to sell her childhood home and combine the funds from his inheritance to purchase a wonderful cottage in the countryside together; his dreams had just about come true. It was a shame there were no children yet, but his love for Ruby was such, that, if they were blessed, they were, and if they weren't. 'Daisy', as she liked to be called, was certainly pro-adoption, but that was a long way off yet.

However, for him, sadly, there was one thing missing; the real icing on the cake, so to speak; that was marriage. Daisy was reluctant to 'tie the knot' until she had reverted legally to her birth name. Phillip tried his best to understand why she would not let him sort that side of things out; it would be a simple procedure, and if there were any children.... Well, he would not push things too much, he knew Daisy well, and he was sure there were deeply set demons at heart.

After a number of awkward conversations, tentative probing, teasing out the knots strand by strand; Ruby eventually admitted to Phillip that she wanted to change her name, but would not feel complete, until at least, she could be sure, she had no other estranged family members. Conflictingly, despite her longing, she was scared; frightened of another rejection. It was every girl's dream to have her father walk her down the aisle, and, in the absence of John Carson, and an unknown parent who seemed to have abandoned her at birth, who would she choose? Certainly, none of the Carson family, she hardly ever saw them. She felt a little silly that it should be so important, but if there was someone... A sense of guilt and shame engulfed her, being true to herself and fair to Phillip had been ignored far too long.

Of course, her beau totally understood, and was relieved to hear her 'confession'. Such was their bond, and a mutual trust of each other; she had eventually agreed to let Phillip, now a successful manager of communications within the General records office, continue the search on her behalf.

Therefore, it was one summers day in the mid-nineteen nineties, the master of detection, came bounding through the hallway, with more than his usual exuberance, and lobbed his briefcase unceremoniously onto the kitchen table.

Ruby jumped, and nearly dropped her wooden spoon into the bubbling stew. He leapt behind her and threw his arms around her waist, kissing her neck affectionately.

Mockingly, she turned within his grasp and splashed his nose with hot sauce. "What did I tell you before!" She laughed. "Don't scare me like that! I nearly burned my fingers! What you so chirpy about then?"

"Beef stew again then; in July? Crikey, it's hot enough in here already, even with that cool air fighting through the window." He chuckled as he rubbed the residue from his reddened face and licked his finger. "Mmm. anyway, forget that; I've only gone and done it!"

This was a term, to which Ruby had become accustomed, used frequently in triumph for any medial task completed. In the main if warranted little attention.

"Beef stew again, sorry; seems like I can't get enough of it lately - Gone and done what? Phil? What are you on about?"

"I found them Dais; I found your real family!"

Ruby froze; visibly paled from the head down as warmed residual of thick gravy seeped down the handle of the spoon and meandered through her fingers, meandering through the knuckled hills. She knew it was a possibility, but she never imagined such a thing could be, and to come at this moment in time, she could barely think it true.

"Sit down Dais, I have it all here. This means we can find out for sure Dais, and even if they aren't around anymore you will know... and then we can be married and maybe those children will come along after all... and we'll live...."

"Phil!" Daisy threw the spoon into the pot, her voice croaked. "Stop it! You are like an old gabbling goose sometimes. One thing at a time, I can't take it all in."

Turning down the hob to avoid desecration of dinner, Daisy moved away from the cooker, slowly lowered herself on the soft, flowery cushions of the old oak dining chair and looked at her partner.

"Now then." She took a long deep breath. "Tell me properly."

Phillip gulped; this was not like his Daisy; quiet and collected. He had expected an eruption, or a denial, even a pot of stew thrown over his head, or at least some excessive response. Instead, she was sat, perfectly still, staring at him, white and expressionless as a solitary ghost.

He retrieved his briefcase, dragging it across the table, dislodging the red check tablecloth and forcing the laid cutlery clattering to the floor.

"Oops, sorry," he garbled.

"Never mind about that; tell me." An undisguised quiver dared to escape her control. Ruby's heart was thumping so hard, she thought it would burst through the constraints of her tightly fastened apron. Her stomach churned, as it had been for days, she felt dreadfully sick.

Pulling the envelope from his case, Phillip opened it gingerly, not quite knowing what to expect. He had thought Daisy would have been as excited as he was. Now, seeing her reaction, was it going to be a disaster? Maybe he shouldn't have pushed the marriage thing; maybe he would lose her. Oh God, what had he done? It was too late to change it now. What will be, will be, and he knew deep down that whatever happened, Daisy would not be really happy until she found out exactly who she was.

"I found your relatives, Dais. Your real mum never married, we know that, but you have some extended family of hers, and I found them for you. Here are their names and last known address. Please tell me I have done the right thing Dais. I couldn't bear it if you didn't want this after all.... and me. Please still want me Daisy!"

Ruby took the letter from his shaking hands and perused the contents. The paper flapped as her fingers strained to hold it still enough to read. Phillip, now speechless and tearful, awaited the jury's verdict with nervous trepidation.

Swallowing deeply, she allowed the letter to slip from her grip, unaware of its journey, as it fluttered in the summer breeze, spiralling downwards, until its demise. Ruby stared at Phillip, her heart still pounding. The realisation was sinking in that she was Daisy, and Daisy with blood relations. It was a minute of two before, much to Phillip's relief, her eyes lit up and a big grin spread across her face.

"I have a family. I really have a proper family. I can be Daisy for real?"

"Yes, you do Dais, and we will find them, no matter what – good or bad – we will find them Dais." Phillip spluttered.

"At least I will know Phil - good or bad. It will be good though, I know it! You know what this means then?" Daisy shrieked.

Before he could answer, it was Daisy, who was gabbling now; Phillip could barely keep up with her outbursts.

"It means, I am Daisy, I am REALLY Daisy. Crazy Daisy, who is in love with the most wonderful person in the world – who I am going to marry – and have lots of babies...speaking of which...there's something I have to tell..."

"Shut up." joked Phillip. "There's something very important we have to do first."

"Like what?" whooped Daisy, who despite her clumsiness and impending confinement, was leaping around the kitchen more adeptly than she had ever done. That is, until she twisted her knee and stopped abruptly.

"Ow!" She giggled. "What do you mean, more important?"

"I mean, you better fish out the letter from the stew before it disintegrates completely and gives us food poisoning." He howled.

"Oh, no! Phil, we might lose the names!" Daisy wailed.

Phillip rushed across the room, knocking a kitchen chair sideways. Ignoring the incident, he flew to his love and grabbed her securely round her waist, hugging her so close she could hardly breathe.

"Daisy! It's okay, I was kidding. I have all the details at work. Don't worry! Whatever happens, pleases say we will be married soon. I can't wait anymore! Mrs Daisy Turner to be!"

Kissing her passionately on the lips, Daisy responded with such tenderness, no reply was necessary; she thought her heart would melt.

Chapter Twelve
The Beating

Prejudice had rarely featured in Molly's life; mainly because very few people were aware of her sexuality and any recollection of the boy that lived with the 'hippy' in the flats, long since faded away in distant memories. In any event, there was such an array of colourful characters residing on the estate, should the manner of her chosen lifestyle ever be revealed, acceptance would come naturally to most.

However, her choice to remain silent only served as a reminder that there was still an element of subconscious shame that lurked beneath the brash exterior; coupled with her overwhelming desire to avoid conflict and protect the ones she loved. Finding her extended family and finally achieving a sense of worth, that had been disguised by a permanent level of false confidence, had made her life just about perfect.

Unfortunately, it did not come without battle, and there were a very small, select group of people, that were not at all pleased that their upper-class, immaculate reputation, was going to be, in their eyes, marred by a family invasion from a load of unsuitable lowlifes. It therefore came as a complete shock, when animosity reared its ugly head one summer late afternoon, a few days before the wedding.

The old, tattered sofa, strategically placed on the uneven patch of weedy grass in her front garden, allowed a perfect view, over the twiggy box hedge, for anyone to observe the ups and downs of daily life in Clover close. Since the on-going deterioration of her mobility, it was Marcia's favourite and most comfortable place to sit; particularly when the weather was warm and sunny. Here, along with

Jacobs, who rarely left her side, they could pass the time, watching the comings and goings of, generally friendly neighbours, interacting only when Marcia chose to display an interest in the latest victim of never-ending chit chat.

Tanya, skipped down the path, twirling her bright yellow bag in circles. Marcia marvelled at her youthfulness and exuberance, still childlike, yet suitably controlled as her daughter tootled through life into her early twenties. Now to be married! Marcia sighed; how proud she was, and how she wished Lily could be here to see it.

Turning her head, hair splaying in all directions, Tanya waved at her mother. "Off to the hairdressers, gonna meet Moll there!" she shouted, excitement uncontained.

"What again?" Marcia laughed. "You bin there a dozen times this week already! Thought they were coming here?"

"Yeh, they are, but I changed me mind again... and there's only so much they can do with your frizzy mop!" she joked.

"Just watch it you!" Marcia, unprovoked, paid no attention to anyone's jibes. "Get off with you! And don't be too long. Bec's has dropped in one of her posh lettuce wot nots for tea!"

Giggling to herself, Tanya went on her merry way. One day, she mused, her mother might remember it was called a salad: not at all posh. Green salad leaves, onion, tomatoes, mixed in oil dressing, topped with a few black olives. And 'one day', her mother might actually eat them. and not insist on picking them all out, throwing the 'little bits of shrivelled poo' into the bin.

After trying countless hairstyles, up, down, curled, straight, jewelled, banded, side-shouldered, braided, netted, a decision was eventually made. An exasperated Catherine heaved massive sigh of relief. "At last! I know you are family and all that Molly, but you would try the patience of a saint."

Molly just laughed, kissed her cousin in a fond goodbye. "Got to get it exactly right. You would do the same if it was your wedding!"

"Definitely!" Tanya picked up her bag. "But it's so mint! Thank you soooo much!"

"My pleasure." replied Catherine, glancing at her watch. "See you Saturday; nine on the dot, will do the lot!" she sang. "Mine included haven't had time to think about that at all!"

Outside the salon, Tanya slipped her arm into her aunt's and the pair ambled along the street, pausing at the bus stop.

"You sure you won't come home for tea?" Tanya asked.

"Will, come back later, got to go to the flat first to see if the old man is still alive, and I have a couple of bits and pieces I have to get."

"It's a shame we couldn't invite him, at least to the evening party." Tanya instantly regretted the comment as she saw the change in Molly's expression, it was a silly thing to have said.

"Tanya! You know dam well what I told you. Edward and Emily wouldn't have him anywhere near them, after the goings on with Patricia. In any case he would ruin everything."

"Yeh, suppose so, sorry; He would probably spike the drinks, then we would all be dancing on the tables!" Tanya lightened the conversation.

"Oh, my gawd, can you imagine?" Molly put her arms in the air and twirled around full circle, kicking her legs in the air. "Percival Smyth-Robinson and that awful girlfriend of his; 'Simone'; stoned and doing the Cancan!" "It would be very funny though...that posh lot getting sloshed, especially that Percival; still can't believe they are relatives of yours Auntie Molly!"

Molly shrugged her shoulders. "Nor me Tanya, God knows why they have accepted me back. Small world isn't it?"

"Sure is! Nice we will be all one sort of family though." Tanya grinned.

Molly looked at the ground to hide her reaction. 'You have no idea what you have just said.' She thought. 'Come on girl, get your act together.'

"Hey Tan!" Composing herself, she ruffled Tanya's new hairdo affectionately. "That's more 'you' I think!"

"Very funny! I'll muck yours up as well then!" She replied, mischievous intentions evident.

The number sixty-two bus trundled along the road, the driver slowing slightly as he approached the stop. George had seen enough of drunken frivolity over many years and was always up for a bit of a singsong; but it was unusual to see it outside a relatively up-market row of shops. But here were two, well dressed ladies, prancing around like a pair of boxing kangaroos. If it weren't for Molly, almost getting herself killed, jumping half into the road, waving her arms madly, he would not have stopped at all.

Leaping, onto the platform, Tanya slapped down her purse. "Hi George! It's us! Don't you recognise me!"

George took off his cap. "Well, I never, if it isn't young Tan – and Molly too. Look at you two posh totties!"

"Yep!" Molly chirped up. "Our Tan's getting married Saturday! We've been to get our hair done and look right smart!"

"In that case," laughed George, "Take a seat, your majesties, this be a free one! Hey folks? She's getting' married. Time for a Tuuune!"

Catherine, put her laden holdall into the boot of her car. Taking a glance at the salon to ensure security, the sound of jolly singing fade, as the bus bumbled on its way to Chalksbury.

"She's getting married in the morning, Ding dong….."

Dylan stretched out on the sofa, happy to be surrounded by empty bottles, overflowing ashtrays and a sea of pot noodle cartons, stuck together with spilt chicken curry. He barely heard the door open as his 'daughter' entered the flat and stood, horrified, staring at the state of the place and trying not to breath.

"Dad, this place stinks, why don't you open some windows and clean it up a bit?"

"Because life is not for cleaning. Life is for loving and grooving and being with friends. Peace is life. Love is life; anyway, if you were here a bit more often it would get done, wouldn't it?"

Molly scowled, walked to the window, pulled the curtains aside and opened the top sash to let in some air. Opening the larger section was out of the question, her father would surely plunge to his death. The room looked far worse in the light of day. Pieces of silver foil littered the floor, screwed with strands of discarded tobacco and cannabis threads. Such was the density of the muddles, what was left of the carpet was hardly visible.

"What friends do you have? Besides Dougie the Druggie. To be honest, I couldn't care less now. I would be, you know; if you were in the least bit interested in normal life, which obviously you are not. Sleeping on Marcia's sofa is the Ritz compared to this."

Dylan did not bite to the comments. He either chose not to comprehend or was in such a state he only heard the mention of food.

"Ritz? Any biscuits going then?" Her father waved the joint, circling in the air, marvelling at the trail of smoke.

Ignoring him completely, Molly stomped into her bedroom. It was a shame she had to come here at all, but the vast amount of clothes she had acquired were far too numerous to burden Marcia's small house, particularly as Tanya seemed to have followed in her footsteps when it came to fashion. There was also a small amount of attire, rarely used these days, which, shall we say, was not suitable for outside activities.

She pulled a favourite yellow sweater from the door and held it to her nose. Thankfully the abundance of air fresheners in her room coupled with the many plastic coverings protecting her favourite outfits, the stale odour wafting from Dylan's habits had not penetrated her belongings.

As always, before selecting her wardrobe for the week, Molly checked inside the drawer of her dressing table. All was in order, paperwork and documents undisturbed. Prescription drugs dwindling, but a couple of packets. She made a mental note to visit the surgery to replenish her supply.

If there was one good thing about Dylan, he would not intrude into his 'daughter's' room; having no respect for anything, or anyone else, at least he had the decency to adhere to Molly's repeated request to. "Stay out of my room, stay out of my business, or I will make sure your any cannabis that I find in the flat, goes down the bog!"

Picking up the brown envelope, Molly hesitated; now was the time. Or will it ruin everything? Either way, it was the last piece to the jigsaw that would complete the picture. With Tanya about to fly the nest, she was sure Marcia would have no objection to taking over the spare room. It would go one way or the other, but it had to be done. Filling the large tapestry holdall with essential apparel required for the upcoming events, Molly checked that nothing was forgotten. All the main wedding dresses were already safely covered and hung on the wardrobe doors in Tanya's room, but she was adamant that the accessories would be just so.

Turning the corner, Molly stopped at the park gates. Gazing across the field at the delipidated swings, the wonky roundabout, randomly coloured with mismatched spray paint, and the fountain, blackened with pollution and age, yet still commanding centre stage. Molly strolled to the monument and sat on the wall, where all those years ago, fate took its chance. She ran her hands through the stagnant water, rarely flowing these days. Smiling, she remembered the good times, the childhood playdays, the laughter of innocence, even the drunken rides, and the numerous times she had to rescue Marcia from one fall after another. Then, there was that night. The night her best friend nearly drowned; the night of uncontrolled, gin-fuelled desire that resulted in the conception of Tanya. Would she change it now? Of course, she made a dreadful mistake that evening, but would she be without Marcia and Tanya? No, of course not; but if she admitted her errors, she may lose them both. But the time had come, the secret could not be hidden any longer.

Deep in thought, she was unaware of the three young men striding towards her, until a sneering voice rudely interrupted her dreams.

Percival Johnson-Smyth-Robinson thrust a fist inches from her nose. Unintimidated, Molly stood upright and faced the intruder.

"Kindly remove your fist from my face." Molly grabbed Percival's wrist and lowered it for him. "I have seen you around before, and your two toffy mates. What do you want?"

Percival shook off the restraint. "We want to give you a warning, you sorry-looking pervert. We don't want your sort in the family, nor at the wedding, nor anywhere near us, do you hear me?"

It was not unusual for Molly to deal with confrontation, it was almost a daily occurrence on the estate, for one reason or another, but never had she encountered an ambush, and NEVER specifically directed at her sexuality.

"What do you mean by that! Who are you to tell me what to do, or what family I should belong to!" Puffing out her chest and pursing her lips, the threatening stare was obvious.

Percival was not to be ignored, and deluged Molly with a barrel of degrading abuse.

"We know who you are, Rodney here, heard Aunt Em talking. It is bad enough having that bastard Jamie, stealing all our money; our inheritance; money that belongs to us. And now you; you pathetic excuse for a human being, and your benefit-land buddies wade in, completely out the blue to ruin it all! You've no right, NO RIGHT AT ALL!"

Molly stood her ground. She could take criticism and mocking of herself, but where her family was concerned it was a no go.

"You just shut your mouth, you upper class twat. Jamie has every right to that money and thinks the world of our Tanya. It ain't up to you to decide. Uncle Edward has seen to that, so just push off. You're just jealous cos we are all so happy and you and your mates have fuck all in your lives 'cept toffy clothes and fancy cars."

The first one to throw the punch was Rodney, knocking Molly backwards, causing her precious bag of goodies flying to the ground. Retaliating with a hard kick to the offender's groin, Rodney coupled his genitals, yelping in pain, taken aback by the manly strength. This only served to incite his two companions as they simultaneously pounced on their prey, forcing her to the ground. Each taken his turn, they laid heavy boots into her side whilst Rodney hobbled forward, regained composure, and placed a foot on her neck.

Try as she did, three men were no match for one masculine girl. Grabbing her assailant's ankle had no effect whatsoever, as he shook the hands away and stamped a footprint on her face.

Molly groaned and spat the blood from her mouth. "I know who... yooou... are. You ain't getting awa...y...."

"Shut the fuck up!" Percival spat down. "One word from you and the whole world will know what you are! And you'll get a second beating, from more than three of us! Finish it off Stephen!" he sneered.

Stephen chortled, an evil sound, relishing the chase. He reached into his pocket and pulled out the knife. "This'll spoil those pretty pervy features!"

Molly screamed, as loud as her weary voice would allow.

Fred placed the gardening tools to the back of the small shed and debated locking the door. Taking a deep breath, he wondered, for the umpteenth time why he bothered. No doubt by the time he came to use them again, someone or other would most likely have destroyed the lock and broken in. Not that they would have stolen the fork and rake, it was the wheelbarrow they normally had fun with. No harm ever came of it, except the odd puncture in the tyre, but it was annoying and tiresome. He was not a young man and relished the impending retirement at the end of the month.

The shouts echoing across the park did not bother him at first. Arguments were of the norm, and he had long since learned not to interfere. It was the screams that disturbed him. Terrified screams of someone in serious trouble. Fred had not run in a long time; he did not even know he could, but something inside him snapped. Before he digested the severity of what he was about to do, instincts took over. Grabbing the fork, he waved it violently in the air, moving as swiftly as his aged legs would allow, towards the group of men.

"Hey. HEY!" he shouted as loud as he could. "What the hell are you doing!! HEY!!!"

Stephen looked up, retreated the knife and stared at the elderly man manically charging directly at them, with the pronged weapon held firmly in his grip. "Well, Well, would you look at that!"

Percival stepped away from Molly, viewing the damage they had already caused. The catch lay there, hoarse screams reduced to gurgled coughing, face swollen, unrecognisable, covered in blood.

"Leave it!" he yelled, breathing heavily from his efforts. "Scarper! It's that Fred, he knows who we all are! We're done here. RUN!!"

Fred threw aside his weapon and knelt beside the victim. "Oh my God, it's Molly, you poor thing. You poor, poor thing." Frantically looking around for help, he shouted. "Ambulance someone! Ambulance!!" But the park was still, devoid of any humans.

Molly tried to sit, her jaw thumped, and her ribs crunched. Putting his arms around her shoulders, Fred looked sympathetically at the broken person slowly regaining some stance.

"No ambulance Fred." she gasped. "No ambulance, am okay. Just help me to Marcia's... if you could...."

"But Moll." Fred protested, "Look at you! You need fixing up!"

"No ambulance Fred." Molly struggled to her feet and leaned heavily on her rescuer. "Those bastards will get their comeuppance; don't you worry about that. Molly ain't gonna be slammed down because of those pieces of shit; and I'm gonna be at that wedding no matter what!"

Marcia heaved herself from the sofa and hobbled into the hallway. "That lettucy thing ready yet? Get some of that ham out the fridge an all, and that margonosey stuff, what d'you call it? You know, Tan!"

Tanya, already anticipating her mother's request had already laid out the three plates on separate trays and garnished them with the food. They rarely ate at the kitchen table, preferring to sit in front of the TV, watching any old rubbish that was being shown. "It's done Mum." Looking at the clock she pouted. "Where's Auntie Molly got too? I've spent ages arranging this nicely. Look; got some beetroot from the shop as well!"

"Marcia!" Fred shouted. "Marcia, come quick!"

Marcia turned around, the days she was able to 'come quick' were long gone, no chance of that, but the panic in Fred's voice made her realise, something was dreadfully wrong. She waddled to the front door as fast as she was able. The sight that met her eyes made her heart leap. Molly, covered in blood, could barely stand. A painful arm clinging to Fred's shoulders, she was supported, as best as he could, by her rescuer's elderly frame as the sorry pair limped up the garden path.

"Oh my god. What the hell has happened to you? Tan, TAN! Come now. NOW!"

"She's been beat real bad Marcia. She don't want no ambulance or nothin'. Can't I get no one?"

Molly shook her head and grunted. "No - really no. Thanks Fred, you did real good."

The worst of Molly's injuries were the bruising to the face and possibly a couple of broken ribs; she was lucky all her teeth were intact, but certainly, the majority of her body was battered and in a fair bit of pain. She still refused to seek medical attention despite urgencies from Tanya. A distraught Marcia cleaned the wounds as best she could, whilst Tanya fumed and demanded an explanation.

"Who could have done such a thing, just before the wedding an all? I will find out, don't you worry, I'll get them. You won't be walking me up the aisle now that's for sure, unless you borrow mum's old wheelchair...Should have kept that mobility scooter...."

Molly shifted in the armchair, making herself comfortable, wincing as Marcia continued to wipe her face.

"She don't need a wheelchair, and that mobility scooter... more trouble than it's worth. I think, the point we ought to think about, it that there is someone in Jamie's family who definitely wants us out."

"Well, they ain't frightening me! Here, get this down you. Weill get to the bottom of it. Wait till I tell Jamie, he will go ape! We'll go to the police an all!" Tanya passed round three tumblers full of very strong gin and not much tonic - medicine for the Gods, as she put it.

Molly tried to speak, but the swelling and soreness hampered any kind of clear vocalisation. Easing Marcia's hand away, she downed the alcohol in three gulps, the anaesthetic seemed to offer alleviation and muffled as it was, she attempted an explanation.

Tanya was furious. "So, you know who it is then? Tell me!"

Molly was adamant. "No, police Tanya; at least not yet. I want to make sure this wedding goes ahead and find out who is at the bottom of all this. I'll be fine, I am going to walk you down that aisle no matter what. It's because of what I am - one of the reasons I have kept it quiet all these years. If it's going to cause major problems, I'll put on a suit and be Martin."

It was then, Marcia decided, enough was enough. Rarely did she 'take command'; her lack of confidence and self-esteem, though steadily built over the years, was still far beyond that required by any leadership role, but everyone has their limits, and this was one of those rare occasions that raw emotion erupted.

Molly and Tanya jolted, then froze, as Marcia's ham-fists came crashing down on the small side table, causing it to wobble and jangle her half empty glass.

"I've had just about enough of all this!" She shouted. "Now, you listen here, both of you. Edward and Emily have said you were alright as you - Molly; Jamie has an all, and from what you say, your other uncle and Aunt are fine with it as well, yes?"

Lost for words, and a little shocked at the outburst, the small audience of two nodded in unison.

"Then, sod everyone else. If Molly ain't good enough as Molly, then I for one, ain't coming to the wedding. Don't even THINK of Martin! Tanya? Your Aunt is going to walk you down that aisle and you are going to be dam proud of her, as much as I am dam proud of you!"

Tanya gawped. "Ma?" Then she, too, drank the remains of her beverage and placed the glass next to her mother's, on the now settled, table.

Putting her hands on her hips, the young bride to be, strolled around the room, being the drama- queen she was, preparing a statement, as if the whole world's existence depended upon the outcome. Perry Mason could not have done a better job.

"Right; for one thing, I am very proud of both of you, and no way am I not having either of you at the wedding! And for another thing, in the absence of my father, who-ever he may be, and may he rot in hell where-ever he is - mother." Tanya scowled, glaring at Marcia. "I need either of you two people that had the decency to bring me up; walk me down the aisle!"

"Don't look at me, Tanya;" Marcia interrupted the performance. "We been through this a million times, I don't know who he was, and don't know where he is! It's never bothered you till now."

"No, and I am not bothered now either; am just saying, I don't give a dam about that piece of scum. I will be proud – proud as punch to have you both at the wedding, and if you can still manage to walk, Auntie Molly, then I want you there as my Auntie, not my uncle."

Of course, it did matter to Tanya. Her wedding was beyond her wildest dreams. Not many on the estate were married, and none were fortunate to have the means to arrange such a lavish affair. A pure romantic, it would have been the icing on the cake so to speak, if her father had turned up and been the handsome gentleman who had been forced to leave her mother for some totally unavoidable reason. She would, of course, never had admitted any of her real feelings for fear of upsetting the ones she loved.

Molly put her head in her hands and cried. So many times, she had consoled Marcia as countless tears were shed. So many times, she had stretched her arms to breaking; to cuddle and squeeze, protect and love. She had always been the strong one, yet also the weakest and she hated herself.

So, it was, for the first time ever, Marcia, reversed the roles and had the gumption to heave herself up from the chair. Using her stick, she walked steadily forward, casting it aside as she reached her friend and place her chubby arms around Molly's shoulders and drew her close.

"It's alright Moll; it's just a couple of idiots, and they ain't going to spoil anything, you see! Safety in family numbers, and there's lots of us!"

Mopping her face, Molly lowered her hands and gently eased Marcia backwards. "I don't care what's happened to me, I deserve it. You don't understand...Pour us each another very large drink," her voice shook. "T-Tanya, get my bag, inside it, there is a big brown envelope, bring it to me."

Marcia protested. "No one deserves to be beaten to a pulp Moll; You are what you are!"

"Oh Marcia, I do – I do – listen to me!"

Standing, Marcia retreated, enabling Tanya to grab the papers. The young bride's heart thumped as she handed the envelope to her aunt. Instinct, premonition, call it what you will, she knew something vital and important was going to be said. With trembling hands, Molly withdrew the documents and passed them to Tanya.

Looking at his daughter, Martin resumed his official standing, and began the speech that had been practised, over and over again, only to stumble at the first fence; he could not recall a word.

"This, Tanya; is a document of trust."

Marcia instantly rebuffed the authority. "What are you on about…? course we trust you, we don't need no papers!"

Molly immediately calmed her. "Listen Marcia. This is important, you might not trust me, or want me at all when you see what it is all about. This document has been with my mother's solicitor - you know, my mother - Patricia."

"YES – we know her name go on…. go on!" Tanya was extremely anxious.

Marcia's face was paling by the minute; she knew, even with her limited perception, something was dreadfully wrong. Never had she seen Molly so broken, and it hurt her to the core.

"A trust is a sort of bank account, and in it, is most of Patricia's inheritance, you know, the money that was left from her business. I spent a little – most on you two of course, made sure you were all okay." Molly picked up the glass, took a large mouthful and swallowed uncomfortably.

"It's a trust in your name Tanya, and you are to have it when I know the time is right; and that is now."

Tanya unfolded the paper and read the first paragraph. It was, indeed, a document, in her name, and figures to the tune of £10,000 stared her in the face.

"W...Wh..t, I don't understand." Her voice almost a whisper. "Why would Patricia leave me money? It's your money!"

Molly squeezed Tanya's wrist, whilst tightening her grip on Marcia's hand.

"B...b...because, she is your grandmother... and I am your father."

If ever a silence fell upon the earth, devoid of any human entity, or animal inhabitant, it was now. Minutes seemed to pass into hours, yet it was only seconds later Marcia's mouth moved, but no words would form.

Evolving from secure roots, nagging thoughts burst forth, and everything fell into place... The beauty of her daughter; the long dark curls; the high cheek bones; the tall slender form; the energy, the exuberance, all inherited from her best friend. Marcia felt stupid, yet strangely relieved. She should have gone with her instincts, but not knowing how or when, she had ignored the signs that were in front of her face all this time.

Tanya threw the paper onto the floor. "YOU WHAT! YOU WHAT!! So, you are telling me, after all these years, that YOU are my father! And you MOTHER! I suppose you knew all along!"

Marcia pulled her hands away from Molly's. "Tanya, I had no idea...well I did a bit... but not really.... you see...."

"I hate you! I hate you both. My wedding is ruined. Everything is ruined!" Bursting into tears, she ran out of the room, charged up the stairs, flew into her bedroom and slammed the door."

Martin tried to stand, but the pain of the damaged ribs, prevented him from following his daughter.

Easing her back into the chair, Marcia pulled away from Molly's grasp and carefully manoeuvred her own position, to enable her ample arms to surround her companion once again. Strangely collected and unusually mature. Never in the whole of her life, had she felt so aware; so, understanding, and above all so warm and calm. It was if all of her life had come together on this very moment. For once, everything made sense - it was a moment she would never forget.

Molly wept; salty drops stinging against raw wounds. "I'm so sorry, I'm so, so, sorry. I've let you all down. I meant to tell you both, I really did, but neither of you would have wanted me. I am shameful, and those men were right. I am just a pervert, an old tart, living on sordid earnings - who can't face up to his responsibilities."

Marcia stared at her idol, her best friend; weak and fragile; tears welling in her eyes; not of shame, disgust or anger; only sympathy, love and adoration.

"I know Moll. I think I've known since we went on that holiday. When you walked to the beach with her, hand in hand. You could have been brother and sister, yet I knew it couldn't be. I don't understand, much do I? I didn't want to ask; in case I was wrong. I didn't know you could ever, or would ever, with a woman or a bloke. You know me; stupid me; I don't know nothin. Responsiwotsits? That means looking after people, don't it? Moll!"

Marcia lifted her lovers chin and looked into her soft brown eyes. "You have looked out for me, since I was a kid. You looked after Tanya, since she was a baby. Don't you see Moll? Without you, I would be in that sodding vase with me mum."

Molly mopped her face, her gaze not leaving Marcia's wonky features for the minute.

"You don't want me to go then?"

"No, I don't. You are staying right where you are. Tanya? Leave her to take it all in. I didn't find out bout dad till mum died, ain't done me any harm has it? She'll come round you see, she will." Marcia ran her hand lightly across Molly's brow and down the blackening skin, caressing the painful swellings with a tenderness rarely seen. "I love you Molly, I love you so much… I said it once before, at the hospital, all those years ago. You are my Molly, you will always be my Molly, and now I know you are Tanya's dad, you ain't never, ever, going away!"

The hugs continued relentlessly, until, exhaustion ensued, ribs complained, and Marcia's arm locked.

Marcia giggled and rubbed her shoulder. "You have to see the funny side really Moll. I don't even remember. You know… or how, till you told me properly. I thought you couldn't…then you never had any boyfriends; you must see, it was all a bit strange I suppose. I never thought much about it. You know me...oh god, you know what I am trying to say, cos I bloody well don't."

Molly sighed with relief, ever amazed at Marcia's acceptance of shocking truth - a painful grin spreading full across her swollen face.

"I suppose you deserve some sort of explanation. I can't really say, I don't know how; I mean I do know - it just, sort of happened. Physically, I still have my bits you know. I used to be able to make things work. Some weirdos like that kind of thing; but that's another story. We were very drunk, that night in the park, when you fell in the fountain. It's all a bit of a blur, but if definitely happened, I remember that much. I thought I lost you and think I loved you very much at that moment. I wasn't really sure who, or what I was really."

"You should have told me before." Marcia reached awkwardly and grabbed the bottle of gin. "All that wonderin' I did; we did. Didn't bother about it much after our Tan came out, didn't seem to matter after that."

"Yeh, I know, I am sorry, I am sorrier that you can ever imagine. I always meant to, then kept putting if off. You had a hard job understanding anything in those days."

"Yeh, I know, come on a bit since then! Oh, shut up apologising, what's done is done. We drunk loads that night, both to blame I reckon. Speaking of which, give us yer glass. Cheers Molly Emery…. Cheers!"

Chapter Thirteen
The Wedding Day

The morning of the wedding arrived all too soon. Tanya had composed an itinerary of who should be where, when, and what for. Even elderly Jacobs has his place amongst the endless list of orders.

Marcia had already 'broken' the rules and spent an extra twenty minutes in the bathroom, much to the disgust of her daughter. The fact that she had been wedged in the bath for fifteen of those minutes seemed to have been overlooked by the queen of the day. The severity of the problem was completely lost on Marcia, who was determined to enjoy the day.

Looking into the old, cracked mirror, combing her sopping straggly locks, Marcia turned her head sideways right, then left. Still the lopsided features, still the twitching eye, but thanks to Catherine's beauty expertise, and endless patience; the normally fluffy covering above her lips and the furry sprouting on her cheeks were no longer apparent. Raising her smooth eyebrows, upwards then down in rapid succession, pursing her lips, then opening her mouth and poking out her tongue, Marcia watched her own strange expressions.

She well remembered the day, twenty or so years ago, when she last assessed her presentation in any great detail. Then, she could not imagine the tiny person inside her, was actually real. Her perception did not allow such thoughts at the time. Now, after all these years, things had changed for very much the better - the quiet, naïve, downtrodden sixteen-year-old, with no self-esteem had progressed to a woman in her mid-thirties, achieving a reasonable level of independence and more importantly, pride.

You could almost say in some ways, the years had been kind to her. Contrary to deterioration of her mobility, there was little change to her face; no onset of wrinkles, at least no more than there ever were, and with the recent hair removal, her skin was rather finer than she could have ever imagined.

'Well Marcia here goes; this is as good as it's ever going to get.' Pulling her pale pink dressing gown around her ample form, she picked up her stick and prepared to be attacked by Catherine with her endless palette of the rainbow.

Tanya, flapping her paper in the air, shouted from the hallway. "Mum! Hurry up, Catherine's waiting to do your hair and make-up. Molly's next to go in the bathroom, god knows how long she is going to take, and quite frankly I don't really care."

Marcia made her way clumsily down the stairs. "I wish you would pack this in Tanya!" she puffed. "You should be glad your dad is going to walk you down the aisle, it's surprising Molly can walk at all. It's about time you dropped this anger, after all, it's your wedding day!"

Tanya put her hands on her hips, itinerary still tightly in her grasp. "I have, haven't I? 'MOLLY' is going to walk me down the aisle, like we always planned, even though she's hobbling. There ain't no one else is there? Unless I want to be ushered up the red carpet by Santa Claus in a matching suit, plopped in a wheelchair with bells on the wheels."

"Don't talk about Bubbs, like that. This is probably the last outing he will ever get. You know what those medical people said… he's gone on longer than they expected. Be grateful he is at your wedding at all!" Marcia had long since learned that standing up to her daughter often resulted in Tanya's impulsive outbursts being re-valued. "Oh, am sorry Mum. It's all this, trying to do everything at once.

Sorry, really, am a bit snappy. Am glad Bubbs is coming, even if he don't know me."

Marcia reached out her hand and placed it on Tanya's arm. "Am sure Bubbs will know. But Molly? She's been through hell. Let it go Tanya, that's all I am asking, just let it go today."

Sombre talk was interrupted by the very person in question. "Right. Bathroom free then? Marcia, you're next for the chop. Tanya? You look like you are done then. Upstairs you go and get into that fabulous dress of yours."

"Okay, OKAY! I got it here on my list. Hurry up Ma, or you aren't gonna be ready on time."

Thrusting the list into her mother's hand, Tanya stomped up the stairs, muttering something intelligible.

Molly breathed a sigh of relief. "Thank goodness for that! She's better off out the way. I hope she calms down a bit. She's completely refusing to talk about the father – daughter thing. I don't know if I should have told her at all."

The look on Marcia's face told Molly, that reminders about whole situation were not really appropriate for the day.

"Aw, sorry Marc. Forget it, am sure it will all iron out eventually. I don't want to spoil your day that's for sure. Please don't be sad."

"Oh, I am not sad about that Moll. Told you before, am glad you are her dad, it's going to take a bit of time, what with the wedding and all that."

"Why are you sad then?" Molly looked worried.

"I don't know what Catherine is going to chop off."

"Oh, Marcia, you are funny. She's not going to chop anything off; it's an expression. You'll be beautiful, you see. Am off to the bathroom, then it's me for 'the chop' next. God knows how she is going to disguise these bruises."

Sitting on the kitchen chair for any length of time was uncomfortable. Marcia screwed up her face and shifted her torso back and forth, whilst Catherine attempted to perform miracles.

"Marcia, please can you try and keep still, you are going to look like Groucho Marx at this rate."

"What's grouchy, that's when you are mad isn't it? I ain't mad, just me bum is hurting a bit."

"A couple of minutes more, that's all. Do you want me to fix on your hat?"

Marcia tried to sound grateful, she was still not sure about the hat. But the girls had said it had the 'wow', whatever that meant. "You just as well, can't get me dress over me head normal times, will pull it up over me arse."

Standing more or less upright, Marcia looked into the hallway mirror; the person staring back at her was unrecognisable. The normal, uncontrollable anemone of wild tentacles, curled around her ears, framing her unblemished skin. Her lips, smoothen with pink satin, bared no evidence of prickly pears. Touching her cheeks lightly, Marica ran her fingers over the unfamiliar surface. It had been a very long time since she wore any makeup, she was no good at that kind of thing.

The girls had often tried to persuade her, but the few times she had attempted application, it always ended with a face resembling Quasi Modo on a bad day, with a body to match. Recalling the evenings of 'disco' fun, Marcia smiled to herself; a bit of lippy and eyeshadow cadged from Molly was about the best she could muster all those years ago. Today, she gawped at the results.

Her dress, necessarily overly large, covered her ungainly form and emitted a kind of elegance in its own way. The lilac flowers, to which Marcia had initially taken an instant dislike, actually looked 'quite alright'. Even the hat looked 'okay-ish; a bit tight, but better that than falling off in the middle of the show. The only thing she was not sure about were the shoes. Matching in colour they were, in size they were not, and pretty uncomfortable at that. However, as she was frequently reminded; she would be sat down most of the time. For now, they were placed by the front door, pain would wait until the last minute.

Mixed feelings came to mind. This was alien, out of her comfort zone. There was no need for all this 'stuff' she did not normally wear, it was not 'her'. Yet, a sense of admiration arose as the unattractive, unimportant woman, gazed upon a different, confident twin.

Her thoughts were disturbed by a knock on the door, followed by a thud of wood upon wood as it was pushed open from the outside.

"Only me!" Mrs Marchent squeaked. "Thought you might want the step washed."

The day her mother's coffin slid out of the house, sledging its way down onto the garden path, was only too vivid. Mrs Marchent had certainly washed the step numerous times to 'ensure' it was all clean for the funeral. Not wishing to risk further chaos; the offer was politely declined. Instead, the friendly old lady was quite content to leave a bright blue bucket and matching mop as 'a little wedding present', before rushing off to finish her endless cleaning of her own abode.

Molly descended the stairs, much slower than usual, owing to the pain in her ribs still presenting itself in abundance. The sight of Marcia, dressed to kill, with a bucket and mop in her hands caused an abrupt halt.

"Marc! You look wonderful! I don't know what to say.

That hat is perfect, I knew it would be....er, not sure about the mop and bucket, maybe you ought to leave that behind."

"Do you reckon? Am quite surprised really. These are from Mrs Marchent, who else? I'll put it in the kitchen with the other bits and bobs."

"Give it here, I'll do it. Hair and make up for me now, fingers crossed Marc; fingers crossed. You go and sit down, before you mess up your lovely clothes."

The few bits and bobs in the kitchen, consisted of numerous presents delivered by kindhearted neighbours. From the old rusty 'Home Sweet Home' plaque to the tiny 'cow' salt and pepper pots; each little item most carefully chosen.

Inexpensive, some second-hand; but all given with good intentions and all equally valued. Tanya was insistent on them being taken to the reception, to stand alongside the elaborate, exorbitant gifts showered by rich relatives more interested in self-image than genuine happiness for the couple. Not that Jamie and Tanya were ungrateful, certainly this was far from the truth. The gifts were much appreciated and far beyond the expectations of the young bride. Although somewhat materialistic, particularly accentuated in recent years, she was still touched by the genuine generosity of the residents on the estate.

Marcia leaned on her stick and endeavoured the return to her comfortable armchair, only to be interrupted by a flurry of jovial activity enthusiastically bursting into the house.

"We're here!!" Tom called out. "Go on Daniel, get on through there! Show them your getup! Becs? Show Marc Sarah's fancy frock!"

Thrusting the poor boy forward, Tom's seven-year-old son looked less than delighted. Dressed in a starchy white shirt, strangled by a massive black bow tie did not help to relieve the nerves of the young page. Pulling the hem of the suit blazer, in the hope it would cover the volumes of trouser fabric enveloping his lower torso had no effect, he still felt a complete idiot.

Three-year-old Sarah, on the other hand, giggled relentlessly, stretched the mountain of frills over her head and proceeded to jump around her mother's legs like a deranged fairy; Becs failing miserably to calm her down. Marcia was in awe of them all.

"Don't you all look so fantabulous! Come in, come and sit down. I'll get the kids some sweets."

At the mention of sweets, Daniel's face lit up briefly.

"Don't you dare do that Marcia; save them for later. They'll get messed up for sure." Becs' witty manner, unoffensive. "You two behave yourselves; go in and sit down. Tom. Take them in, am going to see Moll."

Molly gazed at herself in the small hand mirror. "Guess that's the best it's going to be. Thanks Cathy you've worked wonders, I can do the rest upstairs."

"You look fine, can't do much more with that eye, but looks better than it did." Catherine took off her overalls and packed her bag. "Well, I am off, see you all at the church."

Becs bade her farewells to the beautician and sat down beside a demoted Molly. "You okay? You know you don't have to go through with this if you don't want too?"

Molly stood upright, drawing in painfully. "Am not going to let a few pathetic twats spoil anyone's day; they're the ones with the problem not me. I let Tanya down enough, time to shape up!"

Becs smiled, "Good on you, we are all with you; as a backup or whatever."

Genuinely concerned for Molly's welfare, Tom and Becs were fully aware of the nature of the fight, and both were determined to see justice. For now, the wedding was imminently important. The comment concerning potential disappointment by the bride was misinterpreted completely, as Marcia and Molly refrained from sharing the news of Tanya's parenthood, until their daughter had acknowledged the fact.

"Better get a shift on, car will be here in a bit. How are we on for the timings Marc?" Molly bellowed.

"I dunno, I can't do all that kind of stuff. Ask Tanya" Marcia busied herself with the children, leaving, as always, organisation to other members of the household.

Tom took charge. "Don't bother Tanya, she'll be wanting to surprise us all. Remember Marcia, you are coming with us first, with the kids. Where's those presents?"

"In the truck?" Marcia's face dropped. "Dressed like this?"

Tom reassured her, as he had done several times during the past week. "Marcia, I told you, I borrowed a car from me mate; we done it up. Stop worrying. You wanted to provide the cars for the wedding, so trust me. What's next on the list? Ah…Jacobs….out you go."

The dog sat patiently by the kitchen door, perusing the comings and goings without interest. He was happy enough to toddle outside and amuse himself in the back garden.

Content with the knowledge that Tom was on hand, Molly trudged up the stairs, yelling to confirm her retreat. "See you all at the church then I guess."

Banging gently on his daughter's door, Molly enquired of Tanya's well-being. The staid response was all that she could hope for; a lump lodged in her throat. Resisting the temptation to enter the room, she resolved herself to her own preparation.

It was a grand time when the first of the main party paraded down the garden path. Marcia, supported by her nephew, waved to smiling onlookers. It seemed the whole residencia of Chalkesbury were gathered, most to cheer on the group. A minority, arriving to nose and gossip, were tolerated. Regardless, the atmosphere was one of celebration.

Tom had indeed done them proud once again. The old green Jaguar, rust suitably disguised with ribbon and bows, torn parcel shelf adorned with colourful flowers, stood majestically awaiting their presence.

Marcia beamed. "Aw Tom, it's fantabulous! In we get kids!"

It was a while before all were safely strapped in. Marcia's ample form and Sarah's fidgety nature hampered any kind of graceful entrance.

Tom pulled on his seat belt. "Off we go then! Hey ho!"

He was about to pull away when Sarah piped up. "Need a wee mummy!"

"Oh, for god's sake," Becs replied impatiently, "you went just now."

"Need a wee mummy!" Sarah repeated.

The resulting palaver involved Marcia trying desperately to pass the child over Daniel, who was flatly refusing to move.

Becs decided, an accident was imminent unless either Marcia or Daniel vacated the vehicle.

"Daniel, get out the car, your sister needs a wee."

"Why should I?" Daniel crossed his arms in defiance. "It's always her, isn't it? Took me ages to get comfy in this lot. Can't Auntie Marc get out?"

Becs' face clouded. Daniel knew he had crossed the mark. "Okay, Okay, I'll get out." Crossly he pinged back the seat belt and huffily left the vehicle to sit on the garden wall. His sister barely made it to the gate before she blessed the pavement.

"Look what you're messing around has done now!" Tom leaned across the front passenger seat and shouted out the window. "We are going to be late if we don't watch out!"

The crowd were enjoying the show; some sniggering; some offering words of sympathy and some downright curt. "Look at that! What a shamble, some people can't organise shit. The babs has peed on the path now!"

Sheila, leapt to defend. "Shut up Maud; You ain't one to talk. I saw you the other night, drunk as a skunk, couldn't even get to the front door could you. No wonder you weren't invited to the party."

"Who cares about that?" snapped Maud. "The only reason YOU weren't invited to the church was cos they needed someone to let the dog out!"

"Told you to shut it, Maud. Tan will be out in a bit; wonder what her dress will be like?"

"Ah, I reckon it will be dead tight, and a short veil. What d'you think?"

"She could wear a sack, that one, and still look a million dollars, but I think you might be right Maud!"

The curt conversation exhausted; moods changed like the wind, and all was back to civility in a jiffy.

Becs grabbed her daughter's hand and ushered into the kitchen. Thankfully, the damage was only to underwear and socks. Prepared, as mothers always are, Bec's fished out a change of clothes and quickly rectified the matter. Returning swiftly to the waiting car, toddler in one arm, bag on her shoulder, pushing her son off the wall.

"Get going Daniel, you've caused enough trouble for one day."

"I can't." He replied, hands wedged in his pocket. "I ripped me pants on the wall."

"TOOOOM!" Becs wailed. "Sort your bloody son out, will you? or the bride's going to be there before us."

Tom pulled Daniel gruffly from the wall; the damage was not that bad; dignity could be salvaged. "Make sure you pull down that jacket straight down and it will be fine."

By the time any sense of order has resumed the second car arrived, this time, an immaculate Mercedes Benz. Marcia stared through the Jaguar window; nostalgic and emotional, remembering the day she bought Tanya back from the hospital in a similar vehicle. Charles, now in his early fifties, still chauffeured for the funeral parlour, and although on this occasion it was no surprise that the transport was normally used for more sombre purpose, Marcia was proud they were able to 'do their bit'.

Tanya adjusted her veil for the umpteenth time and ensured the long, curled sections of shimmering hair caressed her body against each carefully designated spot, perfectly complimenting the tanned skin and enhancing the detail of the delicately embroidered fabric. Her tall, slim figure – gifted with closely wrapped covering – could be no more apparent, and utterly stunning. Beyond the curvature of her hips, tightly cocooned thighs stood comfortably together, twins that would embrace the closeness of the gown. Slightly above the knees, billowing clouds of lace floated lightly, brushing the tips of ivory satin with their wisps of albino candy floss.

Standing silently, the young bride contemplated the new life in store. In love, excited, ecstatic, her dreams about to be fulfilled, yet melancholy, apprehensive, with a hint of guilt in leaving the family home. Of course, Molly, even though Tanya viewed her father with utter contempt, he at least, together with her mother, did all they could to allay her fears. She knew deep down, they were right - Marcia would manage. Molly would be there, now on a permanent basis; but she would be gone, away from the little room that had been her whole life. Away from the worn crumpled rug, away from the red ragged curtains, with their little faded stars and no longer able to run to the safe, comforting arms of her bed.

Lost count, were the numbers of times the covers had engulfed themselves securely round, whilst tears had streaked her cheeks, for reasons that seemed insignificant now.

Picking up the small teddy bear, she drew it close to her heart, remembering 'Ganny'; Tanya's eyes glistened, as sad sentiment clouded the happy occasion.

Martin smoothed the pale linen jacket smartly over the matching trousers. His long hair, glossy and immaculately styled, now pulled back into a tight tail, flowed gently against his back. Uncomfortable as he was, he hoped the suit would suffice, and most of all, he prayed Tanya would acknowledge his being. He no longer cared about prejudice and preconceived opinions; the most important people in his life were here, residing in this humble house. Tapping gingerly on the door, he waited anxiously, for behind that wall, more precious than life itself stood his daughter, who he was, or was not, going to lose.

Tanya, outwardly composed, inwardly childlike, whispered a meek "Come in."

Straining to hear the reply, Martin slowly creaked open the door and stepped to face his baby. Complete silence ensued as each stood motionless, neither knowing how to proceed.

Tears pricked Martin's eyes as he took at the sight of the beautiful young woman standing before him, no longer the baby, no longer the child he had rocked and cuddled and nurtured to adulthood. He knew she would now embark on a journey of her own, and she may not be any longer, part of his life.

Tanya swallowed hard, daring not to believe her eyes. "D..D.ad?" she tearfully blubbed. "Dad? Why? Where's your dress? Wh..a I don't understand…"

Martin stood back, reluctant to take his daughter in his arms as any father normally would. Clearing his throat, he attempted an explanation. All the rehearsals of his speech were in vain; he had no idea how to start, then in a few seconds, blubbered the pent-up guilt he had harboured for years.

"I…I am sorry… I can't excuse what I did Tanya. I am so, sorry, I don't know what to say. I didn't want you to be ashamed; ashamed of me, of what I did and what I am. I let you both down. There're things you should know, things I should have told you - my heart belongs to you and your mum. There never was or never will be anyone else. I didn't want either of you to leave me…. I love you both; my life is nothing without you Tanya, please believe me." Martin's voice wobbled, as the leaking droplets destroyed the heavy foundation, revealing the wounded skin. "I am here if you want me, if you don't, I understand, I will go now."

Tanya stared at her father releasing his roller coaster emotions riding dangerously on the track, the words tumbling from his carriage. Not fully understanding the whole of the outburst, her heart pounded against her chest as she struggled to take in his bumbled speech. The exceptional love she had always held for her 'Aunt' suddenly made complete sense. It never was ordinary love, the normal kind evident between Aunt and niece. This binding attraction, felt for her whole life, was not only admiration and friendship; it was love for immediate kin, her biological kin, and standing there, on her wedding day, as any daughter should... she needed her father at her side.

Seeing no response, Martin turned away.

"Dad!" Tanya rushed forward, forgetting the unfamiliar constrictions of her dress, lost her balance and fell against her father. Martin grabbed her in his strong arms, instinctively reassuring and protective.

Drawing in close, Tanya became the child. She felt the same, loving arms that held her when she fell from the swing; the same, loving, arms that picked her up from the path; the same, loving arms that she had known and trusted for all of her short life. What did it matter; man; woman; her heart was taken and complete.

Martin relaxed his demur as the two clung together, it was a moment he would ever cherish. The warmth was different this time, no less loving; just different. Lifting his hand away he placed it under Tanya's chin, raising it to gaze into her eyes.

Speech was difficult. Tanya wept, disregarding the impending results on her flawless look. Martin gently teased the tears away, stroking her cheek lightly with his fingers, disguising the tiniest of blemish. She took Martin's hands in hers and tried to compose herself.

"Dad." She smiled. "Dad?"

Martin answered the question with a quizzical expression, hope daring to spark in his once dazzling eyes.

"Dad." Tanya released her hands, placed them vertically to her sides and took a step backwards. Inhaling a large volume of air, she prepared to deliver her reply as you would expect from the diva she was.

"Dad…Will you do me the honour of walking your daughter down the aisle?"

The grin that involuntarily spread across his face, almost broke his fragile cheekbone, pain searing upward, aggravating the purple bruising under his eye. But the hurt was not felt, pushed aside by feelings far supressing any physical torment.

"Tanya, my darling." It was Martin's turn to retreat and take the stage. Crossing his right arm over his chest, he bowed briefly. "Tanya, I would be proud as punch, to walk you down that aisle!"

Dropping all her airs and graces, Tanya punched the air, hitched up her dress to release her legs and ran to the window - shouting to the waiting crowd below. "Whoopeeeeeee!!!!" she screamed at the top of her voice. "Whoopeeeeee!!!"

Martin responded with the same volume of enthusiasm. "Like father, like daughter…Whoopeeee!!!"

Tanya collected herself and turned. Feigned seriousness unsuccessfully spread on her face.

"There's one thing though Dad."

"Anything my lovely… anything you want!"

"Will you go and take off that silly suit, put on the yellow dress; clip on that mint fascinator, and slip into those very expensive shoes you bought specifically for today. You might be my dad, but you are Molly, after all, and always will be. Make me proud dad; make me proud and walk me down the aisle as who you are. My dad, my Molly!... Oh; and hurry up, we are late." She giggled.

Martin needed no second invitation. "Bride's prerogative" he jibed, and rushed off, as fast as he could, to return to his comfort zone.

As Tanya emerged from the house, linked arms and steadied by Molly; the crowd hushed and admired the beauty of each.

An onlooker dabbed a tissue under her eye, whilst others sighed, mutterings of admiration drowned, as cheers and clapping erupted in crescendo.

The pair walked majestically along the path. Tanya waving like the princess she was, and Molly mimicking the actions. Charles bade them enter the wedding car, and as Tanya bent to slip under the door, she hesitated, lifted her head and faced the clapping mob.

"This is my dad!" she yelled! "My dad!!"

As the car sped off into the distance, the crowd slowly dispersed, until two lingering ladies remained.

"What did she say Maud?"

"I dunno, I think she said she wanted a fag..."

"God, I know how she feels. I wouldn't want to go that long without a puff that's for sure... didn't know she smoked, did you? She didn't 'alf look lovely, a pretty picture that one." Sheila took a drag from her cigarette and draped her arm around her friend.

Maud nodded in agreement. "Tell you what, you come back to our 'ouse; we'll ave a few more fags and a lot more gins... I got a bit of fruit cake as well...after all it's a wedding!"

"Need no excuse for that Maudie.... No excuse at all."

Marcia slowly made her way along the aisle to the front of the church, Tom walked gingerly alongside, ready to help should the worst happen. The mother of the bride was determined to stand as tall as her condition allowed. The scoliosis had progressed, as was expected, and over time, had caused her to bend further forward and hamper full movement in her neck. Today, she felt like the Queen, silently acknowledging the few familiar guests to the left, and nodding awkwardly at the Henley multitude crammed in the pews to the right.

Cyril stood on his tiptoes and peered over the splendid oak; waving as the pair trotted past, pleased to return an acknowledgement of his presence. Of course, he would never have been left out. Saviour at birth, he was not going to miss the wedding of the biggest catch of his fishing career.

Jamie shuffled from one foot to the other. Nervously managing a quick wave to his potential mother-in-law, he returned to wringing his hands and gabbling quietly to his best man.

The cold wooden seats were narrow, not designed for larger beings, Tom had difficulty in ensuring security.

"You okay Marcia?" he whispered.

"Yeh, I ain't done in yet!" The snigger was a little louder than appropriate.

"Ssh."

"Oops... sorry... am alright, not sure about these cushions though. They're a bit lumpy."

"Marcia, they are prayer cushions, they go on the floor to kneel on."

"Well, bugger that, I'll stay on me seat! Where's Dad? Did he make it?"

Tom suppressed laughter. "He's fine, he is outside talking to Becs.... That nice care lady, what's her name?

Anna? is wheeling him in, after he's seen Tanya, so he can stay at the back and see everything better. Becs is going to stay as well, so no need to worry."

Of course, the real reason Bernie was plonked at the rear of the church, was prudent anticipation of Christmas outbursts, in which case, a hasty retreat would be in order.

"Hey Tom, did you see those little bridesmaids? The Henley lot, aren't they sweet? Same dresses as Sarah. Oh, Tom, isn't this fantabulous?"

"Yes, they stood there like angels." Tom's eyes shot to the rooftops.

Daniel and Sarah, on the other hand, were careering around the gravestones, playing hide and seek, and blowing raspberries at any disapproving quest that glanced in their direction.

The mumblings of the congregation diminished, as the final Chinese whisper of "She's here," travelled to the front of the group.

Molly ran her hands over the yellow satin, ensuring everything was exactly in place. Tanya turned to inspect the young supporters, all spaced equally apart, bouquets anxiously held in girlie hands, their nervous and excited grins flickering across their tiny faces. Daniel, on the other hand, with a forced favourable expression, was as good as it gets, for a seven-year-old that would rather be playing football. He pulled his jacket over his ripped trousers and draped the ribbon horseshoe over his wrist, albeit with a slight hint of defiance.

"Ready Bubbs?" Tanya rested her arm briefly on her Grandad's chair.

Anna whispered in her patient's ear. "It's your Tanya. You remember what I said just now? She's getting married."

"Oooh, is that our Tan? Is that you Tan? Cor you look smashin'. You an angel then? In the nativity?"

Tanya gave her 'Bubbs' an emotional kiss on the cheek. "No, I am getting married Bubby."

"Getting married? You hear that, Anna? Our Tan getting married!" Anna nodded, smiled at her patient and whisked him into the church.

Tanya stood tall and took a deep breath. "Ready Dad?"

"Ready daughter."

"Oh, by the way, before we go in, best call me Molly, don't want a scene, do we?" Molly winked.

"Get lost." Tanya grinned. "We'll talk about that afterwards."

Molly, standing relatively erect, pain eradicated by emotion, invited his daughter's arm. In perfect time to the resounding organ, they strode slowly and majestically, to the alter. The pair looked strikingly alike; same height, same slim build, identical shimmering curls cascading each perfect body. Even the purple marring of sadder moments failed to impact upon the astounding beauty both portrayed. Yet the striking similarities were dismissed by the majority of the wedding guests, who's eyes were fixed upon the most gorgeous, attractive, exquisite creature that ever walked the earth.

Marcia shifted herself sufficiently enough to watch the pair. Such joy arose within her soul. The failures, the torment of inadequacy, the long years of mental and physical struggle, had all been a lengthy preparation for this day. She could see her mother Lily, standing at her bedside, rocking the new-born granddaughter, saying how proud she was. Now it was Marcia's turn to be full of pride. This was her daughter, her best friend, her family and what more could anyone want?

Glancing briefly upwards towards the glorious curvature of the immense church roofing; her odd eyes gleaming with happiness, Marcia sacredly whispered. "Ma, I am proud like you was Ma… "

The ornately carved cherubs looked kindly down conveying their spiritual message. "You made it; you survived our Marc. Lily is the proudest angel in heaven."

Bouquet serenely placed in the chief bridesmaids waiting hands, the remaining bunch were unceremoniously ushered to their seats. Becs gave a threatening glare, as Daniel swiped his sister over the head with the equestrian accessory. Her ability to convey, 'once more and you will be banned from watching Manchester United for a month,' without uttering a sound, was blatantly obvious.

Molly took her seat beside Marcia, who was already blubbing.

"It's okay Marc." Molly put her arm halfway round her love. "It's really okay, Me and Tan made up, she's okay about it; called me Dad and everything."

This made Marcia sniffle even more, until a fine lacy handkerchief was stuffed in her face.

"Watch now, the vicar's starting."

From that time on, Tanya only had eyes for Jamie and vis versa, totally absorbed in each other and the service that followed on, miraculously without incident.

Molly and Marcia, hands held together, looked on in awe as their little girl faded into the background and emerged as Mrs Henley, a young and beautiful woman, brimming with confidence and pride, joined in happiness with her new protector.

Molly helped Marcia to her feet, cradling the heavy form as best she could.

"You want me to get the chair?"

"What chair?" Marcia huffed.

"The wheelchair, it's in the back of the car, I got Charles to shove it in the boot of the Mercedes, in case you needed it."

"Need it my arse!" Marcia retrieved her stick. "If you would prop me up a bit, I will walk down the aisle like you did with our Tan!"

Molly chuckled. "We will help each other; my ribs are killing me!" The two linked arms and hobbled towards the magnificent gothic archway.

"Hey Moll?" Marcia beamed. "We did okay, didn't we?"

Molly kissed her life-long companion on the cheek. "We did Marcia; we most certainly did."

"I say," Marcia gazed around at the beautiful carvings. "This church thing is a bit of alright... not my kind of music though."

Molly coughed on her own saliva, Marcia's observations never failing to amuse. "Nor mine Marcia, nor mine...come on... let's go and find Bubbs before he's ushered away. We need him for the photos."

"Wish he could come to the party." Marcia saddened for a moment.

"We all do Marc, but you know how he is, he needs to get back to the care home. He won't remember much later anyway, and we don't want anything happening to him quite yet, do we?"

Marcia hated to be reminded of her father's condition. They all knew it would not be long before they lost him physically, though mentally, they had just about said goodbye already. Breathing a sigh, she cheered herself with the fact that he had made his grand-daughter's wedding.

Turning to Molly, she replied with upbeat mood. "Yes, he does, and it's good he came ain't it? Let's get a photo of us all together - come on... we'll ask that photo-man."

The family groups could not have emerged from such different backgrounds, the gap in social class was immense; yet David, using his expertise in photographing these occasions, seemed to have a knack of bringing everyone close together without issue. He had seen some sights in his time, and this was not unusual. Balancing the large upper class gathering with the small family of the bride was awkward, but not difficult.

The images were captured with care and expertise, as not to overwhelm one side or the other. Limiting the whole group photo to one or two, with many photographs of smaller gatherings had long since overcome any problem. However, it was a first for David, to obtain a snapshot of three generations, one of which comprised of a jolly old man in a wheelchair, dressed in a red jacket and donning a matching hat with a large white bobble bouncing over his shoulders.

Even the unusual request for a specific shot of a beautiful bride crouched beside a minute dwarf in a black pointy hat did not faze him. The scene was stunning, the perfect light accentuating the detail in her dress and her dark eyes, filled with happiness as the ecstatic gaze was returned by the little person holding her hands.

It was the children that were always the most difficult. Having held utmost decorum for the best part of forty minutes, they were now let loose from captivity, out into the grassy fields and freedom. David was lucky to obtain some cracking shots, before the bouquets were ripped to shreds as the inevitable squabbles arose.

Becs firmly reclaimed her offspring and riot act read with stern facial expression.

Elizabeth and Petunia Henley stood side by side, glaring at Daniel's pointing finger. "That snobby one there, shoved her stupid flowers up my arse!"

"I beg your pardon!" Ten-year-old Petunia pouted. "I most certainly did not." Her snigger told Bec's otherwise.

"Anyway, you walloped that horseshoe round me first…Going to get you for that one, you see…"

Edward Henley strode towards the girls, who suddenly switched to celestial beings from heaven.

"What are you two doing? Get on over here, behave yourselves. You can run round at the reception. It's your turn for photos. Look at your flowers Petunia! Re-arrange them at once!" One word from God and they obeyed immediately, as delightful little girls should.

Marcia, tiring, was pleased when the official bits and bobs were complete, and grateful to be carried off to the Henley's house, where she could sit in the shade, laying comfortably on one of the numerous sun beds dotted amongst the trees. Plumped with soft flowery cushions, armed with a large gin and tonic, she felt like a queen, watching everyone enjoying the day. The new Mrs Henley was as energetic as ever, excitedly talking to one after the other, gabbling the same statements over and over again, moving within the happy throng of mingling bodies, who sipped beer and lapped up the sunshine. The young bride happily interacted, without prejudice, and with fellows derived from all walks of life.

Edward stood on the magnificent steps and bellowed over the noise. "Help yourself to buffet spread in the marquee to your left. More drinks available of course! We will all partake of some refreshments and gallons of champagne with the speeches will ensue!! If anybody wants anything else, just ask Julie over there!" He stretched his arm, pointing to a slim young brunette, dressed in a crisp starched white shirt, and tailored black pencil skirt. Julie gave an embarrassed wave and tried to smile.

"What's he on about?" Marcia shifted in her seat. "Who's suing, that's law stuff ain't it? What a time to say that…"

Molly stood giggling. "Oh, Marcia, it's not that. Food's ready that's all; Shall I get you some? Come on Tom, it's bound to be dead posh nosh!"

"Do you have to ask? I'm bloody starvin'. Get us some posh noshy nosh, whatever that is, will give it a go! Need to have a pee first though." Marcia squirmed, raised her glass and laughed.

"Escargot?" Becs announced in her stuffiest voice.

"That's what I said." Marcia jeered. "Off you go! Come on Becs - let's find the lav."

The banquet that enticed gluttony, laid out in abundance. From the basic sausage roll to the glorious salmon, lightly poached and scaled with cucumber precision, the spread was endless. Tom and Molly glanced at each other in approval.

"Goodness Molly, look at all this, not sure what half of it is." Tom picked up a vol-u-vent and held it to his eyes.

"See what you mean. Ah well, we'll get a bit of everything; Jacobs will love the bits we leave."

"Of course! I will go and fetch him in a bit, after the speeches; can't leave him out of all this can we?" Tom piled a vast array of savouries on several plates. Realising it was impossible to balance more than three, he reverted to a more secure two.

"Oh bother; Sarah can pick at mine; Daniel can get his own."

Molly followed suit and armed with enough food to feed the whole of Clover close, returned to a pair of suitably relieved ladies and a pleasantly dry toddler.

"Oh, my god Moll, you should have seen the bog."

"For goodness' sake, you didn't use those port-a-loos, did you? You know what happened the last time you did that; the builder was not happy you bent his wrench."

"Nooo.. in the house silly.... You should have seen it - all them fancy gold taps and smelly flowers. The soaps in the sink were shaped like lots of grapes stuck together and the towels had writing on. Best of all, do you know what? There was even a little toilet for midgets. Where's Cyril? have to tell him bout that one."

"I think he left after the church... and it's a bidet, not a toilet, it's for washing your bum." Molly giggled. "Have some of this food, it looks great!"

Picking at her sustenance, Marcia fired question upon question; so quickly in fact, nobody had time to answer before she bolted to the next.

"What's this black stuff? Looks like mice droppings! And what's this green goo...Why have we got carrot sticks, they ain't cooked."

"Dip your carrots in the green goo, I think it's called guacamole." Tom munched away. "Mmm nice."

"Guacky what? Moles? Not eating them."

"Shut up and eat it, it's not moles, its pears or something. Jamie said the black bits were caviar; it's very posh." Molly savoured her goodies.

Quiet fell upon the small family group as all were engrossed in enjoying the tastes of the elite. Even Sarah sat still for a few minutes, delighting in tuna sandwiches, inlaid with crushed cheese and onion crisps, which she had decided to squash violently into the bread.

Daniel was his usual unenthusiastic self. Being totally fed up with the whole proceedings, he loaded a plateful of food and sat sulking under a large tree.

He was even more horrified when Petunia and Elizabeth, the devil bridesmaids, joined him. Shifting himself sideways as they plonked themselves beside him was to no avail; it was impossible to ignore their arrival. They were strangely polite, but Daniel was suspicious and grunted an inaudible reply to their greeting, inwardly plotting revenge.

Soon enough it was time for the cutting of the cake and speeches. It was impractical to fit everyone inside the marquee; but Jamie had ingeniously rigged up a microphone on the raised steps, together with several expensive, antique Victorian chairs. Edward climbed onto the staged and tapped the boom.

"Ladies and Gentlemen! Ladies and Gentlemen please! May I ask the best man, the bride and groom, to make their way to this make-shift stage, whilst champagne will be served for the toast."

"Ooh, I say!" Marcia tried to re-adjust her position to obtain an improved view. "This is dead posh, ain't it? Who'd 'ave thought! Speeches and proper champagne!"

Tom managed to grab the sunbed as it tipped, avoiding a crash. Unfortunately, Marcia did not stay put and toppled to the floor.

Hoots of laughter followed, as Molly attempted to raise her friend from the ground, only to trip herself. The pair ended up rolling on the ground with glasses in the air, desperately trying to save their alcoholic beverages.

Percival Johnson-Smyth-Robinson sauntered towards the frolicking troop, pausing to gloat as the small band of merry men (and women) regained an element of sensible posture.

Molly straightened her skirt and glared, instantly recognising her assailant. The stern facial expression, serious and threatening, unnerved the solitary criminal. There was no back up this time, those two cowards had declined to attend, for fear of recognition. Resisting the urge to punch him hard, Molly was conscious of the occasion and on no account would she be responsible for spoiling the day.

"Drinks tent now!" She gritted her teeth.

"Where you off to?" Marcia enquired. "It's speeches now; cor! I ain't never seen nothin like it."

"Getting some champers, I'll be a couple of minutes."

Picking up her bag, Molly ran through the trees, short cutting her way to the marquee, reaching the empty bar minutes before the dawdling Percival.

Edward glanced sideways, averting his gaze away from his supporting arm, as he helped his daughter-in-law mount the few steps onto the platform.

"There you are Tanya... where's that Jamie gone? I'll fetch him - shan't be a tick!"

"He's over there." Tanya pointed to her husband, who promptly waved his arms then blew a kiss to his wife.

Edward scuttled off in the opposite direction, much to the bemusement of the bride, who turned to find her father-in-law gone.

Molly filled two glasses with champagne. Glancing around quickly to ensure secrecy, she dropped the tablets into one glass. Quickly swallowing the contents of the second, she refilled her vessel and mopped her sweating brow; The fizz in the champagne weapon seemed endless. Terrified the game would be discovered, she stood, elbows firmly on the bar, arranging her torso to hide the exploding bubbles, as Percival made his entrance.

"If you think I am going to apologise, you have another thing coming. You can't do nothing here, you dare not. I said you aren't wanted and I'm not going back on that. You can't prove anything, so you just as well go back to your crummy little house, on your crummy little estate and leave our family alone." The look on his face was inappropriate for the occasion.

Molly ground her teeth and took a deep breath. Much as she wanted to flatten the pathetic excuse for a human being, she refrained, executing another angle of attack.

"I am not doing anything; I don't want all this aggro; I will stay away, if you promise to leave off the pursuit. I don't want trouble, and I won't press charges." she lied.

Percival was taken aback; he did not expect this response. "W…well. You better make sure you do or else!"

Molly tried to look submissive and handed her victim the spiked liquid. "Agreed, a drink to let it rest then?"

Percival, relishing a confrontation, was reluctant to agree to a truce. Finishing the champagne in one almighty mouthful, he rammed his glass angrily onto the bar. Defeated, he thundered from the marquee; attempting the last show of domination as the tent flat ripped from its hook, falling to the floor, destroyed by unwarranted temper.

Smirking to herself, Molly grabbed a couple of bottles and triumphantly skipped to her family group.

"What's up with you?" Marcia laughed.

"Just nicked us a couple of extra bottles; took me back a bit, we used to do that a lot, given the chance. Give me your glasses all, Let's celebrate like we never have before.".

Marcia certainly remembered those times, at least, most of them. They were good days, but the almost fatal dip in the fountain had ensured future joviality was kept under some kind of control. Simple as she was, there was no way she was going to follow the road that had wrapped itself around her mother for years. She gave thanks to Tanya, for bringing Lily from the depths of destruction, and although her parent's electrocution was tragic beyond comprehension; there was a strange comfort in the fact that the booze did not actually kill her. Sometimes, however, there were occasions when a few glasses were essential, and this, was one of those events.

Tom declined. "Save me some, got to drive in a bit and sort Jacobs."

Marcia smiled at her saviour; "Aw that's nice Tom, am sure the Henley's won't mind. He can meet that Rosy giant, Emily said she were going to let her out in a bit. Sheila and Maud will be at the gin by now, she's bound to forget."

Becs grinned. "Well, my lovely man. Arch is driving Ben over later, to pick up the jag and they're going to give us all a lift back. After you got Jacobs, you can drink all you like! I'm not having much, someone's got to take care of this urchin, but certainly going to enjoy myself. Cheers!"

The content of the best man's speech droned on. Marcia sipped her champagne. "Crikey, I don't understand all that rubbish. When's our Tanya going to speak."

Molly, leaned over, whispering in a low voice. "She won't, it's only the best man, Edward, and the groom. It was

supposed to be me, but given the circumstances, I asked
Edward to do a bit. Save some of your champagne for the
toasts, I'll top it up in a bit. We need to be quiet now."

"Couldn't eat another thing, and in any case, I ain't going
to tip this lovely stuff on my toast when it comes - it will go
all soggy!"

Molly shot her eyes into her head. "Just listen will you!"

Lengthy speeches done and dusted; the crowd were
about to disperse and continue with the party, when Tanya
stood and tapped her glass with the sticky cake knife.

"Ahem…" She swallowed hard. "Ahem… I have a few
words to say if you will bear with me. Then I am going to
throw my bouquet, as we aren't going away until
tomorrow."

Molly looked on unsurprised. Her diva would not let this
opportunity go without forcing herself upon a captive
audience; but no one was expecting the contents of the
forthcoming announcement, least of all her mother and
father. It was a speech that both of them would cherish and
remember forever.

Jamie, stared at his wife with admiration and gave her a
whopping thumbs up. "Go to it Mrs Henley!"

Tanya cleared her throat, before she spoke loudly and
clear. "Firstly, like all of us up here, I want to thank everyone
for coming."

Nods and claps erupted, then subdued as the bride
continued.

"Most of you know my Auntie Molly, she came into our
family many years ago. Without her support me and mum
would be lost in the wilderness. She has also found her own
folks, in all you Henleys and I know that has made her
happier than you could ever imagine. Most of you, by now,

know Molly's situation, and have accepted her as she is, content with the lifestyle she has chosen. Some others in our extended family, unfortunately, seem take great delight in rejecting any human who has found peace and solace. We are all different and deserve respect for our chosen paths. Some of these horrible people chose to vent their own frustration and prejudice in vile ways. Our Molly was a victim of assault, and by nothing short of a bunch of angry animals that should know better. Well, I am telling you now; those bruises on her face are bruises of pride and upstanding. I am blessed with a person, who deserves so much love from every one of us. I am blessed with my Molly, who is my father, and I want you to raise your glasses to my dad.... For, I am honoured to be his daughter."

Molly gasped; shocked; speechless; embarrassed; proud; scared; inundated with an immediate abundance of mixed emotion. She was the subjected to the stares of every member of the party. Silence reigned upon the festivities, save for the distant barking of a frustrated canine.

Tom put down his glass and was the first to start the slow hand clap. No words were necessary as the Mexican wave of approval grew louder as one by one, each guest gestured, some banging their thighs to save their beverages, some lowering their glasses to the ground, or gently placing them on the small round tables before joining in the applause. The noise was deafening.

Tanya descended the steps and walked towards her father, still holding her flowers, stretched out her arms with intended tenderness. Molly moved towards his daughter and the two hugged each other in the centre of the grassy arena, fiercely encouraged by all; save one, skulking in the background. One solitary guest, who fell against a large oak tree, clutching his chest in agony.

"Holy shit!" shouted Tom, clapping as fast as his hands would tolerate. "Where the hell did that come from Tanya? HOLY SHIT!! GO-EE MOLL! GO-EEEEEE!"

Pulling herself away from her father, Tanya skipped around in circle, returning to her childlike manner. "Ready for the bouquet everyone? Here it comes...."

Marcia sat on her sun bed, dumfounded. She did not understand most of Tanya's speech, but the gist of it was, the cat was out of the bag, so to speak.

Drinking the rest of the champagne, she smacked her lips and looked at the empty glass. "Bloody hell girl, that told 'em."

She was about to refill her glass when the bunch of blooms hit her straight in the face, sending delicate petals flying in all directions. Howls of laughter filled the air, as she brushed the colourful slivers from her eyes.

"You're next Ma!" Tanya leaped into the air. "You're next!"

Molly smiled to herself....'you never know.' She mused... 'maybe she will be.'

It was a shame that the arrival of the ambulance put a damper on the proceedings. Edward ushered his brother-in-law into the vehicle, pushing him to the side of a very breathless Percy who was already clinging on to his doting mother for dear life.

"Go to your son. Whatever is wrong with him, get it sorted." he growled.

George wailed. "How can you be so callous? Looks like he's having a heart attack, he might die!"

Edward scowled. "Then he deserves everything he ruddy well gets!"

Slamming the ambulance door, Edward watched as the engine roared into action and the vehicle careered along the drive.

Turning to the surprised party, he lied. "Indigestion; suffered as a child; he will be fine… On with the music I feel, and dance the night away we will!"

The audience gradually dispersed, inebriation in abundance; drama soon forgotten. Airs and graces diminished, as the rhythmic sounds invited people to jig and cavort.

Edward strode towards Molly, bearing a very large glass of fiery red liquid, calmed by a mountain of ice, covered with juicy cherries, and finally topped with a tiny striped miniature umbrella.

Gently pulling her away from her group, he thrust the fishbowl into Molly's hands.

"What did you do to him Molly?" he winked, glancing around to ensure neither of them were overheard.

Molly look aghast, her misdemeanour was rumbled. "What do you mean?"

"Oh, don't worry. I saw you in the bar. I was sort of looking for Jamie." Edward winked again and pulled Molly further away.

"I know what he did Molly. I have ears and eyes in strange places. I know what he is like, a snivelling coward who thinks he's king of the ruddy castle. His choice of - no I won't call them friends - thugs – accomplices, is appalling, his mother has no idea what he is like, and his father is a weak lump of horse manure. I was debating the police, but then, it would have spoilt the day. So, biding my time I was, but you - you seem to have beaten me to it." Placing his unsteady arm over Molly's shoulder, forcing her heels into the grass, he grinned.

Molly, unsure how to take this sudden rumble of her misdemeanours took a swig at her drink.

"You really wanna know?" she asked.

Edward gripped Molly harder. "Yes, I really want to know. Molly me lad, lass, oh sorry… I really want to know, that bastard deserves everything he gets. I won't tell a soul; partners in crime, eh?"

Molly scrunched up her shoulders, Edward was clinging on to her for grim death and she could feel her polished shoes following the submerged heels, as her body was hammered further into the ground.

"He will be okay… after a day or so. I… er… I..er…laced his drink with more than a small dose of my heart tablets. For me they are fine, for him; well, not being used to them, and mixed with alcohol, he will have massive palpitations for a while then it will settle down."

Edward released Molly with such force, she stumbled backwards, leaping out of her static stilettos; narrowly avoiding a fall into a superbly clipped box hedge. He grabbed her arm and saving her from danger, roared with laughter.

"You did what?" he guffawed.

"I laced…."

"I know what you said. How absolutely marvellous! Absolutely spiffing! Wish I thought of it myself!"

"You mean; you aren't mad, you aren't going to shop me?" Molly relaxed

"Not on your Nelly!" Edward put his finger over his mouth. "SSh… mum's the word, let the little bugger stew. We'll deal with the other two another time. Come on, down that drink and join in the dancing. Emily wants to see you as well; she's been so busy trying to get round to everyone."

Molly took a long slurp; the taste was heavenly. "What's in this then?" she laughed.

"It's called, Singapore Sling. I'll give you the recipe another time." Edward reframed his portly form around Molly and marched her off barefoot, to the welcoming arms of revelling party goers.

Marcia swayed a little. "What's that all about Becs?"

Becs looked down at the mother of the bride. "I have no idea Marcia... I have no idea...but Molly's left her shoes, it must be serious."

Tom stopped the Jaguar outside the small house. He pondered for a moment, taking in the eerie silence. Rarely, the house was empty; Marcia's limited mobility saw to that, but no blaring TV, no tittle tattle of voices, no Sheila nosing around; to ascertain if any stranger had dared to infiltrate their castle walls. Even Jacobs had not voiced his usual chord of unrelentless barking, upon the arrival of a familiar human being.

The front door was slightly ajar, normally acceptable. However, on this occasion he was sure it should have been closed, although, its age and lack of maintenance often prevented full security. Walking along the hallway into the kitchen, he expected Jacobs to extend a welcome. The emptiness of the room perturbed him for a moment, then the familiar sound of the dog yapping, reached his ears. Jacobs was still in the garden, but not scratching at the door as expected.

Staring through the window at the unkept jungle, he could see the form of a small being, torso draped in pink chiffon and facial features obscured by the largest purple hat he had ever seen. Jacobs was bounding around, energetic as a two-year-old; certainly not the elderly animal he really was. The newcomer shrieked with excitement as his old, battered ball flew across the tufts. "Fetch it little doggie! Fetch it!" yelled the familiar voice.

Tom knew exactly who it was. Striding through the back entrance, straight across the patchy lawn avoiding the cracked paving, he stared at Dolores with mixed emotion.

"Mother. What on earth are you doing here? I thought you were still in the hospital; you didn't reply to the invitation."

"I am quite well, Tommy. I got a train then a taxi, but I couldn't remember where the wedding was, and everyone was gone by the time I got here."

He hated being called Tommy. It made him feel six years old and brought back unsavoury memories of the mental instability that had consumed his mother, eventually confining her to most of her life in one institution or the other. "You sure you should be here? We didn't get any letters or anything, at least I didn't see any at Dad's."

"Dunno bout no letters. I sent a note, with my friend." Jacobs returned the ball for the hundredth time and Dolores threw it again.

"What friend was that then?" Tom was used to Dolores ranting. Sighing, he was hardly interested in her reply.

"My little friend; you know; Sydney."

"Dare I ask who Sydney is?"

Dolores looked up, her face barely visible underneath the stiff net that disguised her strained features.

"You know Tommy; Sydney; the little bird that eats my crusts. They don't like you not eating your crusts. Sydney likes them and he eats them all up."

Tom winced, he was sadly in conclusion that his mother, was still, as mad as a box of frogs.

"So, Sydney is a pigeon, and you sent him off with a message."

"Of course, I told you, he's, my friend. I tied a little note on his little legs and off he flew. I thought you got it cos it wasn't there the next day."

Jacobs sat looking expectantly at his new playmate. "Nice doggie, what's he called again? Can't remember. Such a nice doggie… Isn't he a nice doggie Tommy?"

"Oh, my lord," Tom cringed. "Well, we will sort all that out later mother. Can't leave you here, come on, you missed the church, but we'll make the rest of the reception."

"Oh lovely!" Dolores jumped up from her seat and held the ball high. Jacobs leapt to grab it, quite happy to be teased.

"Come on then little doggie… to a wedding we will go - doggidy doo dah dum dum…Love a church service we do don't we Freddie?"

"I told you, the service is finished; and the dog's Jacobs - He's crackers; like you - we are going to the reception."

By the time Tom had returned to the wedding party, everyone, consumed with vast quantities of food and alcohol, were either flopped on sunbeds dotted around the garden, chatting rubbish to anyone who would listen, or attempting the Cancan and other impossibilities on the dance floor and anywhere else where there was enough space.

Marcia – suitably relaxed but not totally sloshed – strained her eyes, not quite believing their conveyance. Her odd lid flickered rapidly as she comprehended the arrival.

"Oh my God, it's Delores!" Marcia screeched and the sun bed tipped backwards again, sending her size three one way and her size eight up to the sky.

Molly laughed, "Here we go…."

Becs gently laid a sleeping Sarah onto the cushions. and put her head in her hands.

Tom directed his mother impatiently to a spare chair. "You sit there, mother, I will see if I can get you some food and a drink or something. Where's that dog gone now? He was here a minute ago."

Marcia managed to save herself from immediate death and tried to make her aunt feel welcome, in the most tactful way available to her brain, after you have drunk several large gin and tonics and a more than a few gulps of champers. "Let you out again, did they? Or did you escape, like the last time?"

Dolores took off her mighty head gear, threw it onto the grass and replied with little expression. "Oh, lovely, I do like a nice wedding, don't you Mildred?"

Daniel appeared from behind the trees, sporting a torn shirt, a filthy food-bombed jacket and a thumping black eye. "Is that Grandma? Yes, it is! Daft Delores from the Dungeons of Danger!"

Tom growled, chastising his son for the indiscretion, only to be bombarded with a barrage of excuses, including "'She's potty', you said Dad; and that's what you call her, so why can't I?"

Becs lifted her head and spoke softly the late arrival. "Don't take any notice Delores. You are welcome, you can stay with us tonight, don't you worry." ·

Dolores was more than delighted. "Oooh thanks Betty!"

"What? " Tom spluttered.

"Shut it for once, Tom. We can't do anything now, it's too late. Get us some more drinks and let's enjoy ourselves for god's sake."

Molly looked on, highly amused by the whole situation. She had always liked Delores; okay she was odd; very odd; but weren't they all in their own way? Raising the last bottle of champagne, checking the contents, she sat down beside Marcia and topped up their glasses. Passing the fizz to her life-long companion, Molly freed a hand and took Marcia's gently, cradling it lovingly.

"You know Marc, you couldn't get a stranger looking bunch, could you? Just look at us all; and you know what? Wouldn't change any of them, cos it's who we are, and I love you all."

Marcia squeezed her fingers around the light caresses. "That's for sure Moll; that's for sure, and we love you too."

Tom refrained from further protests and decided to grin and bear it. "Ah well, it is what it is, I'll get some more bubbles and really have a party! If there's some of those sausages left, Jacobs would gobble them up I bet! Where's he gone?"

Marcia grinned, "He won't be far, he's gone looking around, 'spect that Rosy is about, they'll be having a play around."

Dolores squeaked with delight at the thought of bubbles, as Becs tried – in vain – to explain that they were not the kind of bubbles you blow through a hoop.

Tom returned with sustenance and the party trundled on, munching on the remains of the feast and guzzling on the endless supply of booze. Even Dolores seemed remotely coherent as the family merrily engrossed in nostalgic tales of eventful lives.

Marcia took a deep breath, not wanting the day to end. Silently, for a savoured moment, she gazed around her loved ones, and slurred to herself. "Marcia, you are the luckiest woman in the world."

As the night drew to a close, the guests gradually diminished. Some sauntering to waiting chauffeurs, some making their way to pre-arranged rooms within the large house, whilst a few just slept where they were. No one really cared, no one was bothered, it was a wedding, and that's what you do at weddings.

Marcia's party wobbled towards the waiting vehicles, somewhat dazed and weary, contented to be escorted by friendly faces to each abode.

Jamie and Tanya danced romantically alone; the silvery shimmers of the moon flickered across their entwined bodies, twinkling the button pearls and glittering jewels, as husband and wife twirled as one to the serenade of nightingales.

As silence descended upon the Henley household, another loving couple awkwardly consummated affection; Jacobs jumped down from his conquest, ecstatic that he had actually reached Rosie and managed to complete the act at his age. He did not give a hoot that his family had gone home without him, exhausted from his efforts, he chose to sleep under a large oak tree, cuddling into a portly gent.

Jacobs squeaked a soft laboured bark and was rewarded with a drunken arm floundering over his furry shoulder as muffled human mutterings of; "am sorry, Janey....sorry...." snorted around his fluffy ears.

Chapter Fourteen
Shining Bright

Marcia heaved a tearful sigh of resignation as she surveyed the remaining possessions randomly strewn across the bedroom. The years had flown so fast; her little baby, full of life and mischief had progressed through childhood in a torrent of energy and exuberance. It had been difficult to keep up with her at times, but the battles and disagreements were forgotten as visions of joyful memories flooded her mind.

There was Tanya, cocooned in a colourful knitted tabard, banging her head on the roof of the pram, swinging backwards and forwards with each crack of the wobbly wheel as it bumped along the uneven path.

There was Tanya, a cheeky monkey, sat on 'Ganny's lap, trying frantically to grab the bushy eyebrows as Lily rapidly raised them avoiding the grasp.

There was Tanya, greasy sausage in hand, sadly placing it on the coffin in case her 'Ganny' was 'hungy'.

There was Tanya, long locks flowing, papers flying from her swinging bag as she rushed across the playground.

There was Tanya, swinging as high as a kite, fearless and free as Molly pushed her to the limit.

There was Tanya, running along the tiny beach, scattering sand confetti over her long limbs; arms outstretched to the sky, lapping up the warm rays of the sun.

And there was Tanya, a beautiful woman, flawless looks inherited from a beautiful man; a floating angel on her father's arm, gliding to the alter.

Marcia, moved slowly, leaning her full weight upon her sticks; reluctant to discard the support, until she felt securely positioned upon the bed. The room seemed so empty, so bare. Tears ran from her odd eyes, trickling unevenly down her face and onto the irregular contours of her shoulders.

"What will I do now, without you, my darling. How will I survive?" she cried.

Molly, unobtrusively, leaned against the bedroom door, quietly watching the grief-stridden woman. Her friend had held it together nicely, but it had to come, Marcia was distraught.

Unaware of Molly's presence, Marcia jumped as a strong supporting arm thrust itself around her shoulder, quickly followed by another, until Molly had most of the ample form, clinging to her chest.

"It's okay Marc, we'll be okay, I promise." Releasing her grip, Molly put her hand under her friend's odd-shaped chin and lifted it until their eyes met.

"Listen Marc, it will be fine. Tanya's not far; and it'll be like when we was kids, just you and me."

Marcia spluttered words between the sobs. "Yeh, I know, we won't have Bubbs for much longer either. It'll be just you and me; we managed, before didn't we?"

"Yes, we did, and Bubbs is in a good place now. Christmas all the time, what more can you ask for? I'm going to be here now, all the time Marc...come on now... Tanya left you something; she asked me to give it to you."

Marcia mopped her eyes and lowered her arms to receive the small silver box, gently placed in her hands. Carefully removing the lid, the tiny bracelet gleamed as it lounged on the soft cotton wool bedding.

Marcia did not remember a great deal but knew exactly what this was. The bangle that Molly and Lily had given to Tanya on the day she came home from the hospital dangled on her finger as she held it up to the light, as she had done some twenty years ago.

"B..but this is Tanya's, not mine."

Molly smiled. "There's a card, shall I read it?"

"Oh yes, if you could, otherwise it will take me ages and there might be big words." Marcia replaced the bracelet into the box and clumsily re-arranged the coverings.

"It says. To Mum. Please look after my bracelet. I want you to keep it here, so I am never gone away really, and I can still call it my home. Thank you for bringing me up and making me a nice person. I will see you lots and hopefully bring you some babies soon. Love Tanya."

Marcia beamed. "Babies? I never thought of that Moll. We might have more babies soon!"

Molly gave her another hug. "More little Tanyas, no doubt. God forbid!"

"Ganny and Bubbs!" Marcia laughed. "Like an old married couple."

Molly smirked. "Hardly Bubbs. There will only ever be one of him. Think it will have to be Ganny one and Ganny two!"

Thinking on Maria's flippant comment, Molly paused for a moment. There was Tanya, all married and proper, not like all the characters on the estate; perhaps amends could be made after all.

"Hey Marc. Do you think we should get married then?" Molly half-joked.

Marcia coughed. "You serious? How? That'll get the tongues wagging. We don't really need all that do we?"

"Just thought I'd ask; make us a couple, all official like...We don't need to be - well you know.... but yeh, suppose you are right. Have to go back to being Martin then, I guess."

This time it was Marcia's turn to take her life-long partner's hands. Not often did she have the gumption to make any kind of relevant comment, or challenge any of Molly's ideas.

"Look Moll, we are okay as we are ain't we? You want to be Molly, everyone knows who you are now, but to them, you are Molly and no one else. I don't want no Martin – Um – I mean, I do, but I don't… Oh I am getting my bloomers in a right twist here."

Laughing, Molly raised herself from the bed. "Yeh, you're right, for once you are making sense and I am not; but I'm not going anywhere; you will have to put up with me forever. I love you lots see, I really do."

"Aw, I love you too Moll, it's like that vicar said. When you are sick, we look after each other, and when we have lots of money, we give it to each other as well." Marcia pushed herself upwards. "Come on, let's make some tea."

"What money? What you on about?" Molly linked arms and slowly guided Marcia through the hallway.

"He said, I think, something about being sick and having wealth. That's money ain't it?"

Molly kissed her partner on her lumpy cheek. "You mean health, Marcia; Health, and you don't need to worry about money, I never let you down on that front, have I?"

Marcia declined the erratic stair lift and clung on to the banister. "No, you haven't, we manage, we always have, and you don't need to do bits of that funny business either. We don't want that nasty tax person coming here! It's health then! I feel very good actual…."

Before she could finish the sentence, Marica missed her footing and slithered on her behind, down the steps, skimming the well-worn carpet, landing in a crumpled heap on the familiar landing point. Being used to this event on several previous occasions, they both found this exceedingly amusing.

"S..some health Marcia" Molly laughed. "What we going to do with you?"

The gleaming white BMW turned into the small cul-de-sac and drew up outside the tiny, terraced dwelling. Ruby wound down the window and looked at the run-down building. Eyeing the peeling paintwork on the ill-fitting door, and the old sofa dumped in the sparse front garden; she wondered if this really was the place. Double checking the address on the small envelope clutched tightly in her fist; the taxi driver confirmed. 'Yes, this was it. No doubt at all, and should he wait?' Declining, Ruby awkwardly shifted herself and protecting her stature with the cane, stepped out onto the pavement.

Disappointment was far from her mind. Years of searching and questions, yearning for her roots, finally, if documents were to be relied upon, her dreams would either come true, or be completely shattered. Either way, she had to know.

Clutching her bag with one shaking hand, she pressed hard on her stick with the other. It was not often she had to resort to the support, but today, it was as much to steady her expanding frame as to calm her nerves. Staring at the house, she was tempted to turn away. Maybe she should have taken up Phil's offer of company? But no, she must be brave.

Should she go in? After all this time? Would there be a welcome? It was nearly five o'clock...It might be a bit late, and they might not live there anymore; they may not even know of her existence. Maybe she shouldn't go in after all; but then, all these years wasted... she was not about to give up now.

Ruby moved slowly along the path, hesitating, before knocking gingerly on the scruffy door. It appeared, no one was at home, or no one heard. Ruby knocked again, this time, louder. A dog barked incessantly. Thankfully, she ascertained it must be elsewhere and not imminently about to attack.

Molly sipped her tea, it had been several very stressful, but heavenly, eventful days. The macabre bruising on her face still evident, no longer caused physical pain. The purple clouds streaked with rejuvenating sunflower, easing the mental scars of victimisation, allowing the peace and quiet of relative normality to engulf her being. She watched her love contently, as Marcia dozed, comfortable and relaxed, finding solace within the worn indentations of the faded cushions.

The tapping on the door came as no surprise. People came and went, usually bellowing greetings and barging in without invitation; such was the way on Chalksbury estate. This time, however, there was no such calling. The tapping repeated, slightly louder this time. Molly huffed, taking a grim dislike to the disturbance. Replacing her mug on the table, she glanced out of the window.

The person stood gazing at the door looked familiar. Molly blinked, for one minute she thought…. 'No, can't be, Marcia is asleep, must be someone that looks like her; but then no one looks like her….' Molly, intrigued to find out the identity of this stranger, strode along the corridor and heaved open the door.

Ruby stood, pale and shaking, staring blankly at the tall dark stranger, who returned the gaze with gaping mouth.

"Er…" Ruby waved the document. "I am sorry, I think I have come to the wrong house. You are not Marcia, are you?"

Molly gulped, hardly able to answer. The person quaking before her was Marcia, not really curved, excepting an overly large abdomen, the remaining torso was certainly not so big, though the matching eyebrows, identical eyes, hairless cheeks; It WAS Marcia, nonetheless. "No; she's inside. Do I need to ask you…? Who….?"

"I am Ruby, I mean, Daisy- that's my real name. I was adopted….um…Lily, well, she did…let me be adopted…years ago; I am Marcia's twin sister." Ruby relayed the facts as simply as she could, blurting the words with nervous trepidation.

Molly stepped back, visibly shocked. Falling against the wall, clutching her fluttering chest. Barely diverting her gaze from the visitor, she turned her neck awkwardly.

"Marcia? Marcia!!" I think you better come here, like, right now!"

Marcia plodded along the hallway towards the front door. "Who is it? One of those Juoven witnesses again?"

"See for yourself Marcia." Molly squeaked.

Marcia stopped dead in her tracks. She was there, staring at herself. For one fleeting moment she thought someone had screwed a mirror to the door. Her face contorted and her eye began to twitch. The features in the 'mirror' did not correspond.

Neither of the siblings could speak, but their mouths opened and shut with silent communication, until Marcia swallowed hard, then uttered the only words that came to mind.

"Holy shit, there's two of us!"

Anna piled the freshly laundered linen high into her arms and backed into the compact but comfortable room. It was quite dim, but she always drew the curtains early in the day, as Bernie so liked the Christmas lights adorning the little tree that was permanently placed in the corner of his grotto. Placing the sheets onto the chair she turned to her patient, she was not surprised to see him tucked up in bed. Bernie had long since lost track of time and place.

"You're in bed early Bernie, it's barely five o'clock." She fondly glanced at his pale face; his expression of content alarmed her - she had seen these looks many times.

Sitting on the side of the bed, she gently took Bernie's withered hand and cupped it into hers. "You okay my darling?"

Bernie inhaled heavily, but his breathing was not laboured or painful. He shifted himself forward.

"I am at my bestest my dear." He whispered.

Anna moved in closer to hear his words; Bernie was strangely sane, and that was worrying. "You want me to ring your daughter?"

"No need tonight, ring my Marcia and my Tom, tomorrow. They be tired after all that fuss."

"What fuss Bernie? It's not too late to ring." Anna was not taken aback by the brief return of memory, but greatly saddened as to the normal meaning of this phenomena.

"Our Tanya, she got married you know."

"Yes, I know Bernie, we went, do you remember? Not today though..."

"Yes of course, I ain't finished yet my dear... and d'you know something else?"

Anna raised her free hand and hooked up Bernie's second, clustering all limbs together in a ball of love.

"You tell me Bernie; you tell me whatever you want."

"Our Tan is going to have a baby, a baby boy, like Jesus at Christmas - and he is going to be just as special...and d'you want to know something else?"

Anna nodded, her eyes welling.

"Our Marc, well she don't know yet, but she will soon. She had a twin sister you know... She were called Daisy... and she were the strong one...not like our Marc. Lily told me once when we was, well you know, a bit sozzled. I didn't know I was the dad then, Lily kept quiet on that one. She said she had to look after Marcia as she was the runt, and it was only fair that Daisy should have a nice home with people that could give her nice things" Bernie swallowed with difficulty.

"Marcia ain't no runt now, is she? The lights came on for that one in the end - shining bright she is now. She makes me proud as punch she does; and that Molly, she's a rough diamond she is - and do you know something else? She's really a bloke, but she wanted to be a lady. That's okay 'cos she won't let nothing happen to our Marc; I know."

Bernie paused and chuckled. "Now Lily; well, she made me promise not to tell. So, I never did, even though I don't even think she remembered next day. Course I did nearly break me promise when I found out I was their dad. Me and Lil, had some good times you see." Pausing again to refill his lungs, the old man continued.

"Not that I didn't love our Rita, but Lily, well you know what they say - If you meet your one love in your life then you are lucky....and I was. So, it was hard, but I never broke me promise. When I am gone Anna, you make sure that Daisy has come - I know she will."

Anna squeezed her patient's hands lovingly. She was not surprised at the intenseness of his recall, but already inwardly grieving.

"I will Bernie, don't you worry, and I will ring Marcia. You sure you don't want me to ring her now?"

"No, I am happy as Santa Claus on Christmas Day; ring them tomorrow."

"I can stay with you if you like. We can sing carols if you want; shall we do that one you like? Silent Night?"

Bernie looked at his nurse with contentment. "You make an old man very happy my dear. Only one then - am a bit tired, Silent Night will be lovely."

Anna began to sing, fighting back the tears between each word. "Si-a-lent night, Si-a-lent night."

Bernie meekly replied with the second line. "All is calm.... all is bright"

Then, smiling at each other, like two heavenly angels, they harmonised together, "Round yon virgin, mother and child."

Anna stopped, unable to continue as Bernie's voice faded.

"Holy infant so tender and m..."

Looking contently into Annas eyes, he pressed his weary hands lightly against her grip and took a calm, collected, final, intake of breath.

Anna's face drowned in sorrow as she croaked alone, "Sleep in heavenly pe..eace....Sleep in heavenly peace."